MARCH FROM THE FURTHEST LIGHT

LARRY GENT

VIGILS OF THE MYTHS

BOOK 1

ALSO BY LARRY GENT

Lycotta-Verse

The Benedict Forecasts
Be All That You Envy
Never Been To Mars
To Money And A TV
Bedroom Walls That Save Us
The Future Sold Out (Coming Soon)

The TOP SECRET Mac Files
She Who Trains Under Death

Avalon Lost
Lightyears To Go Before I Sleep

Vörissa's Catalyst Online

Expansion 1: The Ashen Downpour
Patch 1.01: New Game+
Patch 1.02: Escort Mission
Patch 1.03: Corpse Run
Patch 1.04: In Another Castle
Patch 1.05: Silent Protagonist

MARCH FROM THE FURTHEST LIGHT

LARRY GENT

VIGILS OF THE MYTHS

BOOK I

Published in Canada by Midnight Reading Publishing, Ottawa

Gent, Larry, 1983-, Author.
        March from the Furthest Light / Larry Gent
ISBN: 978-1-989152-07-2
Ebook ISBN: 978-1-989152-08-9
Copyright © 2024 Larry Gent

Cover Design: Valérie Gent

Midnight Reading Publishing
511 Brittany Drive
Ottawa, Ontario
K1K 0S1

To my wife;

You have been there for me in the best times and in the worst times. You have been my rope when I am drowning and my light when I am lost in the darkness.

Someday, somehow, I will find a way to properly thank you for all of this.

I love you, Val. Not as much as I will tomorrow but more then I did yesterday!

A Land of Beasts

A land constantly assaulted by horrific monsters. Giants and Minotaurs assault villages while harpies attack from the skies. Malicious hags control the seas as sirens lure sailors to their doom. Gorgons turn the innocent to stone as hydras stomp along the country side.

A Land of Gods

High above the mortal realm, meddlesome gods watch the mortals. The benevolent ones give blessings and hope but the malicious ones demand sacrifices and loyalty, punishing those who disobey. Others simply enjoy pulling on the strings of fate and watching the mortals dance.

A Land of Heroes

There are those who take up the shield and spear and set out to protect the weak. There are those who fight the monsters, slay the beasts and defy the gods. There are those who choose to ignore fate and set out their own path. There are those who would earn the title of Myth.

A LAND OF MYTHOLOGY

PROLOGUE

Queen Porphyria paced back and forth in her throne room, each step on the marble floor left a footprint of frost that quickly melted a few paces later. When she reached the farthest left wall, she turned around and paced to the farthest right only to turn around and repeated the process. She grumbled to herself, her annoyance growing with each passing lap. Where was he? Her guest was late. The Giantess Queen was not a patient woman, especially when so much was on the line.

She looked over at the giant who stood guard. He was a gegenees, a six-armed warrior giant race that was loyal to the crown.

"Has there been any word, Aja?"

"No, my Queen," he replied. His voice was rugged and stoic, unwavering in his duty to protect her.

She let out a frustrated sigh, her chilled-breath visible. Nodding, she resumed her pacing. Instead, this time she moved to the hearth. The flame that burned would be considered a torrential flame for the smallfolk but for the people of her size, it was little more than a small burn. It was not a cold day by any means but she, however, brought a chill to the entire castle. The flame began to weaken the closer she got, the flickering becoming more desperate as it struggled to stay lit. Porphyria paused her advance and stared in regret. How she missed her flame. She missed the feel of any flame, to be honest, but she missed hers most of all.

She was born a caculis, a fire-breathing breed of giants. She was their princess. The Caculis Empire was vast and powerful, one that rivalled the might of even the storm giants. Since she was a child she could breathe powerful flames. So strong was the fire that existed inside of her that an entire forest could be burned by her breath alone.

That was gone now, her flame forever robbed from her by the gods. Worse still, any flame she came close to would also be extinguished. Now, as punishment, her flame was replaced with ice and her heart had forever been frozen.

A sudden breeze caught her attention. She turned her head to see dark shadows whip around the room. From every corner and surface, the shadows leapt from their source and dove for the middle of the room. They spiralled together until they took the form of a man standing before her.

"I give you greetings this day, oh mighty Queen," the man spoke. His voice was hollow and seemed to infinitely echo but somehow still held deep charisma. He stood tall, by human standards, but barely came up to her knee. His hair was black as the raven's wing and his eyes resembled coal. He was dressed in ebony clothing that made it difficult to differentiate the cloak from the tunic. A cloth mask was pulled across his face to hide the remainder of his features. Porphyria narrowed her eyes in annoyance. This was not her guest. "I apologize for my intrusion but we must speak."

The gegenees bolted forward, eager to protect his charge but Porphyria stopped him with a wave of her hand. The man who stood before her was dangerous, that was not in question, but he posed no immediate threat to her. Aja obeyed his Queen but he stood firm, his eyes unmoving from the intruder as best they could. He understood not how but whenever the six-armed giant blinked, the human would suddenly be two feet away from where he once stood. It was like his form, even while standing still, was constantly shifting.

"Zagreus, you enter my dwelling without an invitation," she began, speaking carefully. He was only a human but he was one of the most dangerous of his kin. "How did you even come to enter my dwelling?"

Castle Astrape stood high atop Mount Brontt, far beyond the reach of most men. Her intended guest was travelling with an escort in order to safely arrive. This masked man arrived alone.

"How the wind moves is not of any importance," Zagreus explained. "Why it moves is a topic of far more interest."

"I loathe riddles," The Giantess Queen scowled. "Tell me why you are here instead of my intended guest."

"I have delayed your guest so you and I may speak," Zagreus carefully said. "I am here to beg you to stay your hand."

"Of what do you speak?" Porphyria asked.

"I deal in shadows and mystery. I revel in enigma and rumours and from all of that I glean the truth," Zagreus said. "I know why you are assembling your forces and I know what you intend to do. I ask that you change your plan."

"You dare to speak to me as such?" Porphyria bellowed, her anger causing ice to form on the floor and grow up the castle walls.

"Your crusade will not bring your husband back to life."

"King Typhaon is not dead!" She roared. The ice grew swiftly, consuming the walls and moving into the throne room. "I will rip this world asunder in order to free our King."

"And you as well will be ripped in two if you follow this path," Zagreus said, his voice calm. The shadows around him began to ripple. "This is not a threat, your Highness, this is simply a fact."

"The king of assassins stands before me and this is not a threat?" The fire that once lived within her was gone but her rage was still present and it was growing with each breath. "I will crush you where you stand."

"It is clear that diplomacy has failed between us," Zagreus said. Shadows began to swirl around the assassin once more. "This is where our conversation ends, I pray that this choice is not the cause of your inevitable death."

The shadows swirled around him until his form was no longer visible. When the shadows dissipated, his body was gone. Porphyria roared once more.

"Aja!" The gegenees stepped forward. "Find out how he gained entrance into my castle."

"Yes, my queen," Aja said, clearing his throat. "Your *intended* guest has arrived."

CHAPTER ONE

The most devout souls are found on the battlefield
- Castlex Proverb

The night sky was dark and empty, a hungry abyss that consumed everything. It was only the stars, glistening above, that fought back the darkness. They were lonely soldiers, standing on guard against the Dark Lord's invasions. Perigoss, Son of Hylas lay on the forest floor as he stared upwards, admiring the stars, envious of their job. Soldiers were great men, serving their nation with honour and pride. It was something he could never be.

He was born in the hamlet of Dikti, a small town that existed within the reach and rule of Oibalox. The culture, the fashion and the motivation; how it existed in the polis is how it existed in the towns that surrounded it. For Oibalox, there was nothing more important than the military. If you wanted to be a citizen, with rights to vote, you had to serve. If you wanted to go into politics, you had to serve. If you wanted to rise in society, you had to serve. There was honour in serving, for those who carried the spear and those in their family. Anybody could serve as long as they met three criteria: they had to be born in the reach of Oibalox, they had to be fighting fit and they had to be completely human.

Perigoss did not qualify.

Dikti lay well with the polis' borders and Perigoss was exceptionally fit but he was not human, not completely. He was a half-breed. Atop his head was hair fair and silver that seemed to glisten a cerulean blue in the light, and yet his face was completely bare. Despite his age he was unable to grow facial hair. His eyes were golden, his ears came to a mild point and his skin seemed to hold out against the ravages of age far greater than most. He was a man just entering his third decade of living but he looked ten years younger. He was close enough to humans for most but in the eyes of Oibalox, his blood was far too diluted to serve.

There were other poleis of course, ones that were more open to the various lineages of the world, but most did not trust a citizen of Oibalox. When a culture was so focused on war, battle and the honour derived from combat, they tended not to easily make friends.

This left Hakros.

The sudden sound of a snapping twig pulled Perigoss from his mental wanderings. He quickly rolled off his bedroll, grabbed his sheathed sword and swiftly pulled the gladius free from its leather confinements. Quietly, he shifted his body as he climbed to his knees, his blade at the ready. He crept across the forest floor, carefully choosing his steps to remain silent. Perigoss pivoted around a tree, his blade leveled as he readied to strike.

"Careful there, boy," a familiar voice said. "You might poke an eye out with that twig of yours."

"Rarus?" Perigoss snapped his head towards the bedroll that lay beside his own, only to find it empty. "How?"

"Do yourself a favour, child. Do not get old," he said with a chuckle. "I say this not because your body weakens or because your mind wanders. I give you this warning because the worst thing about allowing your body to age is the need to rise from a restful sleep in order to piss. I swear, I do this six or seven times a night."

Perigoss rolled his eyes as he lowered his weapon. He never understood the old man. Some days he could not walk through an empty street without tripping on everything and making as much noise as a marching army and other days he was quieter than a guilty mouse.

Rarus was a priest with grey hair and a full beard. He wore long purple robes and walked with a staff. He was Perigoss' current employer.

"You and I have mentioned this," Perigoss said as he returned to his bedroll. He carefully returned the blade to his sheath. "These woods are dangerous. You are not to be wandering them alone."

"I may be old enough to be unable to sleep through the night," Rarus said defiantly, "But do not think me unable to defend myself."

"And yet you have seen fit to hire a coinling like myself," Perigoss defended as he returned to his bedroll.

"I would be more offended by that statement if you were an expensive hire," Rarus mocked. "Luckily for me, you were not."

Perigoss rolled his eyes. Rarus was travelling from a small town known as Lyrnsi to the polis of Hakros. This trip took them through Torville Thatch, a forest land known for having a variety of dangerous monsters, not to mention a recent bout of giant attacks. It was not the type of area where it was suggested to travel alone, even for one like Perigoss.

"Get some sleep, priest," Perigoss ordered. "We have a long day tomorrow."

No answer came. Perigoss glanced over to see Rarus

already fast asleep.

"You mean to sleep the day away?" Rarus bellowed. Perigoss winced as he came to, the bright morning sun assaulting his eyes as they opened. Shielding his eyes with one hand, he used the other to sit up and look around. The sun had barely risen and yet Rarus was already up, fully dressed and completely packed. Why did the old always get up so early? "Also, you stink like a pig's ass."

Perigoss grabbed his chiton and gave it a sniff. He winced yet again. The smell was bad; very bad. It, along with himself, were long past due for a wash. He climbed out of his bedroll and grabbed his bag. Opening it up, he pulled free another chiton. He gave it a sniff and reached inside for a third, juniper coloured one. It smelled marginally better, which made it the victor. Perigoss quickly changed. He grabbed a brown, leather strap and used it to tie his silver hair into a ponytail, allowing it to dangle behind him. Instantly, a few strands slipped free and fell before his eyes. He flicked his head to the side, moving the hair along with it.

Perigoss grabbed his breastplate and slid it over his shoulders, quickly pulling tight the straps in order to fasten it. Most soldiers wore a breastplate made from brass or iron, Perigoss could not afford that. His cuirass was made from leather, and not one of great quality. He was a coinling, a sword for hire, but he was not an overly expensive one. Work for hire was a difficult task for even the most seasoned of coinlings but for one such as himself, with little to no honour on his name, it was nearly impossible. This meant Perigoss took whatever job was available, regardless of how petty it was. It also meant that there was little coin left for fancy, expensive armour.

Perigoss fastened his sword belt around his waist, slung his shield on his back and finally grabbed his spear. Most soldiers would have a helmet. Perigoss did not. Helmets were a sacred thing in Oibalox. A soldier had to first earn their helm and then prove they were worthy of the polis' markings. He had done neither. Perigoss glanced over at the old man who was impatiently waiting for him.

"Well, are you ready?" He barked. "We have not all day to waste."

The pair of horses trotted contently down the road, pulling a cart behind it. With each bump the cart hit, every passenger was violently jostled. This cart was a version unlike others. It had a rider seat, like most, but where this one differed was in the back. It was an enclosed box with bars over the windows. Instead of carrying objects and goods, this cart was meant to transport prisoners.

The cart hit another bump and the prisoner was violently pitched into the air. She slammed against the ceiling of her box and smashed back down against its floor, letting out a cry of pain.

"Need to hit every bump in the road?" She cried out in protest.

"The prisoner will remain silent," The driver barked.

"Wrongfully accused prisoner," she quickly corrected.

The driver scoffed. He was a gruff, older man with a gut a little too pronounced for his armour. His partner was a younger man, exceptionally tall but thin and lanky. Neither held the commonly accepted body shape for combat, most likely the reason for their current assignment.

"I am innocent," she continued. "This is just a case of mistaken identity. The gods themselves would exonerate me."

"I said shut it," the driver barked.

"Please," she pleaded. "I am not a thief or a warrior or a fighter of any kind. I am just a housewife. My husband must be worried sick over my disappearance and my daughter… she…" Her voice trailed off as she bit back a small fear-filled whimper. "She is only a babe. She needs her mother to feed her."

The tall guard looked through the window at her. The prisoner was a sepia-skinned woman, with long, sable black hair that was done up in several long, dread-braids that ran down her back. Her emerald eyes were wide and vulnerable, tears running from them as she stared up at the young guard, pleading for mercy.

"My wife just had our first child," he shared. "It's a wonderful experience. I…I'm sorry you are away from her."

"Have you yet developed the skill to properly change the baby?" The prisoner asked.

"No, not yet," he answered with a small chuckle. "I am still struggling. Gods help me, I cannot seem to ever make her eat either. But what I can do is make my daughter laugh and smile. There is nothing better than seeing her smile."

"It is a wonderful moment," she replied, producing another set of tears as she spoke. "I will never forget the day my daughter first laughed."

In truth she had no clue. She had never seen her

daughter laugh or watched her husband clumsily try to change their child. This was because both her husband and her daughter suffered from a terrible medical condition known as being fictional. She, however, was a resourceful woman. She was known to overcome great adversity and would not let something as trivial as fact or truth stop her from getting her freedom.

Her name was Scyronna, Daughter of Astyacho but most simply called her Trouble. She disliked that name and preferred to be called Scrya.

"Do not be fooled by her serpent tongue," the driver warned. "They found more blades hidden on her body than what a hoplite carries. She would sooner carve your eyes from your skull then nurture a child."

That was a lie.

She loathed carving out eyes.

The smile on the tall guard's face vanished as he returned to a stern demeanor. He slammed the bars with his arm and growled. Scyra sat back down on her bench, the tears in her eyes instantly vanishing. She did not have high hopes for such an emotional gamble but she would kick herself if she did not at least attempt it.

She was being transported from the farming town of Lusi to the capital of Hakros. Unfortunately, she had been arrested under the accusation of theft. She had profusely denied the claims but found herself wrist-bound none-the-less. The reports stated that someone had broken into the farmhouse of Evipp. This hero, this mythling, was a warbriar. They were a legion of warriors who would call upon the power of trees and plants to strengthen and defend him in battle. They could turn their skin into bark and cover their chest with an armour made from vines. Evipp wielded a blade almost as famous as he was, one blessed with spells that strengthened his own connection to nature. It was called the Bramble Blade and to the right person, it was worth a great deal of coin.

Allegedly, Scyra had broken into Evipp's home. *Allegedly*, Scyra had stolen the famed blade and *allegedly*, Scyra had tried to sell it to an underworld emissary intent on reselling it when she was caught by the town's guards.

Those accusations were clearly false and Scyra would yell that fact from the top of any mountain she could. There was no way she was sloppy enough to be caught by a pair of small town guards. That would be insulting. She was far more skilled than that.

Scyra looked out the box's window. She watched as the landscape passed by. Trees and bushes passed slowly as the horses trotted onwards. The guards were sticking to the well travelled roads, a smart choice in these uncertain times. Not only were bandits and highwaymen a common thing - and definitely not a career path that she had been known to dabble in - but the recent giant attacks had called into question the safety of any travel. Even as she sat and watched, she could see trees damaged in such a manner and at such a height that the only culprit could possibly be giant-kins.

The giants had been assaulting small towns within Hakros' reach and moving inwards. Citizens had fled to the polis for safeguard, its large walls and fearsome military might would allow for protection. Part of Scyra was happy she was travelling to the polis but the rest of her knew what would happen when she arrived.

She would not get to bask in the polis' protection for long. Soon, she would be forced to see the giant's fearsome might up close. Unless, of course, she found a way to escape.

"Hey," she said to the gruff driver, leaning once more

against the window. "I think you and I have a mutual friend in Hakros."

"Unlikely," he scoffed.

"I swear it be true. You and I are both friends with Leonidax."

"Son of Anaxious?"

"Obviously," she confirmed.

"What are the odds?" he replied, genuinely surprised.

Truthfully the odds were very good. Leonidax was a very common name. Everybody seemed to know at least one man with that name.

"Did he ever tell you about the time I saved his life?" she spun. "He owes me a life debt….maybe we can talk about how you can help cash that in."

CHAPTER TWO

Study the heroes of the past to define your future
- Hakros Proverb

The race of men had hundreds of small towns and hamlets scattered across the realm. Each, however, dwarfed in comparison to the five great poleis. Each was a centerpoint of their province's culture, knowledge and development.

Oibalox, the home of might and honour. Ruled by King Cymedious and Queen Anaxxa, their people believed that military might and combat were above all others. Every farmer, soldier and blacksmith was also a trained soldier. Honour came from combat and glory came from victory. All this was done because there was no cause greater than the polis itself. Every man, woman and child lived to better Oibalox. Outsiders, however, were only a burden on the resources.

Athonea, the birthplace of erudition. It was a city-state of progressive thinkers, pious thaumaturges, and skilled mages. A land of free thinkers that elevated intelligence over brute force. They were a vain culture, boasting the wisest of thinkers and the fittest of bodies.

Castlex, the Consecrated Coast. This port-based polis was ruled by the Consecrated Council. One high priest from each of the twelve gods formed the ruling council. A center of commerce and trade, the polis saw great importance in the realm. Yet, the inner politics was a constant dance between all twelve religious organizations.

Yascura, the roots of the world. Unlike the other poleis, which seemed to rise from the destruction of nature, Yascura built around it. Led by the High Druids, this province respected nature and its spirits. To them, there was no dominance over nature, simply learning to live with it. Beasts seemed to walk freely within the polis' streets, unharmed by either its populace or buildings.

Hakros, the land of myth. Unlike the others, Hakros was something far different. Those who were destined for greatness were known as heroes. Those who accomplished great feats became Myths. Their legends and deeds would echo for eternity. Hakros was a polis built for and by the Myths. Nearly every faucet of the polis' inner workings were done so in order to support the mythlings. Even their ruler, the MythKing, did so only as long as he was able to hold a sword and ride a horse. When the day came that he could no longer do either, a new MythKing was crowned.

Perigoss had never before stepped foot inside Hakros. Compared to Oibalox, the polis was far smaller, yet its diminutive size did nothing to lessen its awe. Perigoss had grown up in a province primarily populated by man. Yet, everywhere he looked he saw souls of all lineages. He saw a trio of centaurs walking, a minotaur approaching a gate and a satyr blowing fire into the air.

Perigoss reached out and grabbed Rarus. He excitedly pointed to the satyr. "I did not know that their kind could breathe fire," he said quickly, unable to pull his gaze away as the satyr repeated the act. The old man laughed.

"He can but not in the way you think," he explained with a chuckle. "You see the waterskin he drinks from, it is not water and it is not wine. It is an oil and a very flammable one at that. He spits it from his mouth over a flame and the oil ignites into the large tongue of fire you see before you."

"But I see no torch or flame," Perigoss said.

"Sleight of hand, boy, sleight of hand." Rarus said as he walked forward. "Hidden in his palm is a burning match of some sort."

Rarus had seen such a performance before, yet the satyr's skill was still remarkable. He put his hand on Perigoss' shoulder and gently pulled him away. They made their way through the polis. All around them soldiers, warriors and mythlings of all professions scrambled about. Rarus had not seen such a commotion in many years. Hakros was readying itself for war.

"What are your plans now that I have reached my destination?" Rarus asked as they walked. Perigoss shrugged.

"I have yet to think that far ahead," the coinling said. "I suspect that I will find someone else looking for an escort out of Hakros."

"And after that?"

"Find work coming back to the polis and repeat as necessary," Perigoss said. "There are a great many scared travellers looking for escorts."

"There is more to life than simply making coin in this manner," Rarus said as he subtly steered the pair further inwards.

"There are not many options available to me," Perigoss said with a sour demeanor.

"Look around, boy. Look at all these people. They are afraid," Rarus explained. "The tides of war are washing up on our lands. They need more than an escort who protects them."

"If you mean to convince me to fight then you best

stop there. I will not be a mercenary," Perigoss said quickly. "Oibalox will spend coins on swords-for-hire but there is no honour in it. If I cannot be a soldier, I will not be its pathetic facsimile."

"There are more paths out there than soldiers and mercenaries."

"For one like yourself, perhaps." Perigoss said curtly, ending the topic with a grunt. His entire life was spent hearing comments like this from his father. Hylas was a man who blamed his son's birth for the dishonour of their family name. Perigoss longed to regain his honour but a half-breed life him would always be without option to do so. At best, he had to simply make sure that his honour fell no further. "Where in this polis do you need to go?"

"We are nearly there."

The pair marched in silence for two blocks, stopping in front of a large building. It looked like the cross between a god's temple and a military barracks. It was a long building, taking up most of a town block on its own, but its exterior was adored with stained glass and intricate carvings. Castle Destiny, the home and crown jewel of the MythKing, paled in greatness to this building. Its official name was Typlex Hold, named after the great mythling who slew the serpent-woman drakaina known as Ladelle, but most people simply called it the Hall of Mythology.

Perigoss stared up in wonder and awe. He had heard of the building, everybody had, but fate had not allowed him to stand before it as he did now. Thrice he opened his mouth to speak but no words emerged. Rarus stepped forward to the door, pulled it open and entered. Perigoss swiftly followed.

A well dressed man met the pair. He bowed his head slightly. "I am the hall's steward. How may I help you?"

Rarus returned the bow. "I have answered the call."

"Please state your name and produce the blade."

Rarus reached into his long robe and removed a blade covered in cloth wrapping. He carefully unwrapped it, revealing a small dagger with a curved, emerald hilt. "I am Rarus, Son of Polleas."

"Welcome home, mythling," the steward said. "How may I serve you today?"

"I need access to my display."

"Of course, please follow me." The steward escorted the pair through the building, leading them through the long and winding halls.

"You are a mythling?" Perigoss asked in awe.

"In my youth, boy. In my youth."

As they walked, the trio passed dozens of busts. Each stood on a small podium and was decorated with armour and a helm. On the wall beside each bust hung various weapons. The steward stopped before one bust.

"Will you be needing an escort out?"

"No, thank you," Rarus replied. The steward turned away but Rarus stopped him with a wave. "Wait, where are the calls being answered?"

"Hawkous Barracks." With a final thanks, the steward bowed once more and departed.

"What are all of these?" Perigoss asked. "Are each of these heroes?"

"Each hero who transcends into myth is given an emerald dagger and is granted access into this hall. When they pass away or retire, their gear ends up here." Rarus raised his hands dramatically and spoke with a booming manner, his words echoing endlessly throughout the hall. "This is the hall of Mythlings Past."

Rarus pointed to one bust in particular and Perigoss stepped forward to inspect. The bust wore a golden cuirass, etched with decorative abs, and a Hakros helm. Hanging beside it was a doru spear and a kopis blade.

Rarus the Deathkin.

"You are *that* Rarus?" Perigoss said in shock. "You are the Deathkin?"

Every she, he and they knew about the Deathkin. He had slain more monsters and villains than any other mythling in his lifetime. Some even joked that Rarus was the story that monsters told their monster children in order to scare them into behaving.

"In my youth, boy. In my youth." Rarus paused, hesitant to approach the bust; hesitant to approach his past. "I'm not that man anymore. I never want to be that man again."

"Then why did you come back?"

"When Hakros is threatened or goes to war then the MythKing puts out the call," Rarus explained. "Every hero and mythling who calls this city home must answer, they must return to defend the polis." Rarus shook his head. He was lying to himself. There was something intoxicating about the battlefield. That rush he would feel in the midst of combat was addictive. The sorrow and regret he felt afterwards, however, was like a brutal hangover that never went away. There was a place in the world for heroes and myths, but not in the path he took, not as the Deathkin.

Rarus stepped towards the bust, pulled open a small door in the pedestal and revealed a hidden drawer. He removed a small circular pendant and draped it over his neck. Then he took out a small ring with a rose coloured jewel in the center, slipping it on his right hand. He reached into the bottom and removed a pair of studded-leather bracers. They were pecan brown leather, torn and cracked, with flint-grey studs. The bracers looked like they were on the verge of letting go entirely. He quickly strapped them to his wrists before closing the drawer. Glancing at the hanging weapons, his eyes refused to look upon the spear but hovered on the blade. Reluctantly, he took the weapon and quickly wrapped it in some cloth. Rarus looked over at Perigoss but found him staring at the helm. Rarus' helm was gold coloured, much like his cuirass was, and had a large plume on the top. Etched on the side was the symbol of the Hakros city-state. Perigoss' gaze was a combination of envy and admiration.

"Let us depart, boy," Rarus said as he moved to the door. "I have what I need."

"Wait, you came all this way and you are leaving your weapons and armour?" Perigoss asked in disbelief. "You are leaving without your shield? You are leaving without your helm?"

"I cannot carry them anymore." Rarus paused and sighed. He turned around and pointed at the shield. "If you carry a shield, you do so knowing that you will defend yourself and the warrior next to you. Age has made it so my arms now lack that strength." He held up his staff. "I have spent years unlearning the skills and traits of the Deathkin. I am a priest now."

"Then why answer the call?"

"I am still a mythling. It is my duty and honour to answer such a call," Rarus explained. "But I intend to provide aid in new ways. Instead of killing the enemy, I will keep our heroes alive." He tapped the butt of the staff against the floor and watched as the artefact began to emit a lilac-coloured glow. When the glow faded, Rarus resumed his walk. Perigoss followed him.

"I thought all mythlings were great warriors," he said carefully.

"There are different ways to be a hero or a myth. It does not require a high kill-count." Rarus walked toward a pair of bronze busts holding hands. He pointed at it. "What do you see here?"

Perigoss stepped forwards and read the nameplates.

"Diomestor the Battlebrand and Heruca the King-loved," Perigoss gasped. "These…these are legends. Diomestor slew lamia and beastmen. He led armies and toppled battalions."

"What of her?"

"Heruca was a demon slayer. She had destroyed numerous fiends and mormos. Her deeds had two separate kings bidding for her hand in marriage but she turned them all down to marry Diomestor. Together, they were far more powerful. They could topple giants or overthrow a polis with their reputation alone. The pair stopped the Oibalox-Yascura war without either of them even drawing a weapon."

"Their greatest power did not come from killing," Rarus explained. "It came from love."

"That is a poor example," Perigoss said. "Heruca died in battle and Diomestor exiled himself. If this is the path you wish people to take, I would not use a tragedy as an example." The boy was not completely wrong, a tragedy was not meant to inspire people. However, his facts were out of date. Diomestor had returned; arriving back in Hakros a month ago.

"Why are you telling me all of this?" Perigoss asked. Rarus reached into his cloak and withdrew a small pouch. The coins jingled as he handed it to the kid.

"I paid your 10 coin fee before we left and now I pay you the remaining 10, with five extra as my thanks." Rarus said. "You now have a choice. You can be on your way and continue to scrounge for coin wherever possible or you could join me. There is a war about to begin and they could use your spear."

"I will not fight a war for coin!" Perigoss snapped.

"But would you fight one to protect the innocent?" Rarus asked. "Is there no great honour in protecting the weak?"

Perigoss paused. Oibalox did not believe in the weak. Everybody was strong and everybody fought, however, there were those who had previously fought who had now retired. There was great honour in protecting them.

"I…I would just be viewed as a mercenary, regardless of my private intentions," Perigoss argued.

"Not if you join with me," Rarus explained. "It was no accident that I hired you for this trip. I have heard of you and your skills. I asked around about you. You will make a wonderful hero, all you need is the right tutelage."

In his inquiries, one factoid kept arising over and over. Perigoss had a strong moral code and an unwavering righteousness. Rarus knew that it would only be a matter of time before the kid ended up in the middle of this war with the giants. He would inevitably find himself along the path of hero. The worst thing was with his skills, the kid could be more successful as the Deathkin than he was and Rarus could not allow that.

There would never be another Deathkin if he had his way.

"Join me, Perigoss, son of Hylas, and become my apprentice," Rarus said. "Accept my tutelage and allow you and your skills to be seen for what is in your heart instead of for what is in your blood."

Perigoss just silently stared. Had he really been asked to be a mythling's apprentice? A hero was not bound by lineage. They were not punished for being a half-breed. PErhaps there was honour to be gained from this, especially apprenticing under the Deathkin. He nodded slowly, his smile growing with each rise his head made until the grin consumed his entire face.

"Good," Rarus said. "Then let us begin our journey together by heading to the baths."

"Is this a mythling ritual?" Perigoss asked. "Are we cleaning away our past so we can defend the future? Is it something like that?"

"No," Rarus laughed. "It is because you still stink like a pig's ass."

CHAPTER THREE

A man lives for decades. A tree lives for centuries.
- Yascura Proverb

Blaze General Vulcos marched through the halls of Castle Astrape, determined and full of pride. His valet ran to keep up. Both were caculis giants, with powerful flame breath. Like most of his kind, Vulcos had dark, currant skin with veins that seemed to glow like burning embers. He was adored with jeweled armour and carried a powerful two-handed sword. Vulcos was a renowned military leader with countless victories under his belt.

"Running late again, Vulcos," a voice mocked. As the general turned the final corner towards the throne room he saw a familiar form waiting for him. It was a storm giant, with grey, wind-worn skin and a size that stood nearly ten feet above his own. Valcos scowled. This was the second general in the Queen's forces: Arc General Eurtux.

Before the marriage that united them, there were two major giant empires. One that belonged to the storm giants and one that belonged to the caculis. The king of the storm giants, King Typhaon, wed the caculis princess, Porphyria, and both nations united. On that day two military positions were created. The Arc General, to command the storm giant forces, and the Blaze General, to command over the caculis forces.

Both generals answered directly to the crown but rarely did either enjoy the company of the other. They disagreed with each other on a near constant basis. In fact, the only belief they both shared was that they could do the other's job far better.

"General," Valcos began. "I know not why our Queen summoned you here. The drunkard stumbling that you call military tactics are not needed here."

"You think your cunning will suffice?" Eurtux laughed. "Your military maneuvers would struggle to surprise a child. Scurry away and let the Queen's real military might achieve victory."

"Like the *victory* you achieved at the Battle of Mount Cyrene?" Vulcos mocked. The Battle of Mount Cyrene was during the war between the giant and the gods. The giants had hoped to breach the fable home of the fates, kidnap them and use their magic to their benefit. The gods were waiting and brutally defeated the giants. The defeat in that battle, which had been led by Arc General Eurtux, was monumental in the giants' eventual loss in the war. "You were not even bested by the war goddess. She was busy with more pressing matters. You were bested by Syceux, the nature god."

"Remind me, where were you in that battle?" Eurtux asked. "Oh right, you were a lowly Commander, watching your entire command structure die. Do not forget that I earned my rank. You simply survived long enough to be given it by default."

"And if you had been competent in your job, they would not have died and you would not be dealing with me." Vulcos smirked.

"If you two are quite done," Queen Porphyria barked from inside the throne room. Both generals scowled at each other before entering the throne room. "I want an update on our allies."

"We called forth the Siados Coven," Eurtux began. "The sea hags are sympathetic to our cause, however, the triton folk have proven to be a great resistance. They have slain many of their sea dwelling cetea."

"This loss is unfortunate but it is only a small one. Our alliance with the sirens is already proving successful in weakening the human fleets. It is only a matter of time before we breach Brizzollo's temple."

"The sea-dwelling warriors should not be a threat to you, Arc General. Find me a victory or I will find a new general." Queen Porphyria ordered. Despite her upwards glare, the storm giant still nodded. She turned to Vulcos. "And you?"

"The harpies have joined our campaign," the Blaze General began. "Their aerial abilities will add great support to our attacks. We have also found numerous minotaur bands to join us. The gigas battalion will be arriving in the next few days."

The gigas were giant-kin but at a much smaller size. They stood just shy of eight feet tall, had slate-grey skin and were blessed with the strength of their larger relatives. Their kind were not a long living race, rarely surviving past forty, but they reproduced at the speed akin of rabbits.

"I want our full-fledged invasion to begin within two weeks," Porphyria ordered. "Time is not our ally."

"I would suggest some hesitancy, your highness." Vulcos said. "Our recent attacks have caused notice. Both Oibalox and Hakros have begun readying themselves for war. Hakros has even put the call out for their mythlings to return."

Queen Porphyria stepped forward and Vulcos winced in pain. It was like some force was grasping the life within him and was squeezing it within their palm. With each step closer she got, his pain grew. As she closed the distance to only a few paces, the pain was so great that Vulcos was forced to drop to one knee. He looked up at his queen. Her once-currant skin was now an arctic blue and the pulsing red glow that appeared within her skin, a trait shared by all caculis, had been replaced by a sapphire glow. Vulcos gasped for breath, what little he had suddenly visible to all.

"Hesitancy is not a trait I will allow," Porphyria said, her rage bubbling up once more. A thin layer of ice began to spread across the castle floor. "Our kind was weakened and humiliated in the past. The gods shattered us and now you want to take what little of our pride remains and go cower? In a combat against men?"

Valcos tried to protest but the pain was too great, far greater than any he had ever felt. His life, the burning flame that existed inside of him, was being extinguished and he was fighting with any strength he had left to to keep those embers aglow. Queen Porphyria looked between the two of them.

"You are giants. You are warriors," she boomed. "Never let any god or mortal ever silence or humiliate us ever again." She let out a roar before stepping backwards. Valcos gasped as the grip around him released and air filled his lungs once more. He pushed back up onto his feet. The Blaze General tried to stand tall, despite his weak and wobbly limbs. "You are dismissed."

Scyra sat in her prison cell, alone and bored. Two days had passed since she had been escorted through the town square and tossed in here. Two long days without anything to keep her occupied. For a mind like hers, impulsive and erratic, it was torture. In two days she had counted and named each stone and was in the middle of pairing them off for hypothetical relationships. This level of painful boredom was such a violent shock to her system that it almost made her want to stick to the straight and narrow in order to avoid prison ever again.

Almost.

She looked at the few items she had in her possession. There were a couple of apples and a waterskin. When she was being escorted through the town square, the two guards took to shoving her around in an effort to look strong and important for the gawking crowd. She had used that time to accidentally bump into citizens and allow her nimble fingers to lift and pocket a few items. She grabbed some apples from a vendor and pocketed what she thought was a skin of wine from gawking satyr.

It was definitely not wine.

She paused as she heard the sound of approaching footsteps. Quickly she grabbed the skin and fruit and stuffed them inside her cloth, hiding them within her breasts. Sprawling on the cot, she tried her best to not look painfully bored. She heard the key enter the lock and the door eventually open. A trio of guards stepped in.

"Let's go, thief," the first barked.

"Alleged thief," Scrya corrected. The guard did not seem amused.

"Get up, now," he barked. "Hands forward."
Scrya complied and watched as they bound her wrists together. The guard shoved her out of the cell and pushed her down the hall.

"I hope you got lots of rest," he snickered. "Today you start basic training."

"Why, is it hard?" she asked, feigning ignorance. "I mean if you passed, could not everybody?"

He slammed his elbow into her back, forcing her to her knees. Scrya coughed for air. He grabbed her by her cloth and hoisted her back to her feet. Scrya stumbled into his arms, her hands swiftly diving to his belt. With fingers swift, nimble and stealthy, she liberated the guard's coins and added them to her own collection.

"We shall see if your humour persists after your first day of training, thief."

"Alleged thief," Scrya corrected.

The punishment for thievery varied from polis to polis. In Yascura, they were imprisoned. In Althonea, they were given tasks and jobs to better the community. In Oibalox, a thief would have their fingers or even their entire hand cut from them and in Castlex, a thief would be publicly flogged under the guise of divine cleansing. Scrya knew of more than a couple thieves who intentionally allowed themselves to be caught in Castlex just for that very flogging. She tried not to judge. Each ship's sail was filled by a different gust of wind.

The punishment for defying Hakros laws differed from that of other poleis. They were assigned to a heroic expedition, to fight and battle along other heroes and would-be myths. Hakros believed that a hero could be found anywhere and that reform was always an option. If the thief died on the expedition, well, the problem was still solved regardless. Yet, since the MythKing had declared war, she was not being assigned to an expedition. She was being put on the front line to fight.

Scrya was beginning to see the appeal of the flogging.

Perigoss tried to watch where he was going but found both his touch and his gaze dropping to his new garments. Rarus has purchased him some new clothes, despite his refusal. He had stated that any apprentice of his had to at least look the part. It was a rosewood-dyed chiton with moss-green coloured edging. made from the finest material he had ever seen. The merchant had boasted that the threads were so strong that they could withstand the blade of a knife. Perigoss was not sure how much truth was in that statement but then again, he was not the one paying.

Rarus escorted him past the amassing sellswords and towards the training area. A woman's voice called out his name. Rarus paused as the woman approached. She was clearly a strong woman with defined muscles running down every conceivable limb.

"Rarus," she said, surprised. "Tell me this is not a vision but a truth. Do you really stand before me?"

"Otreax," Rarus said in a fashion of shock that only an old man could produce. "Is that you? My have you grown. You were but a child the last I saw you."

"I was seventeen years old," she laughed, "and on my path to becoming a hero."

"You have done that and then some," Rarus laughed. "Look at you. You were but a twig, now you are a mighty oak. You are beyond worthy of the Ironfed name."

"Thank you for your kindness," Otreax said. "What brings you home?"

"The call was put out," Rarus answered.

"There have been calls before and still you stayed away."

"This one felt different," Rarus said. He paused and looked at his staff. "This one felt defining."

Otreax silently nodded, she had felt it too. Giant attacks were not unheard of. Often lesser-kin would attack small towns for food or to kidnap slaves but attacks of this magnitude, it was unheard of. She nodded her head towards Perigoss.

"Who is the mercenary?" She asked. Perigoss' face quickly became stern and angry. He opened his mouth to speak but Rarus silenced him with a raised finger.

"That is no sellsword," he calmly corrected. "He is my apprentice."

"Oh…oh. My apologies," Otreax said quickly. "Colour me shocked, I never expected the Deathkin to have an apprentice." She awkwardly coughed. "So, how green is the kid?"

"As green as the leaves on Syceux's great tree," Rarus laughed. "He can fight, with great skill, but he has yet to carry a shield for another."

"Understood," she replied. She glanced at Perigoss. "You have a great mentor behind you, kid, but that means shit on the battlefield. Get over to the pit and grab a wooden sword."

"Yes, ma'am," Perigoss said.

"Oh, kid," Otreax said, pausing his run. "This will be a difficult day. You have been warned."

CHAPTER FOUR

A History is kind to those who write it
- Athonea Proverb

Otreax the Ironfed stood in the middle of a large rectangular sand-pit. Dozens of men, women and them stood around, watching her, each holding a wooden weapon in their hands. Otreax paced back and forth, giving some booming speech about honour and skill. Half of it was insulting their previous skills while the rest was about building to something greater.

At least that was what Scrya was assuming. She had failed to put any effort into paying attention. Instead, she was looking at everybody and everything, desperate for some form of an exit. People of all races stood around, watching the Ironfed speak. There were monstrous minotaurs, the aquatic tritons, a couple satyrs and even a pair of centaurs watching, but the one who stook out the most was the myrmidon.

The scribes of lore often speak of how during the Titan-God war, when Cydomea, the goddess of war, was trapped and her forces grew thin, she cast a divine spell upon a large tree. Every ant on that tree suddenly transformed into humanoid warriors. Suddenly, her army was replenished and these new warriors - the myrmidons - laid waste to their foes.

Myrmidons stood nearly seven feet tall, head and

neck above most men, but were thin. They looked like ants who stood upright. They had a carapace outer shell and mandibles near their mouths. They walked without the need for clothes but often wore bandoleers or sashes. Myrmidons were a seldom seen race, often keeping to themselves. Those that left their homes often found themselves, surprisingly, pursuing some artistic avenue.

"Who dares step forth and test their skills?" Otreax dramatically cried out. The loud cry caught Scrya's attention. She looked up and watched once more. Within the sand-pit was a smaller square, the corners of which had been marked by four, chest-high burning torches. Any who stepped into the square would face off against the Ironfed. Scrya happily sat, her wrist bound, and watched. First was some bold warrioress. She quickly had her legs swept from underneath her and was brought crashing to the sand. The second was a minotaur. He was big, strong and wielded a two-handed wooden facsimile but still the Ironfed dropped him. She was far swifter and went for his legs. Chop after chop to his knees brought the beast crashing down like a tree. The third was a human male and Scrya stopped caring. She understood what this was. They would humiliate the most boastful so that everybody trained on even ground.

"How quickly will this one go down?" One guard asked, putting a cup of water down beside him.

"Almost as fast as your wife did when I was over last night," a second replied.

"Shut your mouth before I shut it for you," the first barked.

"I would like to see you try," the second defended.

Scrya quietly reached over and snatched the glass. She was thirsty and they were not using it. Scrya took a sip, the water was far better than the not-wine skin she had stolen. She only looked up when she heard a familiar sandy thud. The third challenger was down. Next was a human man. Scrya was not expecting to take notice of any of them but this one caught her gaze. His hair was silver but as he passed a burning torch the flickering flame seems to transform it into a cerulean shade.

He stepped into the ring with the Ironfed and struck first. He had strength and skill behind his strikes. For the first time since the challenge started, Otreax was giving more than the basic amount of effort. Her blade was quicker, deflecting his strikes and slapping him with her sword before he had a chance to respond, but the man did not fall. Slap after slap and the man did not fall, but he did grow more determined. She watched as the challenger seemed to be able to weave left or right with great skill and ease. That was the Moira Weaving fencing style. She had not seen that in years.

Who was this guy?

Her hands began to shake and a surprised Scrya looked down. She was wrong. Her hands were not shaking, the water was. She snapped her head up to suddenly see the challenger attack again, only this time the speed of his strikes had greatly increased. Otreax barely dodged the first, surprised by the sudden swiftness, but quickly adapted to the second. The challenger, however, did not adapt. The speed had messed with his coordination. He over extended his strike and now he was left off balance. Otreax grabbed the man, flipped him to the ground and then struck him across his exposed chest to keep him down.

The fight was over.

But it was not as one-sided as she has expected.

Otreax offered the challenger a hand and helped him

to his feet. She clapped him on the back, a sign of a valiant effort. Otreax stole a surprised glance at the old priest who just smirked in reply.

Seriously, who was this guy?

Otreax led the crowd in a booming cheer as she limped back to the center. Scrya's eyes suddenly went wide. A limp? Where did that come from? She glanced back at the silver-haired challenger. He had landed a hit and one serious enough to limp her.

Her mind jumped at the possibilities.

"This is the level of fencer we wish to mold each of you into," Otreax explained. "This is the level we exp—"

Her words were cut short as a loud, boisterous laugh filled the air. Everybody turned to the source and stared at Scrya.

"Is that the best you have to offer?" She mocked. "I thought you mythlings were supposed to be great swordsmen, not whatever pale comparison this is."

"So our thief makes herself known," Otreax called out.

"Alleged thief," Scrya quickly corrected.

"You think yourself a swordsman?" Otreax asked in disbelief.

"I am the world's greatest swordswoman. Arm me with a sharp blade and I can win this war for you."

"Care to demonstrate your skill?" Otreax offered.

"If you insist," Scrya replied in a bored tone. She stood up and began to walk towards the square. "But even with my wrists bound, I will still make you go down faster than that guard's wife."

"Hey!"

As she passed by Perigoss, she winked as she handed him her stolen cup. "Here, pretty boy. You look thirsty."

She stepped into the ring. Cheers filled the air and Scrya danced as she drank them all in. She bowed twice and blew kisses into the air as thanks and even flirted with a near-by maiden. Otreax called a minotaur to her side. He wore a breastplate with Hakros' symbols etched into the side.

"Doros, if she runs: stop her."

"With pleasure, Ironfed," he said with a sinister chuckle.

"I need a sword and my bindings cut," Scrya called out. "Perhaps a kiss from the pretty boy back there and several bags of coin from the old man, assuming we are in a giving mood."

Not a soul offered her either the coin or the kiss. Scrya shrugged. No harm came in trying. Someone offered her a wooden sword but when they moved to cut her bindings, Otreax stopped them.

"I thought you could achieve victory while bound?" Otreax mocked.

"I can but if this is to be unfair, perhaps a wager?" Scyra offered. "When I win, you then grant me my freedom?"

"How about you best me first and we go from there," Otreax laughed. She stepped forward to strike.

"Wait," Scrya called. She reached into her chiton and pulled free her skin. "First, some wine!"

She took a swig before tossing it aside. She raised her free hand - as free as it was while still bound - and challenged Otreax to step forward. Otreax accepted that challenge.

Otreax struck first but Scrya easily deflected it. The alleged thief quickly took control and attacked. Her blade a flurry of quick but precise attacks; the onslaught forced Otreax back and the crowd began to murmur.

"You think she is as good as she boasts?" Perigoss asked, sipping from his newly obtained water. He glanced down. That water was just that but somehow it tasted better than ever before.

"No soul is as good as that woman boasts to be," Rarus said with a chuckle. "But there is more at play here."

"How so?"

"Look at her strikes," Rarus said, gripping the staff with one hand while pointing with his other. His eyes began to slightly glow, turning lilac colour in the process. "Her thrusts are incredibly accurate but they always fall just short of striking. They are however forcing Otreax to back-peddle and retreat."

"She is steering Otreax?"

"Perhaps," Rarus replied, scratching his beard. Scrya suddenly staggered her step and lost balance. Otreax quickly took control. Her blade moved to offense and she pushed Scrya back.

"She stumbled," Perigoss scoffed. "This battle is over."

"Perhaps but not in the way you suspect," Rarus said, the lilac colour in his eyes glowing brighter. "The stumble was no accident."

Even on defense, the thief's footwork was impeccable. It was like a dance as she pivoted, twisted and skipped backwards. Each step deflecting, dodging or blocking one of Otreax's attacks. Feeling the heat of a torch on her back, Scrya paused. She waited for Otreax and feigned preparation for a block. Yet as the strike came in, Scrya dropped the sword, pivoted away and around the torch. Now, with the torch between her and Otreax, Scrya dropped to one knee, looked up and spat. A mouthful of oil sprayed outward, touched the flames and ignited. A ball of fire erupted in Otreax's face. She screamed, bringing up her hands to protect her face as she stumbled backwards. Scrya ran forward and made a leaping knee strike, both women dropping to the sand. Scrya reached for Otreax's belt, grabbed the emerald-hilted dagger and pressed it against the Ironfed's neck.

For a long moment, everybody went silent and nobody moved. Nobody even dared to take a breath. They just stared in disbelief. After a long moment, Scrya removed the blade from Otreax's neck and rolled away.

"Ladies and Gentlemen, Them and They, I thank you for all witnessing this fantastic event and my glorious victory." She gave the dagger a spin and a flip as she cut her wrist bindings. She carefully knelt down and placed the dagger onto Otreax's lap. "As was agreed, I have earned my freedom."

Scrya moved to the edge of the sandpit but nobody moved to stop her. She began to blow kisses to the audience, bowing as she did.

"This has been fantastic and you have been a wonderful audience. When you speak of this in the future remember to warn everybody the dangers of calling the pyromantic fencer a thief." She bowed once more. "I wish all of you a pleasant day and best of luck with your.....war."

Scrya turned to run only to find Dorox the minotaur waiting for her. He grabbed her by her shirt and hoisted her into the air. "Where do you think you are heading?"

"You know," Scrya said to Doros, "I think you and I have a mutual friend."

"Unlikely," he scoffed.

"I swear it to be true."

"Lies!," Domos roared.

"You and I are friends with Leonidax."

"Son of Anaxious?"

"Obviously," she confirmed. "Did he ever tell you about the time I saved his life?"

Dorox never let her finish. The sudden slam onto the ground made everything go dark.

CHAPTER FIVE

Live as brave heroes and you shall live forever.
- Hakros Proverb

"Perigoss," A voice called out. "Over here."

Perigoss glanced out across the mess hall. His eyes scanned the hundreds of faces until they landed on the blue arm, waving him over. Perigoss carried his plate of food across the mess hall, eventually reaching the table with his stichos mates. He slid in on the bench beside the triton.

A phalanx was separated into several files, or squads. These were known as stichos. From within his, Perigoss had found friends and allies. Within his stichos, Perigoss was not an outsider. He was an equal.

"Why are you so late getting here?" Lysop asked. He was a triton: a blue-skin aquatic man. The tritons normally lived in towns beneath the sea but some chose to live up on the surface. They were powerful warriors and skilled combatants.

"Rarus had me do extra laps before I fed," an exhausted Perigoss explained. He grabbed his mug and took a long swing of water.

"Remind me of something," Xali asked in a jovial tone. "Aside from all of the extra running, extra training and extra chores, what are the blessings of being an apprentice?"

Xali was a human woman. She had bouncy, ginger

hair and keen, amber coloured eyes. Holding her hair in place were three ceremonial sticks. She was born within the reach of Yascura and the sticks were symbolic items to represent the great tree.

"You failed to mention the extra cleaning, studying and chores," Perigoss laughed. He grabbed a piece of bread and took a big bite. He glanced over his shoulder. A blonde haired woman, a fencer from a different stichos, was stealing glances at him. He smiled in response. As word of his apprentice status had rippled across the barrack, he had been getting more and more notice of late. Some of which was quite carnal in nature. "In all truth, I would be lying if I said the benefits were lacking."

"A man who seeks the fruit of many different trees will never truly appreciate the taste," Xali said with a mocking grin. She didn't believe in the self righteous judgment of others, Yascura was big on free love, but loved the mockery that came with it. "For he will never be focused on the fruit at hand, he will instead be thinking of his next tree."

Luckily, so too did Perigoss.

"Perchance a man simply samples everything so when he finds the perfect fruit, he can be rid of any lingering doubt."

Both laughed.

There was truth within his jest. For the first time in his life he was being seen for his skills and he was being respected for them. Nobody here cared about his blood.
For the first time, Perigoss wondered if there was a life to be made outside of Oibalox.

"Oh, did you pass Boroca or Tik on the way in?" Xali asked, Perigoss shook his head. "Then you have not heard the latest news."

"Which is that?"

"We are shipping out tomorrow," Xali said quickly. Perigoss froze mid bite, disbelief crossing his face. "And I have yet to mention the most stunning tidbit." She teased. "Each phalanx is led by a brigadier and that rank is held by experienced mythlings."

"To whom are we being assigned to?" Perigoss asked. He put down his utensils, not wanting to choke on what would obviously be, based on the build up, surprising news.

"Diomestor the Battlebrand."

"By…the…gods," Perigoss said. "I was not even aware that he had returned from his self-imposed exile."

"Apparently he returned about a month ago," Lysop explained. "Just in time if you ask me."

"We are marching under the Battlebrand," Perigoss repeated, not believing his own words.

"So you heard," a new voice said. Xali looked up to see a bald-headed boy sliding in beside them. His name was Nyreus and he was only seventeen years old. "My excitement is so great that I am twitching as fast as a lightning bolt."

"Figured the kid would be the most eager for the news," Xali teased. Everybody quickly laughed. Nyreus was a fanatic for the mythlings. He knew every rumour, story and legends and was always eager to learn more.

"No details of his exile are known," Nyreus said. "Perhaps there will be a chance for me to ask him about it."

"And perhaps, if there is time, we can get some war in as well," Lysop mocked.

Everybody laughed once more.

"If we march out tomorrow," Pergoss asked aloud, "do we know if the thief is marching with us?"

It had been two weeks since the thief made her sandpit

debut and she had become the talk of the camp. She was being called the Firekissed Thief, but she had rarely been seen since. Perigoss, alongside the rest of the volunteers, had been brutally training for the entirety of the past two weeks but in his spare moments, he could not help but have his mind wander to the woman. It was not her looks that enthralled him, although she was definitely a stunning woman. Instead, it was her personality that he found beguiling. She was charismatic, selfish and cunning. She had fought with trickery and guile. People like her were not common in Oibalox. There were always the selfish degenerates who put themselves above the polis, but they never lasted long in Oibalox. They either fled the polis like scared dogs or quickly perished. Those that fought alone, died alone because no shield was big enough to cover one's front and rear. Those that stood together and fought together, they were unbeatable. This was the Oibalox way. This was the way Perigoss had been raised. Obviously, Scyra had been raised in a vastly different manner, one that was directly in violation to his way of life. She was raised in a manner that should be repulsive to him.

So why could she not leave his thoughts?

Scrya reluctantly walked across the military base under the escort of her two guards. They were the same guards as usual - Myro and Tivar - but unlike before, they were no longer talking to each other. That was her doing. She had spotted the friction between them, centering on Myro's wife, and had decided to turn that small crack into a much bigger wedge, hoping their distraction would produce an opportunity for her to flee.

"Did you do as I suggested?" Scyra asked.

"I did," Myro admitted. "I went home and cooked for her two nights back."

"And, what did your maiden think?"

"She was grateful," he sheepishly admitted, a small blush growing on his cheeks. "She was very grateful. We had a wonderful night."

"And was she in a better mood when you visited last night?" Scrya asked Tivar.

"Stay the fuck away from my wife!" Myro snapped.

"She comes to me," Tivar defended. Both men stopped. Myro shoved his partner and Tivar returned in kind. Scyra smirked as she slowly crept away. Her escape came to a halt as a pair of hands each grabbed her from behind. She looked back over her shoulder and saw the two guards each standing over her, both now far more vexed at her than they were with each other.

"That was attempt number five." Myro said.

"It was far less original than your past idea," Tivar added. "Has the well of inspiration really dried up?"

"You two are both smart and observant men," Scrya said quickly. "How is it you two have not spotted the truth beneath the dilemma that is your wife?"

"Just keep walking," Tivar snarled.

"The problem behind the friction you two share is not due to your wife or her actions," Scrya said. "It is due to the unspoken feelings you each have for the other."

Both men froze. Myro turned bright red as Tivar refused to make eye contact. An awkward silence hung in the air. Scyra hid a smirk.

"I...I am happily married," Myro mumbled, uncertain even as he delivered his defensive argument. "I promised myself to one soul."

"A soul is often a fractured thing," Scrya continued, her tapestry of lies weaving together with each word she spoke. "Venodite says that a soul is only truly whole when two who are in love come together as one."

Venodite was the goddess of love. One had to be very careful when using such a name. Nobody wished to be shunned or punished by the love goddess and find their eternity to be lonely.

"Syceux has a similar thought," Scrya continued. Syceux was the god of nature and was often viewed as an eager suitor of the love goddess. "He speaks about how a tree is made up of three parts. It needs the sun, the rain and the soil. So if it takes three things to make a tree true and strong, why cannot the same be true for a marriage; for love? Perhaps the soul is not made up by two coming together to make one but instead the joining of three."

Myro stammered as he looked for a response but words did not come. Tovar began to nervously pace back and forth.

"Tivar," Scyra began, speaking softly. "No words are needed at this moment but I need you to take Myro's hands into your own." He opened his mouth to object but Scyra simply shook him off. "Take his hands into your own and then stare into his eyes. Myro will stare back and then each of you needs to silently ask yourself one question: Can I really live my life without him in it? Ask yourself that and you will truly know, in your heart, if your souls are meant to be joined as three."

Tivar did as he was instructed. He took his partner's hands into his own and both men looked deep into each other's eyes. Myro was enthralled by Tivar's hypnotic blues as Tivar was smitten by Myro's emerald globes. The moment was long and the rest of the world faded away. Nothing else mattered in that moment; not their duty, not the giants and not even the war. All that mattered was the man that currently stood before them. Myro nodded. It started out as a chin quiver and grew into a full skull movement. A tear formed in his eye. His answer was yes. He did not want to live another day without Tivar in it. Tivar smirked. Neither needed to say a word. Each knew that they both felt the same way.

"Thank you, Scyra," Tivar said without pulling his gaze from Myro. "I do not think we could have come to this realization without your help."

There was no response. Tivar turned his head to the side. Scyra was nowhere to be seen and Myro was missing a dagger.

Scyra bolted across the barracks, her feet moving as swiftly as they ever had before. She snuck behind a building and dropped into the shadows. Twisting her stolen dagger, she quickly cut the bindings on her wrist. Scyra tried to steady her breath as she readied her next sprint. She looked around. Nobody was looking for her, yet. In a few moments her lovebird guards would be on the search, but until then if she ran, she would draw unwanted attention. Instead, she had to blend in. Scyra stood up and slid the dagger in the back of her belt. She stepped away from the shadows and began to casually walk towards the town square. There, she could blend in with the crowd, lift some coins, purchase a seat on the first carriage out of town and vanish into the night. All she had to do first was escape the base.

Scrya saw a small group of volunteers walking and pulled in behind them, walking a step and half slower. She knew not who these four were but she did her best to blend in. The four volunteers were buzzing with excitement, muttering back and forth in half sentences. Scyra looked around. Everywhere her eyes fell upon was filled with a new sense of eagerness and fear. Something was going on and she needed to know what. Scyra caught up with the group of volunteers and leaned in.

"Have all of you heard the news?" She feigned excitement, mimicking their energy and returning it back at them. She had learned long ago that the best way to learn information from a stranger was to act like she already knew it.

"We have," one of them replied. "I cannot believe we're finally shipping out."

"Nearly everybody is shipping out," a second added. "This will be the largest Hakros offensive in…." his words trailed off into nothingness, that or Scyra stopped listening to him.

"And we will be meeting and coordinating up with the Oibalox forces as well," another said, just as eager. "This is monumental."

Scyra's mind raced. A few phalanxes had already been shipped over the past two weeks. They were sent out as an immediate defense against the giants' attacks but this was different. They were no longer simply defending against the giants, they were taking the war to them. Scyra needed to quickly get out of the polis. She pulled away from the group and moved to the base's entrance. Scyra paused when she saw Myro in the distance. She ducked inside the nearest building. She would have to wait here for a few minutes and then try to find a different exit.

The sudden sound of grunts and combat caused her to turn around. She spotted a trio of men. One was watching while the other two were sparring. On instinct, Scyra ducked into the shadows.

"Is this attempt number four?" a voice said suddenly. Scyra turned to see a form standing beside her, a form she recognized. This was Diomestor, the legendary mythling. Diomester was a tall man with a squared-jaw and a charismatic glimmer in his vale coloured eye. He had wavy clay-coloured hair and long bangs that seemed to continuously fall before his eyes. He gently brushed back his locks and hooked them behind his ear.

"Number six," she whispered. "How did you find me?"

"If I dare to speak the truth," he whispered back, "I was not even looking for you. I simply saw you as entered. It was only by chance I was even in this room."

Scrya did not believe in chance. Diomestor had been keen on her. He had come to visit her several times over the past two weeks. It was by his choice that she had not been assigned to the first phalanx being shipped out.

"I am quite glad you did choose this building, however," he said. His voice was soothing and smooth. It reminded her of a fine wine, pleasant to absorb. "It gives me a chance to inform you of our departure tomorrow."

"That detail is rippling across the base faster than a cold," she replied snidely. "Yet the information that I lack is why you find me so special."

"Look at those men as they spar," he said, pointing to the trio. She glanced over. One was a dark skinned man, with an impressive physique. He was the type of man who had more muscles then Scyra ever thought possible. She would be a liar if she said she held no jealousy for the sweat that rolled down his brown skin. The second was a myrmidon. The antman had a sandstone-coloured carapace. Its mandibles twitched as it traded blow after blow with the human. "They are Boroca and Tik. They are perfect warriors. They are the type of fighters that win battles but their kind will never win wars.

"Wars are won by those who can think. Soldiers like them can only ever see the battle ahead of them. They cannot see the angles, they cannot plan five steps ahead and because of that, they are destined to forever win while eternally losing."

Diomestor sadly shook his head. He looked back at Scyra and firmly poked her in the center of her forehead. "You, on the other hand, have a brilliant mind and a swift, capable body. You think with the capability of a philosopher but fight with the skill of a soldier. With you by my side, we can win this war and stop countless others from ending up dead in the dirt long before their time."

"I wish to not be in this war at all," Scyra said.

"The fates have decided differently for you," Diomestor explained. "You will fight in battle. What I offer you is the chance to not die as a nothing thief and instead do something meaningful."

Her mind raced. Diomestor was a charismatic man. His arctic blue eyes were complicated and cunning but beneath them was something honest, something pure. Whatever it was that pushed him forward was something primal, something that existed at his core.

That could be easy to exploit.

Scyra looked at the third man in the sparring circle. He was the silver haired warrior from the challenge circle:

Perigoss.

"What of him?" she asked.

"He is just a nobody," Diomestor said with a shrug. "He is one more soul that will end up dead on the dirt, one whose death you may help prevent."

"Your offer is lacking," Scyra said. "I am not one who concerns herself with the cares of others."

"Then how about coin?" Diomestor said sadly. He had hoped to appeal to her morals but coin would alway work. "I will offer you ten thousand coins to march with me in this war."

Scyra stared at the mythling. Ten thousand coins was a lot of money. She could take that money and vanish. She could be set for life. All she had to do was survive long enough to enjoy it.

"I will make you an offer," Scyra said. "If, by morning, I still exist within these barracks walls, I will join you but if escape is possible tonight, then I will leave and become one with the darkness."

"Seems fair," Diomestor said. He offered his hand. Scrya shook it. "Best of luck on your escape."

"Thank you." Scrya tried to break the shake but Diomestor's grip was too strong. She tried to pull free once more but with no luck. She looked up to see a cunning smile on Diomestor's face. She suddenly noticed wisps of ashen-coloured magic floating around. Diomester was casting a spell.

"Sweet dream, thief," Diomestor said as he gently tapped her on the side of her head. The wisps of magic flowed through his hand and into her skull, filling her mind with fatigue and exhaustion until everything went dark as her body went limp. Diomestor caught her body before it hit the ground.

CHAPTER SIX

Those who fear defeat have already lost.
- Oibalox Commandment

The air rippled with the sounds of boots on dirt. Each step was echoed by the hundreds of identical ones behind it. To most, this echoing march would be unsettling but to Commander Aidox, it was comforting. The gigas commander had marched in such a formation many times in his life, mostly in skirmishes and small battles between clans. Never before had he marched in such a grand army. His kin rarely lived past forty years old, he himself was well into his thirties, but in his life there had never been a grand army such as this. Aidox had proven his skill against gigas and giants alike. He had proved his skills in war against men but only low ranking men and rulers of small phalanxes. An invasion like this would force the greatest of warriors and the most cunning of commanders onto the battlefield. He would finally prove his strength against them all. He would rip them apart, one by one, until they begged for mercy from him. Then he would deny them even that.

The age of men would come to an end and their blood would water the field for a new age to grow.

The best part would be the death of the human tongue. It was a vile, simplistic language that felt like bile in the gigas' mouth, unlike that of the refined giant tongue. Contrary to the words spoken by satyrs, minotaurs or even nymphs, each of which had been learned and spoken by man, the language of the giants was a closely guarded secret. Giants did not teach it to mortals and especially not to men. Giants did not trust men, they despised them, and would not have their eloquent language sullied by the pink tongues of men.

"Harpies!" The call came from Foricu. She was a female gigas; a brutal woman and one of his fiercest fighters. She had blue tribal tattoos surrounding her eyes, and black ink running up and down her arms. Her head was shaved smooth save for the top, where her hickory-coloured hair was formed into a series of twelve dreads that ran the entire length of her back. One dread had been stained cherry red while another arctic blue. With each victory, she would stain another.

The warning rippled across the battalion. The marching men and women came to a halt as weapons were swiftly drawn and shields raised. Aidox glanced up at a dozen winged-women circling in the air. A scar on his chest suddenly flared in phantom pain, the echo of a past injury. Aidox reached up and touched his grey-skinned chest. Long ago, in the early days of his war history, he had been gravely wounded by a harpy, her talons tearing open his chest. He had walked to the gates of the underworld and spoken to Charon, the ferryman himself. It was only by the gods' blessing that he did not board that ferry, instead returning to the land of the living. Since that day. Aidox did not like or trust a harpy. These screeching winged-women were brutal and ferocious but had a brain only slightly more evolved than that of a beast. Yet despite his distrust, they were allies, having joined the great giant army.

Two gigas guards stepped up beside Aidox as a trio of harpies landed before him, the remainder circling above. A small eagle landed on the shoulder of the leader, joining her as she walked forward.

"Commander Aidox?" She asked, her voice carrying a faint screech as she spoke.

"Warwing Xarica," He replied, adding a small growl of his own. "We are honoured to have your numbers joining us."

"We hunger for flesh and battle," she replied. "Give us man-flesh or give us your own."

Aidox growled. Harpies would not dare to make such a threat against the giant battalions but still spoke that way to him. It took every ounce of restraint he had not to rip her apart where she stood.

"My kind will not be touched by yours," he growled. "If you obey my commands, I will grant you a great feast of man-flesh."

The trio of harpies screeched at one another for several seconds before replying. "So be it."

"Then ready your wings and your talons," he growled. "We strike at Pylomia."

Stellia, daughter of Stelios, gripped her doru spear in one hand and her aspis shield in the other. She nervously checked her grip on both, over and over, as she waited, standing in rank and file at the edge of Pylomia village. Her brothers and sisters in war stood on either side of her. Scouts had seen the gigas approaching the small village but there was no way they would succeed. She and the rest of her phalanx would not allow it. They were Oibalox soldiers and they would not accept defeat.

Pylomia was a small, walled village within the reach of Oibalox. It was a farming community but held a nice temple of Cydomea within its fame. It was on the edge of the polis' reach, sitting on the outskirts of the land of men. What few giant attacks it suffered came from the hungry or the bored. Farmers knew how to defend themselves but this was something far greater. Oracles sung of Pylomia's doom. Luckily, Stellia was never one for the insane rantings of an oracle.

Stellia was a young woman with rosewood hair and sun-bleached skin. Her eyes were vibrant and sparkled with a fuschia colour. She was raised to fight and to defend.

Their commanding officer, Lokhagos Mericoi, marched back and forth before them. His hands held weapons identical to each and every hoplite before him. His voice boomed as he spoke.

"These giants have seen fit to march upon us. They wish to crush us beneath their feet and march past us. To them, we are little more than the first stop in an invasion. I say no. I say not this day!" His voice echoed across the phalanx, heard by each man and woman who carried a spear. "I say we turn them away and send them back from whence they came. I say we stand firm and end their invasion before it even begins!"

The soldiers exploded in cheers and cries. They felt invincible and honestly, Stellia felt it as well. They stood at the edge of Pylomia, ready to turn away the gigas and giants. They were the Oibalox Army, the most feared collection of soldiers the world round. Nothing as pitiful as giants were going to stop them.

The cheers went on until the gigas battalion suddenly came into view. They were spotted in the distance, as howls began to echo across the air. Mericoi retreated to the phalanx, standing beside his men. Suddenly, an unexpected sound rippled across the horizon. The sound of flapping wings began to grow as darkness filled the sky. Stellia squinted at first but her eyes went wide as she realized what they were: harpies. Hundreds of winged-creatures filled the sky, their sheer numbers briefly blocking the sun.

This was not Stellia's first battle, far from it. She was an Oibalox soldier, born into battle and raised for it. Stelia held a spear before she could learn to crawl. She was trained in pankration before she could walk and she would sing the paeans - the hymns of war - before she could talk. Yet despite all of that, she would be lying to herself if she did not admit that fear still had the ability to creep into her mind before a battle.

Mericoi barked and the phalanx went silent. A few heartbeats later and singing began. It started in the rear and moved upwards until it reached the front ranks as a roar, like a wave crashing on the shore. The first stage of any battle was the paean. Their lyrics could be heard across the phalanx and throughout the village. Any nervousness that Stellia once held swiftly melted away. Mericoi stood on the frontline, singing as loudly as any man or woman beside him. She was not surprised to see him on the front. Mericoi would often say that it was a lokhagos' duty to lead his troops. He was the first one on the battlefield and the last to leave. A lokhagos did not leave until every member of his phalanx did.

The gigas charged across the fields, roaring as they approached, while the harpies began to soar towards them.

"By the gods," Stellia prayed. "Cydomea, watch over us."

"Ephodos!" Mericoi yelled. The singing came to a halt. "Shields!"

The front lines held their shields in front of them, readying them for the frontal attacks, while the lines further back hoisted their shields upwards, prepared to defend against the aerial attack. The roars and footsteps of the gigas got louder as they approached, until the sound was so thunderous that it eradicated all sound around it.

"Krousis!" The soldiers braced for impact as shield slammed into shield. Steel met steel with a loud clang, one that was deafening. For a brief second, all sound seemed to fade away, leaving only a ringing in Stellia's ears. Suddenly the weight from above drastically increased as the harpies dove down from above, their talons slashing at the shields before flying back upwards. The ringing began to fade, allowing noise to return just as Mericoi cried out once more.

"Doratismos!"

At the Lokhagos' command, spears leapt to action. From behind the shields, spears rapidly thrust outwards. The front lines thrusted horizontally, aiming for the gigas, while the ranks behind them thrusted upwards, desperate to take out the aerial threat. Stellia thrust her spear upwards and suddenly felt the resistance that came from harpy flesh. She pulled the spear free only to feel the weight of a body crashing down on her shield. She tipped her aspis and let the harpy fall to the ground. Two soldiers were instantly on the harpy, their swords running through the beast to confirm the kill.

"Spear!"

Stellia turned to the front. Mericoi's spear was stuck in the shield of a gigas. She handed her weapon forwards. The frontline always needed them more since it was their job to poke and prod with the spears. A prod could force an enemy out of formation, open them to an attack from an ally or even find a break in the phalanx. All it took was one solid break in the formation and the phalanx would fall. Then they could overrun the enemy and slaughter them.

Stellia peeked out from behind her shield. The harpies were still circling, flying down to strike them. Her eyes narrowed as she spotted one, circling like the others but her screechings seemed to have command behind it.

"Javelin!" Stellia called out. A heartbeat later the wooden projectile was placed in her hand. She arched back and flung it. The weapon cut through the air and dove into the harpy's chest. It let out a gurgled screech of pain as it tried to flee.

"Another." A replacement was handed to her and thrown just as swiftly. The second javelin hit the same harpy, only this time in its back. This time the harpy fell.

A cry of pain caught Stellia's attention. One of the frontmen had a spear run through his leg. Despite his injury, the man would not fall. No soldier wanted to be the one to let their phalanx fall. Stellia called out for a replacement and within seconds a female hoplite was there to replace him as two more men pulled the injured hoplite to the rear.
A confident smirk crossed Stellia's face. They were not going to fall on this day.

Aidox smirked to himself. The human phalanx was about to fall. They were resilient warriors but victory was not to be with them this day. Aidox knew of the Oibalox phalanx. He knew of their strength and of their incredible weaknesses. His first thought would have been to flank them but the Lokhagos had placed his phalanx at the walled village's entrance. Instead, he would have to exploit the gigas' strength. The Lokhagos was trying to break the gigas formation with their spear thrusts. He was desperate to avoid the othismos stage of battle. That was where the conflict came down to shield pushing against shield. That was where the gigas strength would prove superior.

Aidox waved and a harpy swooped down to meet him. Xarica screeched. "The archers on the wall are picking us off. My brood is losing numbers and yours seem unharmed. Your tactics are failing."

"Do not question me in the middle of a battle, Warwing," he growled. "Begin the bombardment of stones and then retreat to the air."

Xarica screeched in excitement as she took to the air. Within moments he saw the torrent of stones raining down on the phalanx. Few stones found their mark. The stones, each no bigger than a man's head, simply bounced off a shield and fell to the ground. Like a mistimed collection of drummers, the sound was a chaotic mess of thuds and clangs. Aidox smirked as he picked up his shield and marched towards the battle. Now was the time to prove both his might and his tactical genius.

He had subtly rotated his frontline out, replacing each with his strongest soldiers. Then, at his command, he ordered a push. The strongest gigas all shoved at once and the men found themselves several paces behind where they once stood. Aidox called out once more and the gigas pushed again. Once more the men tried to withstand their shove but lacked the strength. Yet again, they found themselves several paces behind where they once stood. Aidox called out again and again, each command resulting in yet another push that forced the men back. Aidox knew he could not find victory on pushes alone, in fact they could as easily cost him a defeat. His victory would instead come from the stones.

An Oibalox phalanx - or any formed by men - had two distinct weaknesses. The first was the flank. A phalanx was so set on keeping its frontline up that it often left its rear and side vulnerable. The second was footing. Keeping the frontline set and firm required solid dirt onto which you plant your feet. The harpies' barrage of stones were never intended to fell or kill an enemy. They were intended to make the ground uneven and hazardous. When the gigas' pushes forced them back, they were unable to check for footing. They would be unable to get secure ground and it would only be a matter of time before they started falling.

The first was a young human, barely out of adolescence and yet somehow still able to hold a spear. He stumbled backwards, forced out of position by the push, and when he went to place his foot in the dirt, he found only a stone. Suddenly his feet kicked out from beneath him and his arms flailed as he fell. On instinct he grabbed an ally, desperate not to fall, and accidentally pulled them down with him. The gigas pushed again and the situation grew more dire. Unable to reset, the next line looked for solid ground, instead they found a tripped kid. They attempted to step over the kid, stumbling until they too fell. One after another, the hoplites tripped and fell until a pair of shields on the frontline fell with them.

The phalanx had been broken.

Aidox raised his spear in the air, let out a roar, and charged.

Pararrhexis was when the opposing phalanx's formation shattered and the frontline had been breached. This was when combat became a skirmish of slaughter. Stellia longed for Pararrhexis, every hoplite did, but only when they were the ones doing the breaching. Seeing the gigas plow through their frontline was a frightening sight. They towered over men, standing nearly eight feet tall, with a roar that robbed her of all bravery. Worst still, seeing that while knocked down and their backs in the dirt made the horrific sight even more frightening.

Stellia glanced up to see a gigas descending on her. His axe raised high as he readied to strike. With barely a heartbeat to think, she rolled to the side, barely dodging the strike. She rolled to her knees and swiftly drew her gladius, thrusting and stabbing deep into the gigas' leg. He roared in pain as he dropped to one knee. Stellia leapt to her feet and punched with her shield. The edge of the apis, now aligned with the gigas' face, dove into its neck. He gasped for air, desperate to breathe, but never got the chance. Stellia's gladius dove into the side of its skull, ending its life.

Stellia's ears caught the sound of screeching and she spun around. She raised her shield just as a diving harpy slammed into it. The blow sent her stumbling back but this time she did not fall. The harpy flapped its wings as it tried to climb back into the air. Stellia charged forward, taking a leaping strike with her blade. The gladius' edge caught only her wing but it slowed her ascent. The harpy lashed out with its taloned feet, desperate to keep her away, but Stellia was not so easily halted. She slashed again, this time running the blade diagonally across the screeching beast's chest. The slash was deep and the harpy fell to the ground. Stellia leapt over the twitching and screeching body as she looked for an ally in trouble. All around, her brothers and sisters in the phalanx were fighting for their lives and many were failing. The gigas' axes and hammers were devastating attacks. A shield could block one strike but not without consequences. Most shields broke and those that did not, the arms that carried them did.

Stellia's eyes fell upon Mericoi. The lokhagos held his spear in both hands, his broken shield long since discarded. His doru was a spinning blur as he fought. He would run the point through the leg of one gigas before burying it in the neck of another. With speed and grace he would pluck a flying harpy from the sky, forcing it to the ground to die. He rushed from soldier to soldier, helping those he could save to their feet while ordering a retreat. The lokhagos knew they had been defeated, he knew they now had to flee. The priority had become about getting as many of his men to safety as possible. The more her eyes saw, the more Stellia was reminded of how seasoned her lokhagos was. Not only was his skill with the doru beyond approach, he was also veteran enough to know when the battle was lost.

Aidox roared in victorious glee. He had breached the walls of Pylomia and the town would fall, not even the gods could stop that now. All that was left was cutting down what little opposition remained. Aidox cleaved his axe through a charging hoplite's torso. He turned as a second soldier rushed towards him. A forward kick connected with the soldier's chest and sent them flying backwards, skipping across the ground like a stone. These men and women of Oibalox were not even close to a challenge. They possessed as much threat as that of an insect.

Aidox smashed another hoplite with a backhanded swing of his shield. The body hit the dirt with a thud. The gigas slammed his foot down on the soldier's neck, killing them with a sickening snap. He kicked the dead body aside with a sinister smirk. His eyes scanned the battlefield until they fell upon the lokhagos. The leader stood in the middle of the battlefield, ordering his spears to flee. Aidox hoisted his shield and moved towards the man. Mericoi saw him approaching and pivoted towards him. He repeatedly thrust his spear at the gigas but Aidox swiftly raised his shield to block.

"Are you the best that Man has to offer?" Aidox snarled. Mericoi lunged forward, dodging Aidox's swinging axe as he attacked again. Aidox twisted to the side and watched as the spear blew past him. "I find you lacking."

Aidox swung with his axe as Mericoi dodged over and over, each attack in succession missing him by less and less.

"I am Lokhagos Mericoi," he yelled. "I have slayed gorgons, minotaurs and even cyclops. For the honour of Oibalox, I will not fall this day."

Mericoi's spear began to glow, a faint ember-coloured magic emitting from the head. The speed of his thrusts suddenly grew, the weapon becoming a blur. Aidox pulled his shield up to defend but it lacked the size required to protect all of him. Mericoi's spear dove in Aidox over and over, ripping into the gigas' flesh. First it ripped into his axe-hand, then his leg. A dozen lightning fast strikes assaulted the gigas, each ripping tiny bits of flesh from the giantkin. None were ever enough to seriously injure but in combination they were sufficient to force Aidox to his knees, his shield dropping beside the fallen axe.

"This war may not end here," Mericoi yelled as he pulled back for a final, powerful thrust. "But you will not see another battle after this."

Mericoi had the utmost faith in his spear. It was blessed by the goddess of war and blessed with powerful magic. It had seen him through many battles and guided him to victory over and over. His spear had never failed him before, it was not about to fail him now. With the spear aimed at Aidox's head, Mericoi put every remaining ounce of strength and magic into the attack. He thrusted with blinding speed, knowing his aim to be true.

Aidox's hand leapt up and grabbed the shaft, the tip of the spear stopping only a hair's width away from his skull. The gigas' face grew a sinister smirk as an unsettling chuckle emerged. With a sudden twist of his wrist, the spear snapped.

Mericoi stared in disbelief. His magical spear had been broken. He had not thought that possible. Aidox's free hand punched forward, slamming into Mericoi's chest. A loud crack filled the air as the lokhagos flew backwards, stopping only when he collided with a wall and dropped to the ground. Mericoi tried to speak, to stutter out a response, but nothing came. He tried to move, to urge his legs to flee, but no strength was found. He just lay on the ground, broken in body and mind. Aidox returned to his feet and marched forward, holding the broken spearhead in one hand like a dagger.

"The end of your kind begins this day," Aidox said calmly. "This is not some simple raid; this is a crusade. We will march on your world this day and then we invade the realm of the gods on the next. We will not end until all gods, in all realms, are wiped from the face of reality. This is the mission bred into each and every drop of gigas blood." Aidox gently pressed his foot on Mericoi's neck. "When you reach the underworld and finally lay eyes upon your goddess, I need you to give her a message for me." He leaned in and spoke in an ominous tone. "Tell her she will need far greater warriors than you if she ever intends to survive."

Aidox pushed down with his foot, stopping only when he heard a satisfying crack.

Stellia tried to scream but there was no air in her lungs. She just stared in horror, letting the shock quickly morph into an unbridled rage, burning her skin from within. She grabbed a doru spear, discarded or dropped by a hoplite, and ran. The rage and sorrow fueling her, the tears in her eyes blinding her to everything except Aidox. One strike was all she was going to get but that was all she needed. She had slain other gigas this day, she just needed one more. She ran over the body of a fallen gigas and leapt into the air, her voice finally returning as she flew in the air. She screamed as she descended towards him, her spear aimed at his back.

Aidox spun around and slapped the spear to the side as he stabbed with the broken head. What air Stellia was left in her body vanished as the spearhead ripped through her armour and into her chest. Everything seemed to stop and time grinded to a halt. The noise of the battle, clashing weapons and screaming townsfolk, faded away until her own heartbeat, weakening with each thud, was all she could hear. She hung in the air, held there by the gigas' tremendous strength. He pulled her in so close that all he had to do was whisper.

"Whomever you are," he malevolently whispered, "know that with my victory I have taken your honour and that of Oibalox."

Aidox laughed as he tossed her aside, her corpse nothing more than a forgotten soldier.

CHAPTER SEVEN

It is a bold task to end a life that a god created.
- Castlex Proverb

Dozens of men and women silently walked towards the river. They moved without sound; their footsteps were like those of a deer moving gracefully across a forest without disturbing the ground beneath them. Each moved to the large boat that waited at the river's edge. Behind them was pain, suffering and the war. Ahead of them was peace and safety. All they had to do was cross the river on the ferryman's boat.

Stellia looked around. Dozens of familiar faces marched alongside her. Some were the brothers and sisters that she had fought with while others were the villagers she had defended. As she looked even further, she noticed faces she did not recognize and even some gigas walking with her. Stellia paused. Where was she?

Mericoi suddenly caught her eyes. He was standing by the dock, waving her over. She jogged over, nervously keeping her eyes on the gigas that marched behind her. Mericoi smiled as she arrived. She blinked in surprise. His neck was not broken. In fact, his body had no wounds of any kind. She looked down at her chest, there were no wounds on her body either. What was going on?

"You made it," Mericoi said. "I have yet to decide if

that is a good thing or not."

"Wh…where are we?" She stammered. Flashes of the battle assaulted her mind. The image of Aidox stabbing her repeated over and over. "I…I was stabbed. I had a hole run through my chest. I….I…." her voice trailed off as Mericoi placed his hand on her shoulder.

"You did well, Stellia," he said calmly. "You brought the highest honour to your family."

The highest honour? There was only one way for anybody from Oibaiox to achieve that. She looked around once more, eyeing the approaching gigas. She recognized him. She had run her blade through his skull. She had killed him and yet he stood before her. That was impossible…unless……

Mericoi pointed to a barge, floating towards the dock. A hooded man, dressed in long back robes gracefully steered it. Mericoi smiled.

"It's time to go. Elysium awaits us. Those images in your mind will cease the moment we ride the ferry." He reached into his chiton and withdrew a pair of coins hanging around his neck. Stellia did the same, pulling out two coins of her own. "This is the last batch of my soldiers. We can all cross over now."

"You waited for us, sir?"

"I am always the first one on the battlefield and the last to leave," Mericoi explained. "A lokhagos does not leave until every member of his phalanx does."

Stellia smiled and nodded. There was something soothing about what her commander had just done. Even in the afterlife, he was duty bound to look after his troops.

The barge pulled up alongside the docks and a hollow bell rang throughout the air. It was a deep sound that Stellia had never heard before yet somehow it sounded familiar and she instantly knew what it meant. It was time to board Charon's ferry.

Stellia stared at the river. The river styx was black water, void of light. It was a corrupted river, filled with necrotic magic and all of the souls who were foolish enough to try and swim it. Their hands still shot up, desperate to grab anything they could use as a hand hold to free themselves.

A sudden splash of water caught Stellia's attention. She blinked in surprise as two lampads emerged from the river styx. Lampads were a breed of nymphs that served Haluta, goddess of death, and the rest of the underworld. They were stunning looking women, with obsidian skin and wine coloured hair that wrapped around their lithe bodies.

Nothing escaped the River Styx except for lampads.

Each woman carried a handheld lamp that, despite dripping with the water styx, did not seem to extinguish. The lamp light flicked across the land, surprisingly strong for such a small lamp, and when it caught the lampad's hair, each strand seemed to glisten a plum purple. One by one, each of the departed lined up. They approached the ship, handed Charon their two coins and were escorted aboard by one of the lampads. Stellia watched as everybody boarded; soldiers and civilians, male and female, man and gigas. When it was her turn, she stepped up but was stopped by a wet hand. Stellia looked at the lampad as she shook her head.

"This is not your time, Stellia, daughter of Stelios." She spoke softly, her words were like the echoes of musical notes, dying in the distance and consumed by the shadows.

"Kelaria," a hollow voice asked suddenly. "What are you doing?"

"I apologize, Lord Charon," she defended. "But a spark of life still exists in this one. Her body yet lives."

"The soul has moved on while the body remains," he repeated. "Separation exists for a reason. Her body will have a duty to fulfill on its own."

"My lord," Kelaria pleaded. "You mustn't."

"Because you are special does not allow for you to make others as such," he ordered. "Now do what is required of you."

"I…I…" The lampad's voice trailed off and she stood still. For several long moments she pondered. Then, she definitely shook her head. "I will not do as you say, Lord Charon. I will do what is required of me."

She turned back to Stellia and slammed her palm into the dead soldier's chest. A glow of black, necrotic energy moved from Kelaria into Stellia. The lampad began to speak quickly. She spoke faster than Stellia had ever seen a mortal do but somehow she clearly understood each word the underworld creature spoke.

"Find your body and return to it. Your task is not yet complete. You need to stop the betrayer." The underworld around her started to violently ripple and shake as a force from behind her desperately tried to pull her away from the barge. It was like a cosmic line was tied around her waist so she could find her way back through the labyrinth of life and it was reeling her in.

"I need you to find someone," Kelaria frantically said. "When his mind is ready, I need you to give him this message."

Pain ripped through her chest. It was so great that it forced Stellia awake. The woman screamed as consciousness returned to her. She opened her eyes and breathed deeply, regretting both actions the moment they occurred. The bright sun burned her eyes and the breath caused agony in her chest. She put her hands on the ground and pushed herself to her knees. As soon as she could, her hands immediately went to her chest. She frantically pulled off her damaged cuirass and pat her body. She was searching for the spear wound but none was found. She pulled open her chiton and looked down. A weird scar weaved between her breasts. As she delicately ran her fingers over the scar, a weird spark of magic rippled from it.

What the hell had happened to her?

Stellia racked her brain as she searched for an answer. She remembered being stabbed and then…nothing. Next thing she knew, she had woken up here, on the dirt. Yet her brain felt cumbersome and hazy, like the morning after a night of heavy drinking. There was much in her memory that she could not access and it was frustrating.

Stellia sighed and climbed to her feet, ignoring the agony in her limbs as she did so. She looked around. Pylomia was decimated. Buildings burned before her, bodies were scattered and there was not a soul, man or otherwise, to be seen. Pillars of green smoke hovered above the decimated town. The gigas had razed the village and had moved on. Stellia shook her head, not allowing herself to dwell on this loss. She needed to leave and it needed to be quickly. She needed to find her allies and warn them of what was coming. Oibalox had no clue of the gigas' true strength, let alone that of the giants. She grabbed her cuirass and frowned. With the large hole in the chest, the armour was useless. She tossed it aside, pausing to look at the corpses that lay on the ground and dropped to one knee.

"Cydomea," she prayed out loud. "Please forgive me for what I'm about to do."

Stellia walked from corpse to corpse, each a fallen member of her phalanx, and took their equipment. She took a gladius from one, a shield from another, a doru spear from a third and blood-stained cuirass from a fourth. There was great honour to be buried with your spear and shield but Stellia was robbing them of that and she would eventually be punished for it. However, that was something she would deal with later. Right now, she had to save as many souls as possible or there would be no one left. She moved to the village's exit but paused, something was not letting her depart. She turned around and found her eyes falling upon the spearhead that had caused her near-end: the remnant of Mericoi's broken spear. Despite her attempts to ignore the weapon that almost killed her, Stellia found her attention being drawn to it. Like a beating heart, it seemed to pulse with magic, over and over until she relented. Stellia walked over and picked it up. The spear head - and the tiny portion of the shaft still attached to it, was bigger than a dagger but smaller than a shortsword. For the first time, she got to actually examine the magical weapon. The spearhead was not made from a metal of any type. It was a talon, a claw from some unknown beast. Stellia rolled her eyes as she attached it to her belt. She did not want this weapon but it seemed to want her. Now was not the time to argue with an inanimate object, especially since it looked like she was losing. She had to warn the others and she did not know how long she had been unconscious for. Using her doru for support, Stellia exited the walled village and started her long walk.

Blaze General Vulcos heard the sound of his name and looked up from his desk. He had been reading reports and comparing them to his maps. He nodded as a steward walked into his tent.

"Blaze General," the caculis said. "I have more reports for you."

Vulcan nodded and pointed to the pile beside him. The steward gently placed them on top. As the steward left, a second giant came in. This was a thosa, a race of giants that lived in the vast sand-filled deserts. They were a giantkin lineage that were adept with blades and spells.

"What can I do for you, Brigadier Nezzor?" Vulcan asked, tired and impatiently.

"Pylomia has fallen as expected," he calmly informed. "The gigas eagerly raided the town and the temple."

"I would be very surprised if they had not," Vulcan curtly replied. "Why does this information require a hand delivery?"

"I know the gigas make up a crucial number of our forces but I have concerns," Nezzor explained. "They are skilled and brutal warriors but I wonder about their allegiance. Commander Aidox is dangerous."

"I certainly hope so," Vulcos said.

"Not like that, General," Nezzor explained. "They… they cannot be controlled. They fight alongside us solely because it benefits them. Once that ends, they will turn on us."

"That is a challenge for another day," Vulcos said. "In the meantime, we become the bow and we use them as the arrow. We will aim them towards the poiles and watch the destruction."

Nezzor hid his scowl. He despised the gigas. They were dishonourable warriors and lesser giants. They were not to be trusted, in any form.

"I will pair them with the giants moving on Oibalox."

"You will do no such thing, Brigadier," Vulcos said sternly. "The caculis will be leading the march on Oibalox with their forces. Assign Aidox's troops to the march on Hakros."

"You assign them to my invasion?"

"I do," Vulcos said, finally looking up from his desk. "The MythKing and his forces are dangerous and numerous. You will need every available blade and spear in order to slay the MythKing."

Nezzor let out a small growl. He did not need their numbers. His troops were sufficient enough to achieve victory.

"Your ego has been wounded. I understand this, but think this not as an insult, Brigadier," Vulcos explained. "This victory is too crucial to allow pride to get in the way. We cannot take any chances with this invasion."

"Of course, General."

"And if, by some chance, the fates decide that Aidox will not survive the battle," Vulcos said with a sinister grin. "Then all the better."

Nezzor smirked, eagerly nodding in agreement.

"Firstly, secure Ogre's Path and One-Eyed Way. Those points will be crucial for our flanking."

CHAPTER EIGHT

Old Men declare wars but it is the young that fight them.
- Athonea Proverb

"Formation: halt," Diomestor barked. The marching troops came to a stop along the forest road. He looked up at the late afternoon sky, the sun well into the western sky. "Our march ends here for the day. Domos: front and center."

"Sir," Domos said.

"Get me a couple sentries to stand watch as we set up camp," Diomestor ordered. "I also want a couple scouts doing the rounds. Feed them first and send them out."

The minotaur grunted in understanding. He turned away and walked down the line, pausing by Tik. "How are those legs of yours?"

"My legs function properly, sir," the myrmidon clicked. It was often said that the ant-folk talked peculiarly, unnatural to that of mankind. In truth, their bodies were not built in the same fashion. Their own language was a series of clicks. They struggled to speak with the same flow as others, often finding solace and comfort in proper word choice over the complications that were slang.

"Good, take Nyreus and get a bite to eat. I want you two on scout duty."

"I will accomplish that task as requested." Tik grabbed

the kid and pulled him from the line.

"The rest of you," Domos roared. "Break and make camp. We are done for the day and sleeping here for the night."

"Oh joy of joys," Scrya said sarcastically.

Scyra could not decide which she loathed more: marching or sleeping outdoors. Marching was endless walking that ended up with sore legs and tired feet. Worst still, somebody always started singing during a march and they were never the ones who had the ability to do so. Outdoor sleeping, on the other hand, was disgusting for a woman of sophistication like herself. People wanted her to sleep in the uncomfortable dirt, soil her fine clothing and eat dried, tasteless rations. It was unbecoming.

Diomestor was so generous as to offer her the chance to spend the last four days doing both.

The lochos - or war band - of warriors had been marching every day since leaving Hakros and frankly, Scyra was tired of it. They were walking north, to the edge of the giantlands. These rocky plains, hill-filled lands and vast mountain ranges acted as the home to many of the giants.

When the giant-god war had come to an end, many punishments were given to the giants. Their leader, King Typhaon, had been locked in the underworld and the giants found themselves pushed from the lush lands of men. They fled into lands so harsh that even the gods dared not dwell. There they hid in the mountains, the deserts and the snowy tundras. These lands were harsh and unforgiving, killing many of the unprepared giants, but those that did survive had just grown stronger. As the giants began their invasion of Hakros, they would have to cross Ogre's Path and One-Eyed Way. Hakros was sending troops to both in order to slow them down.

Rarus found a fallen log and sat down upon it, making loud sounds of relief as he took the pressure off of his legs. His breathing was heavy and laboured. Perigoss walked over.

"Are you going to survive the night, Master?" He asked of his priest. Rarus just rolled his eyes.

"Are you going to ask that same question every time we make camp?"

"For every time you make those dad noises, I will re-ask the question," Perigoss said as he took a seat beside him.

"Has anybody ever told you that you are an annoying shit?" Rarus laughed.

"Many people," Perigoss replied. "But none more than this old man who asked me to be his apprentice."

"How about we consider that request a senior moment and forget it ever happened?"

"Sadly, that is not an option," Perigoss laughed. "You are stuck with me."

"So this be my burden." Rarus laughed. He handed his bag to Perigoss. "Go set up our sleep accommodations. I demand a warm bed with a warmer man to join me in it, preferably one with strong knees, an eager mouth and a vigor that only comes with youth."

"How about cold dirt with the surrounding scent of sweaty soldiers?"

"It will have to suffice," Rarus said. "When you have completed that task, see if any of our marching men and women are injured."

"Yes, master."

Perigoss took both his bag and that of his master and walked away. Rarus watched him go. When the kid was distracted elsewhere, he closed his eyes and willed the magic from his staff alive. A small haze of lilac magic moved into his arm and travelled across his body. A sense of rejuvenation rippled across him and he began to breathe easier. He was ashamed to admit it but this march was harder on him than he had ever thought. The younger man he once was would have found this no challenge at all. His age, however, was doing its best to be known. He was relying on the healing magic in his staff more than he had ever expected to. Keeping him walking was not the intended use of the Staff of Last Breaths, but he was sure that Haluta would not mind too much.

As he watched Perigoss and the other young warriors, Rarus found his mind wandering. As a man of his age often did, he looked back at his past and the path he took to get where he was. Once he had been a feared warrior, a master of fencing and bringer of death to his enemies. Now he thought of himself as a master of magic and a healer. He was a protector of life and an escort of souls.

In the aftermath of a battle, when beasts and man lay dead all around him and he was one of the few survivors, his mind finally gave out. Gone was the desire to fight and slay. His desire for fame had suddenly evaporated. On that day, he hung up his weapons and walked away. He found love with a man named Neilo and took to a simpler life. The pair lived in a small village, days away from the polies. Decades passed and sickness hit. A plague swept his home and many died. Rarus spent weeks watching those from his village get weak until their bodies eventually gave way. The village had no healer or priest. Rarus did what he could, using his battlefield medicine, as primitive as it was, to aid where needed but those limited skills could only lessen the pain, never halt it.

Then the plague came for Neilo.

Rarus did everything he could but there was no cure. He cried to the gods and begged for aid but none could be found. When Neilo passed away, without a priest to give him last rights, Rarus prayed again. This time he prayed to Haluta, the goddess of death. He did not insult her by asking for her to relinquish his husband's soul. Instead, he asked for her to escort his partner's soul to the afterlife.

That was when she made herself known to him.

The faint mew of a cat was heard in the distance, rippling across the air until it appeared in his home. The feline, black as night with sparkling jade eyes, rubbed itself along his leg. Rarus pet the cat and fed it what little food he had. While the cat contently fed, a whisper emerged from the shadows. These were the words of the Death Goddess. She offered Rarus a new path in life, a new direction for his days. No longer was he to take life, instead he was to prevent death. Only those who cherished life could fully embrace the rewards of the underworld when it was their time. For those beyond saving and for those who were destined to pass on, it was his duty to guide them there.

This was to be Rarus' path. He was to become a death priest.

There was no honour or goodness that came from ending a life before its time, he had learned that the hard way. When the time came for his own soul to cross over, he would pay for the many sins of that nature he had committed. In the meantime, he wanted to make sure that Perigoss did not make the same errors as he. He refused to allow the kid to err in the same fashion he had.

War had the ability to bring out the worst in people; it would tug at the darkest part of each of them until they crossed a line from which they never could come back. Those would be the souls forever haunted by the actions they took during war. Rarus did not wish that on any soul and thought it his duty to teach them such.

He just wished that such a noble cause had required less walking. His legs were killing him. Worst still, he had to piss again.

Scyra reluctantly walked through the camp, a plate of food in her hand. Her eyes scanned the camp, watching as the light faded away, as she eyed a possible escape. It was a habit now, constantly looking for an exit, but she found herself lacking the motivation. Diomestor's words hung in her mind.

He is one more soul that will end up dead on the dirt, one you may help prevent.

The thought would not shake free. Scyra had lived her life caring only for herself and that was not shaping to change. She was here for the coin and nothing else. She had no guilt in her, not now and never again.

Seeing people chatting amongst themselves by the fire, Scyra walked over and plopped down beside Lypos, nodding to the triton. She shovelled souvlaki into her mouth as she looked around the fire and recognized a few faces amongst the dozen or so who sat there. She knew of Lypos and Xali and recognized the stunning form of Boroca. Her eyes fell upon the form of Perigoss and found her cheeks turning red. She quietly blessed the gods for the night sky to hide her embarrassment.

She did not know what it was about the silver-haired warrior that she found so appealing. It was not based on physical attraction. While he in no way had a poor physique, Boroca's chiseled body was far superior. Boroca was the type of man she would ride for a night or two before vanishing with their coin. She was the type of woman who rode so skilfully that it left men confused as to if they were eager to introduce her to their mothers or ashamed to and truthfully that was the way she liked it.

Perigoss, however, was something different. She knew next to nothing about the coinling but still found him enthralling. It was frustrating.

"Your love is so obvious." Boroca said loudly.

Wait, what? Scyra looked around in stunned panic. What was he talking about? Love? That was not possible. That was not…..was it really that obvious? She thought herself stealthier than that.

"Yeah," Xali said sheepishly. She placed her hand on the thigh of Nikka, the woman sitting beside her. Nikka had tawny beige skin and merigold-blonde hair. She had a great deal more muscles than any woman, or man, had any need for. She was the larger of the two women but still she seemed to lean on Xali's shoulder. "We were wed only a week before we enlisted."

"I was there," Lypos bragged.

"I knew not that you two were acquainted before this," Boroca said.

"We were not," the triton admitted. "Their marriage, however, was quite public."

Boroca raised an eyebrow in confusion. Xali just chuckled.

"We met at the Heklious Tourney," Xali admitted. The tournament was held every three years. It was named after the mythling known as Heklious, a man known for his legendary twelve labours. Unlike the Olympics, the Tourney focused solely on combat sports, the biggest draws were the fencing and unarmed fighting competitions. "We locked blades as opponents. With each strike we saw the truth of each other. By the time the battle had ended, Venodite had blessed us with love. We married at the Tourney's end."

"That was so romantic," Perigoss said. Xali grumbled an embarrassed, undecipherable response and thanked the gods that the darkness covered up her blush. "There is no greater binding of souls than the euphoric bliss that comes from combat."

Silence filled the air as everybody turned and looked at Perigoss. A few seconds later everybody burst out in laughter.

"If there was any remaining doubt that you hailed from Oibalox," Nikka laughed, "it has since faded away."

Perigoss smirked and thanked the gods that the darkness covered his blush of embarrassment. Since leaving home, he had learned how his cultural beliefs were viewed as near fanatical dogma. He disagreed, of course, but it still was a little embarrassing. The same, however, could be said for each polis' culture. Some mocked the do-nothing philosophers, the political priests with their insane declaration or the tree-loving druids. Each had their embarrassing elements.

"So I take it with a comment like that," Xali teased, "you do not have anyone romantic waiting for your return."

"I have no one," Perigoss admitted with a frown. He had no one, romantic or otherwise, waiting for him since his father's passing. His mother had passed away when he was young and his father had honorably died in battle just a few seasons past. What pain he had from being alone as a half-breed, he did his best to hide. The last thing he desired was pity from others.

"What about our fun-loving thief?" Xali asked, glancing in Scyra's direction. "Does she have a love?"

"Never for more than a night or two," Scyra responded. "Then I leave them with pleasant memories and longing for a repeat."

"Do you leave them with their coin?" Nikka gruffly asked. Everybody chuckled, including Scyra herself. A rustle of swords caught each of their attention. A dozen soldiers rushed out of the camp, weapons in hands. Nikka turned back to her fireside gathering. "What do you think that is about?"

"Another few eidolons perhaps?" Xali suggested.

Eidolons were spectres; returned souls from the underworld. While not a common occurrence, souls and bodies could return from the dead. If a soul returned without a body: they were eidolons. Ghostly warriors with the ability to flutter across a battlefield. The stronger the warrior before death, the stronger the eidolon after death. A more common occurrence were the adeiazo, a returned body without a soul. If a soul passed on before the body had, it could roam the world without a face, forever a soulless husk.

"Whose wisdom caused us to choose a haunted woods for our campground?" Boroca jested. The group laughed once more.

Scyra winced as she lethargically walked in the morning light. The sun was barely up in the sky and for some horrific reason, she was up and walking across the stone-filled, rocky terrain. It was a despicable treatment bordering on torturous. If there was a positive, it was that she was not marching, but she could see that blessing at such an early hour. Diomester had summoned her and a few others to join him as they scouted ahead. One-Eyed Pass was a road that came down from the mountains, crossed through a small valley before arriving in the Hakros farm lands. The giants would use this very path in their march. It was Diomester's job to stop them.

Scyra spotted Diomester in the distance. She yawned as she approached him. Her eyes narrowed as she saw ashencoloured wisps of magic swirling around the palm of his hand. They formed a still image of a woman. Scyra slowed her approach. The man was obviously casting a spell of some sort but she did not want to bother him.

"You've arrived," Diomester said as the wisps suddenly vanished. "Join me."

"If you insists," Scyra yawned.

"There," Diomester said as he brought Scyra and the scouts to his side. He pointed to a small valley path with rocky cliffs on either side. The valley had two entrances. One came from the mountain while the other was from Hakros territory. "We'll face them there."

Scyra found the nearest rock and plopped down upon it. She let out a loud yawn, too tired to take notice when a couple of soldiers approached Diomester and began chatting with him. One would point and mumble something as another would wave in disagreement before mumbling a response of their own. Scyra paid little attention because frankly, she had little care. She raised an eyebrow as she saw Nikka approach her.

"Thief," she mumbled.

"I have a name," Scyra yawned.

"I know," she replied as she sat down beside her. "But you have yet to earn it."

Scyra blinked in surprise recognition. She had not heard such talk in years. She had not heard of that since she had left her home, since she had left the seminary.

"You are from Castlex as well?" Scyra asked, finally fully awake. "For which god did you attend Ithoma?"

Castlex was a theocracy and the self-appointed religious center of the world. It was the home of the Consecrated Council, a ruling council made up of high priests from each of the twelve gods. One of highest honours that any citizen could achieve was to attend the Ithoma Seminary. It was a school for religious teaching, theology and combat. Those who graduated were great priests, powerful paladins and defenders of the realms. It was tradition in Ithoma that names had to be earned. Every student was a nameless squire until they had proven their piety.

Scyra enrolled in the seminary when she was a teenager. Unsurprisingly, she did not graduate.

Nikka frowned, not out of frustration or anger, but simply out of habit. Xali had often commented on her *resting glower* face. "I went as a student of Venodite."

Scyra blinked in surprise. This muscle bound warrioress was a disciple of the love goddess? Normally their kind were flamboyant, promiscuous dandies who adorned themselves in roses and fruit. They were the kind that chose only the finest quality clothing and the sweetest of food. Nikka, a strong, battle-forged woman who wore only the most practical of clothing and struggled with public displays of emotion, was the literal polar opposite.

"I remember you," Nikka said. "You were the church of Psophious' prize student."

"I think you have mistaken me for somebody else," Scyra yawned. "I am not the schooling type."

"The prized student rises to the top of the seminary both in fencing and theology. She was thought to ascend to the priestly studies," Nikka continued.

"The woman that you describe sounds nothing like myself," Scyra defended.

"Then one day, the prize student broke into the Seminary's library, pilfered their rarest tomes and scrolls. She then fled into the night, never to be seen again," Nikka explained. "She sold them to wealthy private collectors for large piles of gold.

"That…..may sound a little like me," Scyra nervously replied.

"She is currently one of only four people permanently banned by the Seminary," NIkka continued. "Ironically, she is the only one of the four with a bounty for retrieval and return."

"I'm…I mean…she is banned but they offered a bounty to bring her back?" Scyra said, sitting up. A scheme quickly began to brew in her mind. "How big is the bounty and what would you say to an alliance if I cut you in at twenty percent?"

"No, I would not bring you back for the bounty and then help you escape," Nikka said sternly. "Especially not for a measly twenty percent."

"You are on board," Scyra said with a smirk. "So all that remains is finding the correct percentage."

"So why did you do it?" Nikka asked, fighting the smirk on her face.

"Assuming the person of which you speak was in fact myself," Scyra began, "Then that person probably saw a truth from which she could not come back from."

"There was a lot of praise and hope being cast your way," Nikka explained. "We all knew who you were."

"Allegedly," Scyra quickly added.

"And if truth were to be the sole words that passed

through my lips," Nikka said, "then I would be remiss to say that some of us were relieved to hear of your departure. We were tired of being compared to your greatness."

"My greatness is pretty overwhelming," Scyra said with a chuckle.

"Allegedly," Nikka added. The pair chuckled together.

"Do you ever practice your studies?" Nikka asked. "Do you still train in the Seminary's fencing or casting?"

"Casting? Oh, not at all," Scyra chuckled. "I have barely even attempted a spell since my alleged departure. I doubt if I could remember how to summon any magic, assuming I still had the ability to do so." Nikka raised a dubious eyebrow but Scyra just shrugged.

"Scyra," Diomester called out. The thief looked up and saw the mythling calling her over. The thief climbed to her feet and walked over. "I need your opinion on the matter."

"You want a thief's thoughts?" Domos said in disgust.

"That I do," Diomester said with a smirk.

"Well, I think you are big, tall and obviously possess great strength," Scyra charismatically said. "But what you possess in god-like power, you lack in bathing. You have the stench of a swine, Domos."

"I mean your opinion on the field of battle," Diomester said, desperate to hide his laughter as Domos growled. He pointed to the valley-path. "What do you think?"

Scyra looked at the path and studied the rocky cliffs on either side. She took a long moment of thought. Tha pause gave her the illusion of wisdom and intellect but in truth it allowed her mind to wander. She glanced up at the birds fleeing from the mountains and wondered if there was a way for humans to fly. Could someone build a pair of wings that would allow them to take to the sky? But how would the feathers be held together? Wax was the first ingredient that came to mind.

"Well, what do you think?" Diomester asked. Scyra blinked. Her mind had wandered too far and she had gotten too distracted. "We plan to meet the marching cyclops at the valley's mountain mouth, preventing them from entering."

"The middle of One-Eyed Pass will allow you to force them into a smaller phalanx," she began. "But instead, why don't you meet them at the valley's Harkros mouth. That way you could put archers on the top of the rocky cliffs. They could pick off the giants before they get close."

"That is dirty fighting," Domos growled. "It would not show our strength, simply our cowardness."

"I prefer the term cunning," Scyra corrected.

"The giants will not fight with honour or fairness," Diomester said. "They are larger than us and possess the strength to match. We must find a way to even the fight."

"I will not sacrifice who I am simply to achieve victory," Domos growled.

"And I will not sacrifice any of you simply to maintain some illusion of honour or strength," Diomester said. "Your lives mean more than victory and honour. Do not be so ready to throw it away because Hakros wishes it."

Domos growled again as he glared at the thief. He was not fond of this thief. Where was her heroism?

"Domos: go back to grab and move the troops forward. We will hold the line here." Diomester said.

"If I may," Scyra said, a wicked grin forming across her lips. "A new idea has suddenly sprung to mind."

CHAPTER NINE

War provides no prize for second-best.
- Oibalox Commandment

The afternoon sun beat down upon the silent gathering of soldiers. Not a soul said a word and not a beast made a sound. There were no birds singing or bugs chattering. There was no tussle of the grass or whistle of the wind. There was just silence. It was like the earth itself knew of the battle that was coming and even it feared the outcome.

Scyra had never before been in a military phalanx on the cusp of a battle. She had never witnessed the chill that somehow existed, even under the midday sun, before a battle. The men and women of Diomester's command each sat silently, preparing both their minds and bodies for the battle that was about to come. Boroca stretched his muscles and readied his limbs. Lypos silently checked his gear and that of Nyreus'. The triton had taken it on himself to make sure that the kid's first battle would not be his last.

"Where is your dagger?" Lypos asked. Nyreus patted his belt but found nothing. He gave the triton a sheepish look. Lypos rolled his eyes and drew a small dagger. "This is a dagger from my home river. When my kind sets out, we take a piece of coral and fashion it into a dagger. Upon our return, we return the dagger from where it came." He handed the weapon to the kid. "I intend to do the same with this, so do not lose it."

Nyreus nodded as she carefully placed it on his belt. The kid let out a large breath before speaking. "I'm scared."

"As am I," Lypos calmly admitted. "My kind have a method to imbue courage and strength." He handed the kid a waterskin. Nyreus took a swig and violently coughed. What lay inside was not water but the strongest, vilest liquor head ever tasted. "That was for the courage."

"And the strength?"

Lypos began to sing. It was discordant singing but still sounded soulful. It was a triton song that brought hope to the kid and all others who heard it.

> *Talli-fah-ohh*
> *Nolla torum-nay*
> *The currents of our home*
> *Guide our path this day.*
> *Talli-sin-ohh*
> *Nolla Bokl-nay*
> *From a river to an ocean*
> *Growth will always find a way.*

Xali hummed along. She had never heard the song before yet somehow she knew all the words. She continued to hum as she checked her quiver of arrows and her bowstring, for what could easily be the hundredth time this afternoon. Beside her, Nikka knelt on one knee, her head bowed as she silently mumbled a prayer. Her hand began to emit a pink glow as she summoned forth her god's magic. Nikka was a champion and each champion could summon small amounts of magic to protect themselves and others. Nikka stole a glance up at her wife. Seeing Xali was distracted, Nikka reached up with her glowing hand and grabbed her wife's rear, seductively squeezing it. Xali looked back at the warrior and gave her a lusty look, thinking the grab was little more than a lecherous squeeze. Xali did not know that Nikka had sacrified her own arcane protection to give it to her. Xali gently grasped Nikka's head. She desperately wanted to feel the touch of her wife's lips but as she glanced down and saw that Nikka's head was at the exact height of Xali crotch, the archer had yet to decide exactly where she wanted to feel the touch of Nikka's lips. After a long moment, she reluctantly pulled Nikka to her feet, deciding to match Nikka's lips with her own.

As she watched, Scyra felt the pain of longing and regret. Not at the kiss - not completely at the kiss. It had been too long since she had felt the carnal touch from either gender. She felt the longing and regret from the spell. Scyra had lied to Nikka. She knew exactly how to cast a spell, she simply could not. Every day, for years on end, she tried to cast even the most basic of cantrips but with no success. Whatever blessing the gods once gave her, they no longer found her worthy. She was one of the scorn; those abandoned by all of the gods. Eventually, she stopped trying but the longing still remained. Casting magic was a feeling unlike any other. It felt fulfilling. It was like how a warm cup of tea warmed one's entire body on a cold, chilly night. The spell did the same but on a spiritual level. It was an assurance that the gods were watching out for you; that they cared about you. That assurance no longer existed for her.

Scyra glanced over at Perigoss. He was currently tying two coins to a cord which he then put around his neck.

Scyra shuffled closer.

"What is that?" she whispered.

"It's a brelok," he explained. "It is for our passage to the underworld."

Scyra gave him a confused look. Perigoss just smiled. He pulled two Oibalox coins. Their currency were octagon silver coins with a hole in the middle.

"In Oibalox, every man, woman and child is a soldier. Everything in our culture supports these soldiers, even our coins," Perigoss explained in a whisper, not wanting to disturb Lypos' song or everybody else's preparation. "When the time comes that any of us dies in battle, we want to greet Charon with the two coins needed to cross into the underworld. So our coins are minted in a way that they can be tied to a cord and worn as a necklace. We walk into battle wearing our keys to the underworld around our neck."

Scyra nodded in understanding. It seemed like either a grim look on battle or a complete acceptance of their fate. She was not sure which was healthier.

"Did you want one?" Perigoss asked suddenly. Scyra stammered for a few moments before simply nodding. Perigoss pulled a length of cord from his pack and began threading it between the two coins. Scyra watched closely, feeling a swelling in her chest as she did. Perigoss tied the cord into a knot and then tested its strength. Satisfied in its hold, he held the brelok in two hands and leaned forward. He reached over her head and draped it around her neck. As the tips of his pinky fingers gently ran down either side of her neck, Scyra felt a tingling sensation that made her skin shiver and the hairs on her head stand on end.

"Thank you," she whispered.

"Perigoss, to me." Perigoss looked over at Rarus and

nodded. He gave Scyra a smile before departing. He stopped before Rarus and raised an eyebrow. The priest simply frowned. "Are you ready for this fight?"

"I have been in a battle before, Master," Perigoss reminded him. Rarus just shook his head.

"This is different. It is not simply fighting bandits or monsters; this is war and this is a phalanx," Rarus explained. "This will be unlike anything you have ever experienced."

"The theory is still the same," Perigoss defended with an annoyed tone. "I protect those beside me with my life and kill anything that tries to stop us."

Perigoss suddenly felt the slap of Rarus' hand on the back of his head. The priest then grabbed the kid by the chin and turned him so their eyes met. Perigoss blinked in surprise as the look of sorrow and regret that hung on the priest's face.

"There is more to war than just killing," he said quietly. "There is more than just dying. You must never forget why you go to battle, why you fight and you must never forget who you are." Rarus released his chin. He took in a deep breath before speaking once more. "War is a vast ocean, dark as a moonless night and endless as the midnight sky. Each battle is a violent wave that rocks you further off course until you can no longer see the shore. Who you are is like a lighthouse, guiding your path so you can safely find your way home. Few who lose their way at sea are ever able to reach land again."

Perigoss stared at his mentor for a long, silent moment. He was not fully understanding Rarus. What did it mean to lose yourself in war? He was from Oibalox; he was built for war. Yet despite that, he would keep the priest's words close to his chest. There was a saying in Oibalox. Take to heart the words of an old soldier.

"On your feet," Domos loudly barked. "Grab your shields,

steady your feet and take your position. It is time for a fight."

As his giant feet walked down the mountain path, Captain Kruzza could not help but curse his fate. He hated the mountains and more importantly, he hated the idiot kin that lived in them. He was a thosa giant, one of the sand-dwelling kin, and he missed his desert. The mountains were windy and cold and, if he was being honest, the rocks hurt his feet. He missed the soft and warm sand; he loved how it was coarse and got everywhere. Yet, by the ill-blessing of fate, he was in the mountains. He had been tasked by his brigadier to fetch the cyclops and the laestrygonians, both lesser giants, and escort them into Hakros. Another thosa captain had been ordered to do the same but with the ogres and ettins. Neither of those giant-kin stood high in their kind's cultural standings. They lacked intelligence and cunning. Cyclops were impulsive brutes, ogres were dumb and laestrygonians were gluttonous, man-eating beacons of vile stench. He could not stand being near any of them. The cyclops and the laestrygonians bickered, fought and complained the entire march. They were quickly wearing down the last nerve of Kuzza. The sooner he linked up with the rest of his thosa forces, the more of his sanity he would retain.

"Capt'n," a cyclops said, speaking in the giant tongue.

"We are not there yet," Kruzza roared. "If you ask again, I will slay you where you stand."

"Men," the cyclops repeated. "There be men ahead."

Kruzza looked forward. Standing at the mountain's mouth of One-Eyed Pass was a phalanx of men. They stood firm, shield and spears in their hands. A few paces ahead stood one man. A small sinister smirk crept across Kruzza's face. A low chuckle grew from deep within his chest, rising until the unnerving sound escaped his lips. Kruzza brought his troops to a halt. He marched forward, on his own, to meet the commanding human.

The thosa stood twelve feet tall and had a skin tone that matched the desert sand of which they dwelled. He looked down at the diminutive human that stood before him.

"You would do well to move out of our way, human," Kruzza spat, lowering himself to speak in the human tongue. Humans did not deserve the honour of a battlefield discussion but Kruzza still offered. The betters were the ones who tried to raise the stature of others, not those who kicked them while they were down. That being said, when this discussion turned to violence then Kruzza would not halt until he had ground their bones beneath his boot.

"I am Diomestor the Battlebrand. I have slew lamia and beastmen. I have led armies and toppled battalions," Diomestor boasted. He stared up at the thosa, the giant standing nearly double his height. "I cannot stop you from crossing but I will slow you down. If you attempt to cross, you and your forces will regret it."

Kruzza bellowed out loud, the laughter echoing across the mountain. He shook his head in amusement. "Your words are bold but do little to hide your inadequacy. Your forces will die this day."

"Not before I slay a great number of yours."

"Let me break him myself," a voice spoke in the giant tongue. A laestrygonian stepped up out from behind. Kruzza moved to stop him but thought against it.

"Feast on his bones," Kruzza replied as he stepped

backwards.

The laestrygonian was a ten-foot corpulent giant. His gut was bulbous; a seemingly endless mass of noxious, rancid folds of skin. Each step the giant took caused every inch of skin to ripple. Its usual dimwitted look was replaced by that of hunger, putrid drops of drool hung from its lip. In its hand was a stone lashed to a large tree branch.

The rotting stench was the first thing Diomestor noticed. It assaulted his nose, caused his eyes to water and even burned the skin on the inside of his nose. Diomestor stepped back a few paces as he tried not to vomit. The laestrygonian chuckled as he walked forward. Diomestor reached to his back and drew two blades. Each was a gladius, one had an emerald stained handle with a matching jewel at the butt of the pommel. The second was an identical blade, except the handle and the jewel were magenta instead. This was the blade of the departed Heruca the Kingloved.

The laestrygonian swung his makeshift club with a horizontal strike, hoping to remove Diomestor's head with a single swing. Diomestor waited until the last second before he ducked. The laestrygonian roared and swung again, this time with a vertical swing meant to smash the human into the ground. Once again Diomestor waited until the last second before he dodged to the left. The club smashed into the ground with a thud. The laestrygonians were powerful creatures and their swings had the speed and power to match. However, they were not warriors. Their attacks were sloppy and their bodies revealed their attacks long before they even began. Laestrygonians were little more than drunken brutes brawling in a tavern.

The laestrygonian swung again, only this time Diomestor dashed forward. His two blades slashed across the laestrygonian's leg, staggering its step. He pivoted around and did a double slash deep into the laestrygonian's gut. The skin tore open, its innards started to flow outwards and a stench even worse than before filled the air. Diomestor found his chest convulsing at the vile, rancid stench. It was like rotting, maggot filled meat had somehow permeated the air. Diomester dropped to one knee as he struggled to keep his last meal firmly within his gut. The laestrygonian dropped its club as it desperately tried to stop his innards from escaping, holding his guts in with his large, bulbous hands.

Diomestor glanced at his magenta blade and whispered towards it. "Finish this, Heruca."

Diomestor pushed himself to his feet and thrust his wife's blade upwards, starting from beneath the laestrygonian's chin and forcing it into the giant's brain. He pulled it free and quickly leapt backwards, the laestrygonian falling to the ground in a putrid thud. Diomestor retreated backwards, flicking the blood off of his blades before returning them to his back.

"Turn now and flee while you still can," Diomestor called out. "And while you still have honour left to regain." Diomestor walked back to his phalanx. He was swiftly handed a spear and a spear. Standing on the front line with a grin on his face, he simply bellowed.

"Shields!"

The phalanx snapped to attention, their shields slamming in front of them while their spears readied for an assault. Kruzza looked down at the dead laestrygonian. Cursing, he drew his blade, roared for his troops and charged forward. Diomestor smirked.

"Xali: let them loose."

"Yes, sir." Xali smirked. She called up her gaggle

of archers, ten in total, and as the rest of the troops dropped to one knee, the archer stood tall. Xali drew an arrow and quickly notched it. As she pulled back, so too did every other archer. "Aim for the knees."

Ten arrows flew across the valley, diving into giant flesh. Some only hit the gut or arm, others were knocked away but the lucky one dove directly into the knee of a sprinting giant. The beast would lose its footing, trip and fall to the ground, suddenly blocking the path for those behind it.

Diomester subtly moved the phalanx back a few paces as the archers fired again. With each volley of arrows, another giant would fall to the ground and the phalanx would pull back a few paces more. Some giants would climb back to their feet and fight through the pain but the damage was already done. They had stumbled and slowed the charging horde.

Kruzza was livid with anger, at both the humans but mainly at his idiotic kin. They were tripping over each other like newborn children just finding their legs. This would never happen in a thosa march. He did his best to keep his eyes on the archers. They were succeeding in slowing him but he would not let them fall or trip him.

"Boulders!" Diomestor yelled suddenly.

Kruzza slid to a halt and looked around. He was no longer at the mountain's mouth of One-Eyed Pass. The human phalanx was at the Hakros mouth and he and his first wave of giants were standing in the middle of the valley. He glanced up and saw several humans on either side of the rocky cliff, each behind a large boulder and eagerly pushing it down the hill. As the dozens of stones bounced down the cliff, hurdling towards him, Kruzza realized what had just happened. He had been so focused on the archers that he had not realized it when the humans had subtly retreated to the other side.

They had lured him to the center and now rained down upon them with falling rocks. Kruzza willed his inner magic to life and summoned forth what little sand was around. His magic pressed the sand together into a blade and shot upwards. It found a boulder about to collide with him and split it in two. The piece still slammed into Kruzza and dropped him to the dirt but left him reasonably unharmed.

Boroca, Domos and others cheered as the rocks smashed against the giantkin. Few died in the attack but dozens were on the ground, their bodies broken or bruised. Diomestor stepped ahead of the phalanx, raised his spear into the air and ordered the attack. The phalanx dissolved as the men and women under his command rushed forward. Nikka ran up the body of a fallen cyclops and thrust her spear downward, running it through its solitary eye.

All around her, her allies were doing the same. Each swarmed a fallen giant and swiftly stabbed it until it no longer moved. The giants were bigger and stronger but Diomestor had still brought them down to their size. Realizing what was happening, those that were capable did their best to climb to their feet.

Perigoss spotted a laestrygonian returning to its feet. He gripped his spear tightly as he charged the giant. He ducked beneath a clumsy swing and thrust thrice with the spear. The first ripped into the laestrygonian's leg, slowing its movement, and the second ripped into the laestrygonian's arm, slowing its attack. His final attack ran through the fat giant's gut, hoping his blow would be as effective as Diomestor's slash had been. But as he pulled the weapon free, he noticed the giant unphased. In fact, his fat, bulbous gut barely showed signs of a wound. How strong were the blades of Diomestor?

Perigoss barely had enough time to raise his shield as the laestrygonian's fist punched towards him. The monstrous hand, sweaty and stained with dirt and blood, slammed against the wooden shield. Perigoss closed his eyes as the inside began to fracture, the splinters bouncing off his face. He thanked that the laestrygonian's wound had slowed the attack or he would have never been able to protect himself. Perigoss stepped out from behind his shield and thrust again, this time tearing into its neck. The laestrygonian fell to the ground, choking on its own vile blood as it gasped for air.

Nyreus ran towards the sand giant. He thrust with his spear, hoping to get a second kill, but as he got close a foot shot out and caught him in the chest. Nyreus flew backward and bounced across the ground. Kruzza called for the second wave of giants to attack as he climbed to his feet. He brought his blade around just as the triton spear of Lypos came at his face. He knocked the weapon aside with his steel and brought it over his head as he attacked again. Lypos rolled out of the way just as Nyreus ran forth. The kid, ignoring the pain in the ways only a teenager could, charged the giant leader. All of his training took over as his muscles moved without command. The kid's spear moved swiftly and accurately, aiming directly for the giant's chest. The steel tip collided with the giant's armour with a loud twang. Such a blow did not feel pleasant but it left Kruzza unharmed. Kruzza slashed again and caught the kid across the chest. His cuirass split under the force of the giant's strength and once again Nyreus found himself slamming against the ground.

Xali drew two arrows from her quiver as the next wave rushed forward. Most of the other archers had already switched to a blade. She had chosen to remain with her bow. She was swift with her draw, swifter than most others with an edge. Holding her bow horizontally, she notched one arrow, drew, released and notched a second all in just a few heartbeats. Each of her arrows found a new home in the gut or legs of a giant but as a roaring cyclops charged towards her, Xali turned her bow vertically and notched another arrow. A horizontal draw allowed her to pull the string back as far as the nose on her face. She preferred it for close-range combat. A vertical draw allowed her to pull back as far as her ear, giving her far more power in her shot. With the added strength, the third arrow ripped across the air and dove into the cyclops' eye, instantly halting his charge and snapping back his head. Xali drew two more arrows from her quiver as she scanned for her next target. Her eyes fell upon Kruzza. The sand giant stood over a wounded Nyreus.

"Nikka: the kid!" Xali called out. She swiftly let loose one arrow after another, both at Kruzza's direction. Nikka turned her head and bolted. She ran towards Kruzza at full speed. Xali admitted that there were many times that she wished for Nikka to slow down and take her time, at this moment she was thankful for her wife's remarkable speed. Xali notched arrow after arrow and let them loose, moving forward between each shot.

Nikka bolted as fast as she could towards Nyreus. Nobody deserved to die in their first battle and Nikka would make sure it did not happen this day. As Xali's arrows flew past her, Nikka could not help but smirk. Not once had she ever been not thankful for her wife's nimble fingers.

Lypos rushed forward with a spear thrust of his own

but much like the kid's, it too harmlessly bounced off Kruzza's armour. Lypos, however, had enough experience to know when to dodge and pivot. After a harmless attack like that one, Lypos needed to move lest he be run through with a blade. Kruzza's blade cut only air as the triton thrust once more, desperately looking for a gap in the giant's armour. As a barrage of arrows bounced off of his armour, Krazzu turned just in time to see Nikka's shield colliding with his knee. The leg buckled and the giant stumbled about, desperate to keep his balance. Nikka pivoted around and struck again, this time aiming for his other leg. Her spear dug into his shin, tearing off flesh as she pulled it free, but the giant did not fall. Instead, he lashed out with a backhand, colliding with Nikka and sending her spinning into the dirt. He grabbed her by the legs, hoisted her into the air and then slammed her back onto a rock like a hammer into a nail.

Xali screamed and rage overtook her. She ran forward as fast as she could, firing a non-stop stream of arrows. Discarding her bow, she finally drew her blade. Gripping it with both hands, she leapt into the air as she tried to stab it into Kruzza but the giant had other plans. He grabbed Nikka's spear and stabbed it into Xali's chest, the two meeting midair. For a moment, Xali hung in the air, propped up solely by the spear in her chest, until Kruzza flung her aside like a discarded apple core.

Kruzza turned back towards Lypos when a blast of lilac magic slammed into the giant's chest. He flew backward, landing a dozen feet away. Lypos turned to see an exhausted Rarus, leaning on his staff to stay upright. "Th..that took a lot out of me."

"Are you okay?" Lypos asked.

"See to the archer," Rarus snapped as he hobbled over

to Nikka and knelt by her. Tears rolled down the woman's face as she lay unmoving.

"Xali," she cried. "Is she okay?"

"Where does it hurt?" Rarus asked.

"I feel no pain," she admitted. Rarus' eyes went wide in fear. That was not a good sign. He had to act swiftly. Closing his eyes, he clutched the staff tightly with one hand and put his second on her chest.

"If this be not her time please aid me, goddess," Rarus whispered. The glow of lilac coloured magic suddenly appeared. It started in the staff, moved through his hand and into her body. For several seconds Nikka's body began to glow like the staff until suddenly she screamed in pain. A smile crept across his face. At this moment, feeling pain was better than feeling nothing at all.

"Take it eas—"

"Xali!" Nikka rolled to her feet, screaming in pain as she did. She stumbled to the ground but defiantly pushed herself back up. She rushed over to the fallen archer. "How is she?"

"She ...she's okay," Lypos said, clearly stunned. "There is not a wound on her."

Xali sat up, gasping for breath. She turned and slapped Nikka across the face before grabbing her hand and passionately kissing her. "Those defensive spells are meant for you, not me."

"Get the kid and Nikka and pull them back," Rarus ordered. "I'll find the rest of the wounded."

"I can still fight," Nikka protested but Rarus cut her off.

"Do as you are told! This is still a battle!"

Perigoss raised a shield as he blocked the swinging club of a cyclops. The repeated blows had forced him back a few inches and caused his arm to go numb. He swore as the cyclops pulled the weapon back, readying to strike once more. It collided and his shield shattered; wood flew in various directions as he was knocked to the ground. Perigoss tried to scramble to his feet, desperate to escape and rid his arm of the now useless defense that weighed it down. The cyclops let him do neither. Instead it pressed its foot on top of his leg, trapping him. Perigoss kicked at the leg over and over, desperate to free himself. The cyclops raised its club once more, this time aiming to strike at his head. With little other option, Perigoss readied himself for one final kick.

Scyra was not liking battle. Normally she thrived in moments of chaos, she could always find some way to benefit. Short of simply surviving - which was something she was quite fond of doing - there were few benefits to be gained in battle. She was no stranger to fencing but her skills were against humans, not giants. Her style of fencing was based around speed and grace, not brute strength.

Scyra swiftly dodge a laestrygonian's attack, doing so with grace and ease, as she retreated further into the fallen stones. She could gracefully leap from stone to stone. The giants could not. She watched as a lunging laestrygonian tripped over a stone and fell face first into the dirt. Pinching her nose with one hand, Scyra dashed to the fallen brute and stabbed into the back of his head.

Suddenly her belt began to shake. Surprised, she glanced down, desperate to figure out its source. Her hand dropped to her water skin. It was shaking. She blinked in surprise. What was going on? It was like the time her cup of water shook when Perigoss was fighting in the training pit. She snapped her head up and somehow her eyes instantly fell upon Perigoss. He was laying on the ground, a stunned look on his face as she stared at a fallen cyclops who lay beside him, an equally stunned look on the one-eyed giant's face. Suddenly both remembered they were in combat. As Perigoss tried to climb to his feet the cyclops punched him, forcing him back into the ground.

Her legs moved before her brain ordered it. Scyra leapt across the battlefield, her sword in one hand and dagger in the other. She flung the dagger forward, burying it into the cyclops' eye. Perigoss scrambled for his spear. He grabbed it, turned around and finished the cyclops with a thrust to its skull.

Scyra bounded over to Perigoss and offered him a hand. He readily took it. "Can you walk?"

"I'll make do," he replied. "Let me retrieve your dagger."

"Do not bother. It is now covered in eye juice." Suddenly Scyra began to smirk. "Besides, it is not my dagger. I swiped it off of Domos."

Diomestor's twin blades were a blur as he fell another laestrygonian. As the putrid body fell, he looked around. All across the field, his troops were killing the giants but not without cost. Many were injured and some had already been pulled off the battle. In the distance, Kruzza was picking himself off of the dirt and signaling for the third wave. Diomestor had pushed his luck with this battle. His job was to slow the giants and thin out their numbers. He had done just that.

It was time to leave.

Grabbing a horn from his belt, Diomestor gave it a blow. The long note echoes across the battle, signaling their retreat. One by one, the men and women of his phalanx began to disengage and depart the battle, each retreating into the distant woods. He glanced at Kruzza and gave him a mocking sword salute.

"Flee you coward," Kruzza roared.

"Next time we meet will be your last," Diomestor said, speaking in the giant tongue. "You will die like the cyclops and the laestrygonians, disgracefully in the dirt."

CHAPTER TEN

Whoever stands for their polis cannot be called wrong.
- Oibalox Commandment

Stellia, daughter of Stelio, ran across the farmlands. Her legs pushed as hard as they could and she swiftly traversed the landscape. She came to a halt, a brief pause as she tried to reorient herself. It had been nearly three days of constant running, yet as she came to a pause, she found herself barely out of breath. She looked around, eyeing the Phenious River. At her current pace she was only a few hours away from the town of Mikha. Originally she had been heading towards the polis of Oibalox, desperate to warn them of the number that the gigas alone possessed. Yet she found herself being pulled in a different direction. The broken spearhead of Mericoi seemed to direct her elsewhere. Stellia could not explain how, but the closer she got to Oibalox, the stronger the desire to go to Mikha grew in her mind until it was all consuming. She could think of nothing else and when she tried to fight it, somehow she still found herself walking towards the farming town. Eventually, she just surrendered to the urge and the spearhead seemed to pulse in satisfaction.

Mericoi claimed his weapon was a gift from Cydomea, the goddess of war and patron deity of Oibalox. It was not an unusual claim. Every Oibalox warrior who had a sword, spear or shield with magic claimed it a gift from the goddess. Few actually were, simply being minor magical weapons. Perhaps, Mericoi's weapon actually was the exception and Stellia was being guided by Cydomea but for what reason, she had yet to decipher.

Stellia let out a small yawn. She was not exhausted from the running but sleep had suddenly proved difficult. Dreams assaulted her mind, flashing images of Mericoi's spear being stabbed into her chest over and over. It did not make for a restful sleep.

The sound of snapping branches caught Stellia's ear. It was not the small snap of a fallen twig but instead a commanding crack of a large branch being snapped from its tree. Stellia dropped to one knee and moved towards the largest form of cover she could find. She ducked behind a large tree - ignoring the irony of that action - and carefully peered around the trunk. She saw a trio of lesser giants smashing their way through the trees. They were cyclopes. Stellia frowned, they were an unusual sight in Oibalox territory. The one-eyed blunders tended to stay near One-Eyed Pass if they ever descended from the mountains at all. Mikha, however, was the farming town that bordered Hakros and Oibalox and sat uncomfortably close to the Pass. Seeing a cyclops meant that the lesser giant-kin, of all types, had indeed joined the invasion.

The cyclopes barrelled through the trees, laughing as they broke and smashed anything that drew their ire. Stellia watched them and frowned. They were coming in her direction. There would be no way to sneak around them. She would have to face them or flee and she was far from a fleeing mood. Stellia gripped her doru tightly as she readied her legs. She nervously checked her piecemeal collection of equipment. The cuirass did not fit properly, the spear was meant for a man a head taller and the blade on her waist felt – off. Yet it was all she had and it would have to make due. She waited for them to get closer before striking, readying herself with each of their steps. Stellia leapt out from behind the tree and ran towards the trio as fast as she could.

The first in her sights was a startled cyclops with a makeshift hammer. Her doru leapt first, thrusting upwards into the cyclops' arm. She pulled her spear from the limb only to thrust again, this time digging into Hammer-clop's peck. The beast screamed in pain and annoyance as it stepped backwards. Stellia felt the thump of the ground as a rotund cyclops approached from the side. Fat-clops tried to grab her with its plump fingers. Stellia slapped away the first hand with her shield, an action that made the giant-kin pull its hand away with a shake and then suck on his fingers in an attempt to make the sting vanish. Stellia thrust her doru once more, this time aimed at Fat-clops' gut. The spear ripped into the rotund gut and Stellia gave it a twist before pulling it free. The third cyclops, welding a large tree branch in both hands, ran towards the fight and took a swing. Stellia, who stood before Hammer-clops, dove out of the way and rolled to her feet just in time to see the branch slam into the groin of hammer-clops.

Tree-clops roared as he pivoted around. He took another two-handed swing at Stellia. She tried to dive out of the way but the swing was far faster than before. Caught off guard, the branch barely missed her. Tree-clops roared once more and swung again, the tree moving even faster still. This time Stellia was unable to dodge in time. She raised her shield, closed her eyes and braced for the devastating blow.

But it never came.

As she opened her eyes, Stellia found herself nearly fifty feet away from Tree-clops. She glanced down at her body and saw her arm, now an opaque spectral limb, swiftly re-forming into the flesh and blood she was used to.

What in the underworld had just happened?

She glanced back at the trio. Hammer-clops was on the ground, clutching his groin as he vomited into the dirt, Fat-clops was holding his wound in agony and Tree-clops was staring at the point where Stellia once stood, confused as to what had just happened. Suddenly Fat-clops pointed at her and yelled to the others. Stellia flung her spear forward, the doru diving into fat-clops' eye. Tree-clops barrelled towards her, his lumbering steps shaking the leaves as he swung his branch once more. Stellia rolled beneath the swing and swiftly drew her gladius. She slashed at Tree-clops' leg but as the blade tore through flesh, she saw a ghostly visual echo, fol-lowing behind the blade. The spectral echo caught up to the weapon only when it stood still.

What was going on? What had happened to her?

Tree-clops dropped to one knee, the joint making a thud on contact, and Stellia's attention was snapped back into battle. She thrust her blade upwards and ran it into the back of its skull. Stellia turned towards Hammer-clops. The brute was starting to climb back to his feet. Stellia began to run towards it when her body shifted. Suddenly every inch of blood, skin and bone on her body dissolved into spectral mist as she flut-tered forward, rematerializing right before the cyclops.

Hammer-clops began to scream in the giant tongue, a language she knew none of, but one word rang true in any language.

Eidolon.

Stellia thrust her echo blade into hammer-clops' eyes and twisted, watching the body twitch before going still. She withdrew the weapon and looked around. All three cyclops were slain, their bodies little more than food for the carrion eating coyotes and crows. She stepped back and allowed herself to fall butt-first onto the dirt. She stared in shock first at her limbs and then at her sword. What had happened after Pylomia? She remembered falling in battle but then waking up, an once-thought corpse, abandoned on a battlefield. Had something happened in between? The cyclops had called her an eidolon.

Did that mean she was dead?

Stellia ripped off her armour and pressed her hand against her chest. She felt the beats of her heart, swiftly beating from the aftermath of battle. She was still alive. Oibalox taught that if a heart still beat, then a soldier still lived to fight. Stellia shook her head and quickly scolded herself for her selfish thoughts. She was an Oibalox hoplite. She was not allowed to think of herself when others were in need. The polis came first; self came second. Stellia pushed herself to her feet and took in a deep breath. She aimed herself towards Mikha and took off running.

Commander Aidox brought his marching phalanx to a halt. His legion of gigas all stopped in unison as the wings of harpies circled above. He stared across the bare fields that separated him and the town of Mikha. Standing in the field, acting as the village's guardians, were a phalanx of Hakros soldiers. Their well-armed numbers stood in a phalanx, carefully eyeing the gigas numbers. A woman stepped out from within the phalanx and walked towards the center of the field. Aidox eyed the woman. She was clearly strong, the many muscles on her body were evidence of that truth. The gear she carried was of fine quality but had many battle-earned imperfections. She stopped in the center and waited. Aidox departed his phalanx and walked forward to meet her.

"I am Helmene, the Oakbred," she boasted. "I have slain a hydra, bested the sphynx and protected this world from the horrors of the next."

"I am Commander Aidox, leader of the gigas legion," he replied, playing along with the human's asinine introductions. "I have brutally murdered hundreds of your kin. Are you so ready to die that you walk ahead of your phalanx all by your lonesome?"

"This battle will not greatly affect our war. If I win, you will retreat, regroup and return with higher numbers. If you win, I will retreat further into Hakros," Helmene explained, a lack of luster in her voice. "There is no sense in either side losing massive numbers of troops this day. Especially when we can save them for more crucial battles."

"So what do you suggest, tree-breeder?" Aidox asked in a mocking tone. "We both walk away and call the day's duties complete?"

"I suggest we settle this in single combat. The winner takes Mikha and the loser flees. What say you?"

Aidox stared at the woman for a long moment before simply shrugging and nodding in agreement. Helmene turned around and waved her spear in the air, shouting at the top of her lungs. "We will have single combat!"

The humans and gigas roared and cheered. Helmene turned back to Aidox. "So which of you petty humans will I be facing?"

"You will face me," she declared. "Who do you choose as your champion?"

Aidox glanced over at his troops. A sinister part of him wanted to choose the runt of their phalanx, embarrass the human warrior with the weakest of his kind. Instead, he decided on himself. The sadistic joy of pain and suffering would belong to him and him alone. "You will face me."

Both sides cheered once again. Aidox turned his head to his phalanx and called out to them.

"Foricu, break out the booze," he roared. "Allow them to drink while they watch me fight."

Foricu started handing out vials of booze to each of gigas soldiers and to each of the harpies that descended to partake. Aidox pulled the flask from his belt and pulled free the cork. He offered it to the human woman. "Care for a swig?"

Helmene took a sniff and instantly recoiled. It smelled vile and almost like pure alcohol. For a moment she was shocked that their kind could drink such a thing. Then she remembered who they were. The gigas were uncivilized warriors. They had no concept of taste. It would be like pouring very fine wine for a dog. She shook her head no and Aidox simply shrugged. He took a swig before returning the cork and the flask to their original place. Helmene raised her shield and aimed her spear at Aidox. The gigas commander made no similar motions. He just stood there, staring at her.

"I may have failed to mention," Helmene said smugly. Flames ignited on her magical spear. "I also slew the legendary giant known as Tiahoka. His blood now fuels the magic in my spear. You will not stand a chance against me."

Tiahoka was once an infamous caculis, one of the greatest warriors of his kin. He was feared the world over until he was slain two years ago. Aidox smirked. He never would have thought himself ever to be standing before the slayer of Tiahoka. He burst out laughing. It was a dark and sinister laughter, one that suddenly unnerved Helmene.

"Tiahoka was once the fiercest of all giant kind. Then he got sick," Aidox explained, a sinister smile creeping across his lips as he spoke. "He got so ill that he was barely able to lift a boulder. Tiahoka was a fraction of the giant he once was. He was due to die, slowly and painfully. Instead, he decided to wander into the kingdoms of men."

"What?" Helmene stuttered, confused. "Why would he do that?"

"He wanted his death to matter as much as his life," Aidox explained. "He wanted to die in combat but more importantly, he wanted to aid in the invasion. He knew giants would march on mankind. He cursed the fates that he would not join. Instead, he decided to aid the giants by giving the myths of men an incorrect measurement of our strength. He let all of men think that he, the sickest of the sick, was the benchmark for giant strength."

Helmene's firm stance began to weaken with every word that Aidox spoke. That battle was the longest and the most difficult of her entire life. She had been celebrated as a hero for her heroic killing. She had earned the rank of mythling from that deed. Hakros had drilled her for weeks, trying to learn the true strength of a giant. Their entire military defence was based around that knowledge. Surely, Aidox was simply lying to her, messing with her mind as he attempted to weaken her resolve. Even if he was speaking the truth, there is no way that a giant's true strength could be that much greater than that of a sickly Tiahoka.

"You will not scare me!" Helmene dashed forward, lunging with her spear. Aidox grabbed her spear and pulled, yanking her off balance. His foot fired out, sneaking past her shield and catching her in the chest. The kick sent her flying backwards, her shield and spear dropping from her hand while in the air. The humans went silent in shock as the gigas cheered. Aidox walked over to their hero, grabbing her flaming spear on his slow journey. He looked down at her cracked cuirass and smiled. She was trying to breathe but each attempt was laboured and caused pain.

"Look at you, so desperate for life even as the very gift of it brings you unbearable pain. If there was ever a metaphor that so perfectly described your feeble kind, you would be it." Aidox stepped on her neck and gently pushed down. "I bested you without a shield or a spear. I bested you with just my foot."

Helmene gasped again, desperate for air but none was coming. Aidox pushed down with his foot but not enough to let her die, not yet. Aidox glanced up at the harpies.

"Give the humans a drink of booze, so they may taste their hero's loss." The harpies screeched as each flung a vial at the human warriors. The vials harmlessly smashed against the shields but their contents splashed across the entire phalanx. Aidox looked down at his bested foe and grinned. "Are you ready? Your troops are about to die."

"You…promised…single…combat." She gasped for air beneath his foot, pushing out what few words possible. Knowing hers was already lost, she pleaded for the lives of the men and women under her command.

"The concept of single combat only works in a battle for territory." Aidox ignited his stolen spear and watched the flames glow bright. The burning flames caused a flickering light to perversely dance across his face, somehow making him look even more frightening. "We are here to wipe your pitiful species from the face of the earth."

Aidox flung the burning spear forward. From the

ground, Helmene watched as the spear left a burning tail as it soared across the air, flying towards her phalanx. The spear bounced off of a shield, harmlessly falling to the ground, but the hungry tongues of flames reached out and lashed the fallen booze. The spirits instantly ignited. Suddenly, blue flames burned all around the human phalanx, viciously feeding on the flesh of each man and woman caught within. Tears rolled down Helmene's cheek as the screams of pain filled the air.

"When you meet Charon, tell him that he will need a far bigger boat." With his final word, Aidox firmly pressed down on Helmene's neck, smiling at the satisfying crack.

CHAPTER ELEVEN

Win or lose, we all return to nature eventually.
- Yascura Proverb

Xali crept through the trees, her feet making not a single sound as she moved. Her steps were so soft that they failed to even damage the forest floor. She had learned long ago how to be one with the forest, how to read all of its signs and to survive off of its gifts. She had learned how to be a ghost amongst the trees; a glimmer just outside of one's view. Perigoss, however, had not. For every silent step she took, his paces were loud cries. In truth, his steps were not so clumsy. He was skilled enough in stealth to hunt but compared to her and the silence that she was used to, his steps were like deafening roars.

Xali dropped to one knee and waited for Perigoss to catch up. The pair had been assigned ahead of the phalanx to act as scouts. Xali reached down to the forest floor and gently picked up a snapped twig. She eyed the surrounding area. Grass had been flattened, branches had been snapped off and chunks of tree bark had been hastily torn from the trunk, not on purpose but was done in a manner that suggested that a creature - possibly a deer - had been so desperate to flee that it cared not if it accidently bumped into a tree. Her first thought was giants, scaring the wildlife off, but she internally disagreed with her own assumption. Giants were not stealthy. If they had been approaching then the deer, and whatever other wildlife were nearby, would have fled long before the giants got close. This was different. This was a fear based on something primal.

A faint scent wafted past Xali's nose. She could not quite place it but it felt familiar. Flashes of memory danced before her mind. Images of her father, a stout man with a love of the drink, appeared. He was a man who whenever he had a spare moment, he would partake in drink and always in excess. It did not matter what the spare moment was. Perhaps it was the time before work or during the hours when he was to watch her and her brother. Xali remembered a moment when her father was cooking a meal. He set the food to simmer on an open flame and decided to drink while he waited. He passed out and the food just sat there, endlessly cooking until it burned to a crisp. That moment was seared into her brain. She would never forget the smell of black smoke and burning flesh.

By the gods.

Xali jumped back to her feet and took off running towards the scent, all hopes of stealth vanishing from her step. Perigoss blinked in shock and bolted after her.

"What is wrong?" he cried out.

She did not answer. Instead, Xali just prayed that she was wrong, that her memory had failed her like it so often had her father. As she reached the forest's edge and slid down into a crouch in the long grass, she cursed. She stared out over the village of Mikha and its surrounding farmland and watched in horror as flames consumed it all.

Mikha was burning.

Rarus had discovered, in his later years, that he was not a difficult man to make happy. Give him a place to sit and something to eat and he was content. As he sat upon a fallen log and happily chewed upon a freshly picked apple, there was little else he needed or wanted in that moment. Diomestor's phalanx was currently at a break. Aside from a few rotating scouts, each spear and sword were sitting and eating much in the same manner. They were waiting on the return of Xali and Perigoss. The phalanx had been marching together for only but a week but Rarus already noticed the groups and pairings forming. A small number seemed to circle around Xali and Nikka, the make-shift parents of the group, dealing out wisdom and guidance. Many of the younger spears tended to flock towards Lypos, the makeshift mentor who was teaching them how to survive. Some even flocked towards him, looking for religious comfort. Unsurprisingly, Rarus had seen several examples of bodies finding partners with whom to share their warmth. The phalanx had only suffered a few losses and a couple injuries during their battle but that seemed enough for the soldiers to want to find comfort and joy in the present. War reminded them that there was no guarantee of a tomorrow. Rarus noticed that even Nyreus' attention was being drawn towards an archer named Enior. Rarus found himself a tiny bit envious. For a relationship, he needed someone who had the same level of life experience as him, but for a night of passion there was little better than an inexperienced, energetic nineteen year-old. What they lacked in skill they made up for in enthusiasm, vigor and a desire to prove themselves. Rarus was about to scold himself for his lecherous thoughts when Perigoss and Xali suddenly came into view. They emerged from the tree and were running at full speed towards them. Rarus pushed himself to his feet and walked towards the camp's center.

Xali and Perigoss ran past the patrols and bolted directly towards Diomestor. The pair slid to a halt. With heaving chests, they swiftly explained. Rarus could not hear what was being said but clearly it was not good. Diomester loudly cursed. He stormed towards his kit, lying by a tree, and grabbed his shield and swords.

"Perigoss: stay here. Domos: Get these people ready to move," Diomester barked. He turned to Xali. "Lead the way."

The pair ran off into the woods. Rarus walked over to his apprentice. The kid was breathing heavily and sweat was rolling down his face. Rarus handed him a pouch of water. The kid took several long sips between gasps for air.

"What is going on?" Rarus asked.

"Mikha is burning," Perigoss replied. He shook his head, trying to shake the horror from his mind's eye. "The gigas army ripped through it and burned it down. They have mostly moved on but some remnants still remain, torching and pillaging." Perigoss looked up at his master, pain all across his face. "There are still people there, crying out in pain. I could see them. I could hear them."

"Mikha…is burning?" Boroca asked, as he approached. His voice was cracking and stunned. "That is my home. I…I…I was born there. I grew up there." Suddenly his eyes went wide. "Mother! Father!"

Rarus put his hand on the brawler's shoulder and whispered his condolences.

"We have to go," Perigoss said suddenly. "They need our help."

"I am going with you," Boroca quickly added.

"Both of you need to calm down," Rarus said quickly.

He looked between the two men. "If you run in without planning, you will only cause more trouble."

"I cannot simply stand here and do nothing," Boroca snapped.

"I know this. Trust me, I know this loss," Rarus reassured. "We cannot do anything until Diomestor's return. Make use of that time; figure out what needs to be done."

The two men nodded and began talking amongst themselves. Rarus turned away and spotted Domos. The minotaur walked around the makeshift camp and was swiftly readying the troop.

When Diomestor returned, all of the food had been stowed and all soldiers were on their feet. He took a look at Domos and shook his head.

"Mikha is burning," he said loudly. "We need to move and we need to do it swiftly."

"Understood," Domos said. He turned to the troops. "Drop your gear and bring only your weapons and shield. I want three groups. We will move quickly and swiftly and descend upon the village. We will save the people of Mikha."

"Belay that order," Diomestor loudly corrected. "We are moving further inwards."

"You mean to abandon Mikha?" Domos asked in shock.

"The war council knew that the giants would attack Mikha after One-Eyed Pass. We were supposed to stop them," Diomestor explained. "However, the council knew not the speed of the gigas. They are moving too swiftly. We have to move inwards, at a faster pace, in order to save the other villages."

"Sir...."

"If we fail to weaken and slow the invading armies,"

Diomestor snapped, cutting off the objection. "Then when they reach the polis proper, Hakros will not be strong enough to defend. They will fall."

Domos glanced at Rarus. Both shared a look of confusion and sorrow. Both of them were not strangers to war or battle. They both knew what had to be sacrificed in order to achieve victory. This was not it.

"Where do we march to?" Domos asked.

"We will march around the Pharian Fields and make our way to Aornya," Diomestor said. "We will have to move swiftly so be prepared to hustle."

Domos let out a loud, thunderous agreement as Rarus slinked towards Perigoss. The kid was trying to be quiet as he chatted with Boroca. Xali and Nikka had joined them.

"Do not dare tell me what I suspect you are about to," Rarus said sternly. Perigoss shook his head.

"I am very sorry, Master, but I must," the Perigoss defended.

"You mean to abandon your fellow troops?" Rarus asked.

"That is my home," Boroca snapped.

"Xali and I saw innocent people in that village," Perigoss explained. "They need help. They cannot defend themselves. We can help them."

"We go in, save the people and then we rejoin the phalanx in Aornyna," Perigoss continued. "We can move faster as a few than they can as many."

"There is only a small gathering of gigas troops stationed there," Xali finished. "It is nothing beyond what a few of us can handle."

"Tell me why?" Rarus said, staring his apprentice deep in the face.

"There is no honour in simply letting those people die. This is not glorious combat, it is a slaughter," Perigoss said. Rarus frowned. That was not the answer he was hoping to hear. The passion in the kid's eyes flared as he spoke. "If we can protect them then we can save their honour. We can save their lives. We need to save them."

That was close enough.

"Okay, I will be joining you," Rarus said. Perigoss opened his mouth to argue but the priest shook his head. "Some may be injured. You will need my healing."

"Good. That makes five," Boroca said. "We just need to escape without Domos watching."

"Leave that to me. Form up in the phalanx's rear and be prepared to sneak away." Rarus said. He stepped away and made eye contact with Domos. He subtly nudged his head first toward Perigoss and then towards the rear. Domos nodded in agreement. He walked down the line of the forming masses, stopping only when he reached the thief.

"Take your position in the rear," he quietly growled, thrusting a shield into her hands. Scyra looked up at him with confused eyes. They never let her be in the rear, they were always afraid she'd run off. She opened her mouth to speak but he growled her to silence. "Take your position in the rear. Stick with the priest and do not let me regret this."

Scyra blinked as her mind raced. Something was happening but she had yet to figure out what. Doing as she was told - there was a first for everything - she moved to the rear. There, she found the priest, Xali, Nikka, Boroca and Perigoss. Suddenly she began to understand.

"This will be our sixth," Rarus whispered.

Scyra walked to Perigoss and handed him the shield. "I think this was meant for you."

The six raced across the vast farming lands as they sped towards Mikha. Boroca led the charge with Perigoss close. Nobody strayed too far behind. They passed several farm houses and noticed that their fields had been torched. Some had sickly, pine-coloured scorch marks while others still burned with an unsightly fern coloured smoke emerging in the distance. Each instance they passed left Boroca more and more uneasy. Even Rarus seemed to be unsettled by the green-coloured sightings.

"We're stopping here first," Boroca said as he pointed to a small farmhouse. The house and barn seemed undamaged but the farmlands had been burned to the ground. As they passed the barn, Perigoss noted the corpses of several slain lambs and goats. Boroca quickly approached the house, forgoing any caution. He leaned his spear against the house and carefully pulled open the door.

"Stay away!" A voice called out from within. "I have an arrow notched and aimed directly at the door."

"Father," Boroca called out. "I beg you not to fill me with arrows."

"Son, is that you?" the voice asked.

"Yes. Is mother there?"

"Boro?" a female voice cried. "I am here and safe as well.

Boroca walked inside, going to greet and hug his parents. Perigoss lowered his spear as he looked around. The destruction rippled on for as far as he could see and it was devastating. Mikha looked to be on the verge of total destruction. If these flames could not be controlled, the village would be burned off the face of the world. He had never seen such destruction before.

"Why is there green smoke?" Xali asked aloud. Perigoss shook his head, he did not know. He was just as confused. "I have never seen that before."

"I have," Scyra quietly admitted. "Green flame."

"By the gods," Rarus quietly whispered. "Why does this village have green flame? It is far too dangerous for the average person and it has no use in farming."

"What is green flame?" Perigoss asked.

"It is also called war fire; it is an alchemical mixture that can burn anything," Scyra said quickly. "It burns with a green flame and can consume nearly anything. Some say it can even burn atop water."

"It is a tool of war and nothing else," Rarus said.

Boroca emerged from within his childhood home with his parents in tow. He was a tall man, standing head and shoulders above most other people. His parents, however, were just as tall. His father stood taller than Boroca and his mother was no slouch either in the height department.

"Thank you for coming, son." his father said, clapping his hand onto Boroca's shoulder. "But you have to be careful. Bandits have descended upon the town as well."

"I will." Boroca hugged his mother before retrieving his spear. He turned back to his renegade six. "Let us move swiftly."

The six nodded goodbye and moved inwards. They stopped at buildings, checking for survivors and battling any looters they came across. As they reached the town's edge, the group ducked by the nearest building, using it for cover. Nikka leaned around the corner and peered into the village.

"We have a couple harpies circling and perhaps a dozen gigas," She whispered. "We move in swiftly and do not pause. Xali goes for the air while Boroca and Perigoss stick with me. We will be heading towards the biggums directly.

Rarus and Scyra: keep our flanks covered."

Everybody silently nodded. Perigoss reached to his neck and checked that his brelok was in place. Nikka summoned pink magic to her hand. She glanced at Xali but found only a scowl waiting for her.

"Do not even think about it," the archer scowled. Nikka sheepishly nodded and pressed the glowing hand to her chest.

"Are we ready?" Boroca asked. Everybody nodded. "Then let us move."

The six bolted out around the corner and ran into the frey. Xali swiftly drew and notched arrows as she shot them upwards, aiming at the harpies. Nikka and Perigoss targeted the first gaggle of gigas and attacked. Boroca's spear was first to strike, a new-found vigor and speed filling his soul. His thrust caught the gigas by surprise as it tore through its arm. The brute stumbled backwards, shocked at the attack, and roared to his allies. Boroca silenced him quickly with a second thrust, his spear diving into the brute's mouth and up into his head. Despite his speed, the roar still echoed throughout the town.

Nikka was next in line. She ducked beneath the strike of a gigas axe and struck with her shield. She slammed it against the giantkin's left knee and watched as the leg buckled. Nikka pivoted back to a stand and stabbed her spear into its neck. She did not have time to watch it die. By the time she withdrew her weapon her attention was already focused on the next gigas, charging in at high speed alongside Perigoss. A pair of arrows whistled past Perigoss' head and dove into the charging gigas' knees. The brute tripped over his legs and stumbled to the ground, crashing into the dirt with a loud and heavy thud.

"Injured townfolk," Rarus called out. "Cover me."

Xali nodded. She pulled three arrows from her quiver and quickly notched one. Despite every instinct in her mind and body telling her to protect her wife, she knew had to care for more than just her. She watched as the priest ran over to a couple bodies on the dirt. He slid in beside them. His staff began to glow with lilac-coloured magic, the same he had used to save her wife. The harpies suddenly screeched, their heads snapping towards the priest. They were attracted to the magic. Xali pulled back on the drawstring and aimed upwards, readying to shoot the diving beasts from the sky, when she suddenly felt the thud of a charging gigas coming directly at her.

"Scyra: the priest." Xali could not deal with both threats. Xail pivoted toward the gigas and let loose the first arrow. The next pair follow in rapid succession.

Scyra ran toward the priest and quickly flicked out a dagger and tossed it. She hoped to catch the harpy mid-flight, but the eagled-eyed beast spotted the flying steel and pulled up from her dive. The dagger missed by only a hair's width. The harpy furiously flapped its wings as it screeched loudly. Scyra continued her charge, transferring from a run into a leap. She slashed at the harpy, her gladius cutting through its wings. Scyra hit the ground and swiftly rolled away, avoiding the furious talon slashes. The thief shifted her stanced and dove again, avoiding the attack of a second harpy. She rolled up and lunged, thrusting her blade at the first harpy. Her steel ran through the screeching torso. Scyra pulled the blade horizontally as she withdrew, cutting along its midsection. She brought her steel up and quickly tried to slap away the talons of the second harpy. Scyra was always a swift one, in body and mind. She had not the strength of Boroca or Domos but she was good at avoidance - in combat, relationships and in life. So when the talons slashed at her, Scyra used her steel to block the few she could not dodge. A blast of lilac magic slammed into the second harpy and sent it crashing to the ground. Scyra glanced at the priest and gave him a thankful nod. He nodded back before returning to his injured pair.

Scyra's eyes fell on Perigoss. He was surrounded by two gigas and doing his best to fight them off but his struggle was becoming more apparent with each passing second. Scyra bolted toward him to grant assistance. As she ran forward, she found her mind loudly protesting. What was she doing? This was not her usual approach. She was not a head-on type of combatant. She preferred to avoid direct combat and instead resort to trickery and guile. So why had she chosen her current action?

Perigoss raised his shield as a gigas hammer slammed down against it. The blow was powerful and instantly he felt the repercussion in his arm. He was barely able to duck as a gigas sword slashed at his head. Perigoss back stepped a few paces and thrust with his spear. It was a clumsy attack, with no real purpose but to hopefully keep his foes from advancing. Sadly, it did not work. Hammer-gigas continued with large, arching brutal strikes while sword-gigas tried to run him through. As the hammer connected once more with the shield, Perigoss found himself knocked on his ass. He looked up as the sword lunged at him.

The sword never made contact.

Scyra dashed in and slapped gigas steel aside with her own. Standing before the fallen Perigoss, she brought the blade upwards, deflecting the second and third attack.

"Do you mean to lie in the dirt all day?" Scyra jested.

"When did you learn how to use a sword?" Perigoss replied in kind as he scrambled to his feet.

"Why must I remind everybody, over and over," Scyra sarcastically replied. "I am the world's greatest swordswoman."

"And here I was still thinking you were a coward," Perigoss laughed. "A stunning one but a coward none the less."

"Cowards tend to live longer," Scyra promised. She pointed her sword as the gigas began to move once more.

Hammer-gigas arched his arm back to swing once more. Perigoss stepped in with his shield raised. The hammer connected again but as the gigas pulled his weapon back, Scyra attacked. Her blade leapt in. A quick slash caught the inside of the gigas' hammer arm and tore along the tricep. As Scyra attacked the hammer-gigas, Perigoss pivoted around her back, his shield catching the sword before it could cause harm. His spear instantly leapt over the top of the shield, snapping at the sword-gigas like a hungry serpent. Scyra and Perigoss fought side by side. When the hammer attacked, Perigoss moved in to block. When the sword slashed, Scyra deflected. No words were spoken but they worked as one. When one flank was left vulnerable, it was covered by the other. As a gigas attack was deflected by one, the other would step in with a cursory strike on an arm or leg. None were strong enough to end a battle in one blow but each chipped away at their strength and speed until the gigas slowed enough for a final strike.

As the final gigas fell, the two stood there with heaving chests while gasping for air, they realized that four gigas lay dead around them. They had not even notriced when a fallen one had been replaced. The two had just kept fighting.

"Priest!" Both heads snapped over. Boroca lay on the ground, his cuirass cracked and the warrior struggling to breathe. A freshly slain gigas lay beside him while Nikka stood over him. Rarus bolted across the town square, running towards the fallen ally. He clutched his staff tightly, willing the magic to activate. By the time he reached the fallen, Lilac magic had already begun to billow around the priest. Rarus moved his hand slowly as he began to mend the insides of the dark-skinned warrior. Perigoss looked around. The village still burned but the attackers - what few were left alive - had fled.

The sudden sound of a large explosive blast filled the air. Perigoss snapped his head in the sound's direction and spotted a large ornate building - obviously a temple - burning. The kid took off running. He ignored his exhaustion and just pushed forward. As the temple got closer, he spotted a pair of men exiting the building with arms full of stolen goods. Both men spotted him but each had a different reaction. One dropped his gear, pulled free an ill-kept blade and charged directly at him. The second took one look at Perigoss and sped away in the opposite direction. Perigos shifted his grip of the spear, holding it like a javelin, and fired it forward. It soared past the sword-bandit and dove into the leg of the fleeing man. He crashed into the ground, dropping his stolen goods into the ground. Without slowing his run, Perigoss drew his blade and screamed. He smashed his shield into the bandit and sent the man flying backwards. The bandit hit the ground, hard, but quickly scrambled to his feet. He slashed at an approaching Perigoss but his attack was quickly parried. The bandit had no real training. His attacks were weak and frail. The bandit grabbed his blade with both hands, thinking it a more powerful attack, and swung again. Perigoss deflected the attack, slammed his shield into the bandit and once again knocked him to the ground. He kicked the sword away from the bandit. Perigoss pressed the tip of his steel against the bandit's neck, drawing a single drop of blood. The bandit begged for mercy.

"Leave, now," Perigoss said as he withdrew the tip of his blade. The bandit scrambled to his feet and bolted away. Perigoss turned back to the burning temple just as another form emerged. It was a woman wearing a patchwork suit of armour, obviously stolen or looted. Worse still, she wore a helm that she had not earned. Perigoss charged the third bandit, looking to knock her to the ground with a shield slam but just as his shield was about to hit, she brought her shield to meet it.

Shield slammed against shield and neither side moved. Perigoss blinked in surprise. He had pushed with all of his momentum but the female bandit was not budging. He pushed harder, putting each ounce of his strength behind it, but still she did not budge.

Until she did.

Using a burst of speed, she suddenly removed her push-back and stepped aside. Perigoss was suddenly off balance and stumbled forward. The bandit grabbed him by his shield and twisted, flinging him to the ground. He thudded against the dirt, shocked and surprised, but shook it off. Scrambling back to his feet, he slashed and her blade met his with a loud clang. She slapped his sword aside and lunged in with a speedy thrust. Unlike the other bandits, this one knew how to use a blade. Her strikes were fast, accurate and her intention was well hidden by her limbs. Whomever this bandit was, she knew how to fence. Perigoss used his shield to block the attack and returned with his own. No longer needling to hold back, his strikes became faster. The bandit blinked in surprise as the blade became almost a blur. She twisted away, narrowly missing the taste of steel. She sidestepped and attacked again.

One moment ago, Perigoss had been standing beside her. The next moment that Scyra looked, he was gone. From the corner of her eye she spotted him running towards the temple. She sighed and shook her head. Do-gooders would always be doing good. With the gigas and the harpies gone, what trouble was left for him to get into?

Then her waterskin began to shake.

She had yet to figure out what exactly caused the event but she had learned enough to realize that this meant that the kid was in trouble and, most likely, he was in over his head. She bolted towards the temple, passing a pair of terrified looters who were desperately fleeing. As she turned the street corner, and the temple came into view, her eyes suddenly fell upon the sight of a fight.

Perigoss and some unknown woman were eagerly fencing. She slid to a halt and watched in stunned silence. Two blades moved at a blurring speed. They clashed against each other, bouncing off a shield or missing entirely but the blades never struck their opponents. Scyra had seen high-level fencing in her past - allegedly - but this was something different. This was fencing perfection. When one took a step, the other countered. When one struck, the other parried. When one baited with a weak opening, the other feigned commitment. Worst still, they seemed to fight with the same Oibalox-ian style. If the Oibalox maestros of fencing were to teach a class on perfection of fencing, this would be it. It would be a terrible lesson filled with Oibalox propaganda and radicalized beliefs but it would be a study of this fight.

The longer the two fought, the more Scyra started to distrust what her eyes saw. Suddenly the woman's body and gear was becoming translucent and when her limbs moved, Scyra swore she saw an echo of her movement, still lingering in the air. It was like when she was a child, holding a half burnt stick and waving it around in the darkness. The seared end still burned red with embers and the burning glow seemed to leave a burning tail in the sky. Scyra used to write her name in the sky and feel like the grandest sorceress in the land. Even Perigoss' body began to move in ways that she had never seen, Scyra suddenly scolding herself for how often she had studied his body from afar. The moves he was performing had not changed, they were still the rigid and formulaic Oibaloxian strikes, but somehow they had evolved. Not only were his strikes and forms faster but somehow they seemed smoother, more flowing. It was as if he was no longer trying to walk up a stream but had decided to flow with it. Scyra blinked as Perigoss' blade began to shimmer. It never seemed to properly change colours but in the flickering flames of the burning town, she swore that both his hair and blade began to transform to a cerulean shade.

In a blink of Scyra's eye, the woman warrior vanished, only to reappear behind Perigoss. A solid strike to his back was all it would take to drop the warrior but somehow Perigoss twisted at the last second, transforming a devastating blow into a glancing one. Angry, the warrioress kicked the off-balance Perigoss and sent him crashing to the ground. The kid bounced off the dirt once, but before he hit again his entire body twisted. He landed in a three point stance. The woman was angry now, there was no hiding that fact. Her blade transformed into a spectral weapon and she lunged forward. Perigoss' gladius was now entirely a cerulean colour. He brought the weapon up to block and the two blades collided with a deafening, metallic clang. The warrioress was shocked her attack had been blocked and Perigoss was surprised to see himself still alive. The pair disengaged, each nervously staring at one another, unsure as to what had just happened.

"Whomever you are," Scyra said as she approached, her blade out and leveled at the unknown woman. "I would strongly suggest that you end this battle. You are now outnumbered and worse still, you face the world's finest mistresses of the blade. If you still wish to pursue this fight, you now face me."

Scyra really hoped she did not want to continue.

"Nothing you steal here is worth your life," Perigoss said, panting for air.

"You think me a bandit?" The woman protested. "I am no such thing. Do not cast your dishonour upon me. I am Stellia, Daughter of Stellios. I am a hoplite of Oibalox."

Perigoss lowered his blade and stepped back, Stellia's words cutting deeper than her blade ever had. Scyra, however, was not so eager to simply accept her words. More than once she had claimed herself to be a hoplite. In her past she had also claimed to be a farmer's daughter, a gem merchant, an oracle, a princess, and, more impossible of them all, a virgin handmaiden. She was not about to believe this woman on her words alone.

"I care not what lies you speak but I—"

Scyra's words were quickly cut-off as Stellia's blade leapt up. In the blink of an eye the steel was pressed against her neck. "I will not have the honour of my word or my blade called into question. If you want this fight to continue then we shall."

Scyra let out an annoyed sigh as she gently pushed the blade away from her neck. This woman was telling the truth. Only the citizens of Oibalox spoke with such levels of pomp and idiocy. "You are a little off course, hoplite. This is Hakros territory."

"I know where my feet walk," Stellia said sternly. Her voice seemed to lessen slightly as she continued. "I simply know not as to why. I have been guided here by visions."

"You abandoned your phalanx?" Scyra asked. Stellia's blade leapt up once more, returning to Scyra's neck. Stellia opened her mouth to protest but Scyra shook her head and pushed the blade away yet again. "This conversation will go far swifter if we can speak without the steel."

"We can talk about this later," Perigoss said. He pointed at the burning temple. "We need to save whomever and whatever we can."

Both women nodded and all three moved toward the temple. As they approached, all three of them grabbed their water skins. They were planning to douse themselves with its contents with the hopes of adding a layer of protection from the flames. Yet as all three opened their skins they found each was already bone dry.

CHAPTER TWELVE

If we do not eliminate war, it will eliminate us.
- Athonea Proverb

With the fires finally at a calm and the town at a brief moment of rest, the six plopped down on the ground, exhausted. Several hours had passed since they entered Mikha and they had not stopped moving the entire time. On habit, Rarus reached for his staff and tried to will the magic forth, looking to revitalize his body with its arcane touch but the lilac magic that came forth was dull and miniscule. The staff needed time to recharge. Rarus had spent the past few hours healing anybody who was injured, for which there were many, and his staff had run dry. A magical item like his could never run out of magic - not easily at least - but it could run very low from overuse. It would take a few days for the magic to properly refill. He would have to rely on his own strength for the next little bit. While he had been tending to the wounded, the others had been combating the flames, evacuating the temple and safely securing artefacts and items of importance.

Rarus looked up as Stellia approached. She was the Oibalox hoplite that the kid had stumbled across. She had been helping them for the last few hours. She pulled off her helm and nodded to the six. Rarus nodded in return, giving her permission to sit.

"Do you need some water?" Rarus offered. She nodded and graciously accepted his skin, taking a long swig.

"If you would excuse my questioning," Stellia began. "But what are your plans after this? Where are you six heading? I assume none of you are so honourless enough to permanently abandon your phalanx."

"Be careful of your words, priest," Scyra said with a scoff. "This one likes to speak with her steel upright. She is very judgemental for one who walks without her own phalanx."

Stellia's eyes narrowed in disgust as she glared at the thief. Every instinct told her to draw her blade but the last thing she wanted to do was to prove Scyra correct.

"We will be returning to our phalanx," Boroca said. "The gigas are moving inwards towards Hakros. We will not let them or any other giant take our city."

"Then why are you not with them now?"

"We were not going to allow any other person suffer either," Boroca answered.

Stellia frowned. This thinking was unlike what she was used to. She was from Oibalox. The priorities of the Oibalox came before the individual. If you better the polis, then you better everybody's lives. No small village was above all of that. No village was worth abandoning their phalanx.

"The gigas are a frightening force," Stellia explained. "We faced them at Pylomia. They have harpies with them and god knows what else. We were unprepared."

Rarus' eyes suddenly went wide. He recognized a look in Stellia's face. It was guilt, not for something she had done but for something she had not: she had not died. He knew the feeling, he had experienced it himself. Many nights he had cried from guilt, wondering why he lived when Neilo did not.

"How many are left?" the priest carefully asked. Perigoss' eyes went wide and Xali let out a gasp. Understanding suddenly rippled through the remaining three.

"I do not know," she said, fighting the sorrow from surfacing. "But I do not think it is many."

"What are your plans then?" Rarus asked.

"If you will have me, I wish to join you."

"For what purpose?" Rarus asked.

"I want to run back to my polis and fight in its defense. However, I feel myself drawn elsewhere. I feel like I've been drawn to this band." She glanced down at the broken spear that hung from her waist. "Now all I want is to run my blade through Aidox's neck," she said sternly. "The gigas commander deserves to die and I plan to send him to the underworld."

"You are more than welcome to join us," Perigoss said quickly. "There is no spear greater than an Oibloxian one."

Rarus nodded but inside he was torn. He knew this mentality; when the desire for revenge overshadowed everything else. It was not a desire unknown to the Deathkin but it was a dangerous and toxic one. Rarus looked down at the earth and silently spoke to the death goddess.

"Not only must I steer the boy down the proper path, now you put her in my visions as well?" He silently prayed. "I think you may have overestimated my abilities."

One of Mikha's priests approached the six. The priest was thankful and gracious, bowing several times as he sang their praises. "We would have lost everything if not for your intervention. The fates were wise to send you to us this day. It matters not which god you worship, on this day you have earned the thanks of all of them."

Rarus rolled his eyes. Even though he was a priest himself, a holy man in service, he could never stand the rhetoric. To him it always felt so disingenuous. No man ever revealed his true self by speaking in the words of another.

"Boroca, our prodigal son," the priest said. "We are forever blessed to count you in our numbers and forever thankful for your return. You will forever be a hero to our village."

Boroca just sheepishly nodded. He stammered to find the words in which to properly reply but he found none. He forced an awkward smile.

"Because of you, our temple stands strong."

"That is an aspect that puzzles me," Nikka said suddenly. "They cause an amazing amount of damage in this village. They pillaged and torched everything but left the temple for last?"

"The temple suffered great losses as well," the priest explained. "They pillaged and looted the temple for hours as the rest of the town burned."

"They did the same in Pylomia," Stellia added. "When I came to, the village was in a state of pure destruction but the exterior of the temple was left mostly unharmed. The same green smoke hovered in the sky above."

"That is what I feared," Nikka replied. Her face scrunched up as her mind raced.

"I know that look," Xali said. "You are worried about something - something bad. What has your mind at such unease?"

"Is the temple safe to enter?" Nikka suddenly asked of the holy man. The priest nodded. Nikka stood up and pointed to Scyra. "Thief, you are with me."

"I am?" Scyra asked, a little surprised. It was a sentiment that Xali shared. "I did not know you thought of me in that fashion and lest we forget, your wife is sitting right there."

Nikka and Xali both scowled. "Shut up and follow me."

"Wow, this is a poor start to our relationship," Scyra mumbled as she reluctantly climbed to her feet and started following. "Perhaps you would do well to know that I do not enjoy lengthy walks upon the sand and much prefer bottomless mugs from which to drink wine."

"I have some serious questions about this temple," Nikka said, "and I need your eyes and your deviousness."

"Why does nobody ever want me for my body?" Scyra lamented.

Stellia stood up. She had questions of her own and she assumed that the temple would aid her in discovery. She needed to know why the spear wanted her here. Stellia quickly followed. Rarus waved his apprentice over.

"I want to know what they are thinking. I think it will be vital for the war," he said sternly. He held that look for a few heartbeat before a smile crossed his lips. "But I have pushed myself to the point of exhaustion so I will send you instead."

Perigoss rolled his eyes and followed, taking Boroca with him as the pair jogged to catch up.

Stellia sped up her pace until she fell in step with Scyra. She leaned in and spoke softly. "You still have your brelok on."

Scyra eyed her with confusion. Stellia spoke like it

was an embarrassing thing, like a lace undone or a loose strap. Stellia raised an confused eyebrow.

"You are not from Oibalox?"

"By the gods, no," she loudly protested. She stopped when she saw the quickly sterning look on the hoplite's face. Scyra flashed an innocent smile and tried again. "I mean, no. I was not lucky enough to hail from that glorious land."

"I am sorry. I made my assumption on the brelok."

"Perigoss gave it to me," she explained. "He said his people wear them into battle."

Stellia's face carried with it a look of stun. She had not expected that. She had thought Perigoss to be unattached. An Oibalox citizen rarely gave a brelok to an outsider. It just was not done except for the more intimate of cases.

"So why is it bad that I wear it now?"

"We wear those into battle so we may be ready to meet Charon if we fall," she explained. "There is an acceptance of our fate when we wear them. It shows our preparation for the honourable death. However, if you wear them outside of battle, it shows that you are a coward who fears death."

Scyra frowned. In a twisted way of thinking, there was some logic behind it. The only problem was that it made no sense. Everybody should fear death. Scyra was quite fond of living and planned to remain in that state for as long as possible.

"Thank you for explaining," Scyra said, pulling the brelok over her head. She quickly shoved it into her pouch. There was no sense in insulting Perigoss' culture after he had shown her kindness by sharing a part of it with her.

The group entered the stone temple. The white material stood strong despite the scorched marks that covered the outside. Perigoss walked into the temple and looked around.

He had been in Oibalox temples before, grandiose buildings depicting their righteous victories, but this was nothing like those. Most of the temple's decorations and artefacts - those that weren't smashed and destroyed - were for Opato, the god of farming and harvest. It was common for farming communities to pray to the deity with hopes that he would bless their crops.

He wordlessly glanced at Stellia and she nodded back. Neither of them were comfortable here. The war goddess was paramount; she was above all others. Despite the good they did, this still felt wrong. Both quietly reached into their belongings and began to run their thumbs over their breloks, thanking Cydomea for their victory.

"To what god was the temple was in Pylomia for?" Nikka asked.

"Cydomea," Stellia replied.

"I feel like we could have guessed that," Scyra replied with a distant voice. It was the type of response that came when one only gave half of their attention to the conversation. Stellia narrowed her eyes at the thief but eventually shook it off. She glanced back at Nikka. "Why do you ask?"

"The gigas arrive and decimate each temple," Nikka began. She continued her theory but Scyra paid it no mind. She was distracted.

Something did not feel right.

Scrya looked over the temple. Her eyes darted everywhere as she desperately tried to pinpoint what it was that made the hairs on the back of her neck stand on end.

Focus.

The words hit her thoughts like a brick and caused her to visibly flinch. The voice - albeit one of her mind's own making - was from her past and one she was none too pleasant with reliving.

You are of a mind that everything is easy because you are far swifter than most. The true test is what happens when a task actually requires your effort.

Gibus, High Priest of Ithoma Seminary.

He was a priest of Psophious and eventually was her direct teacher. As Scyra rose through the seminary, excelling at nearly everything with little effort, Gibus was the one who took interest in her. He was the first that said she was limiting herself. He saw so much potential in her and pushed her to try harder and as much as she regretted it, Scyra bought into his ideology. He was an intoxicating soul, especially for an old man with a long greying beard, a mind full of wisdom and knowledge, a lifetime of charisma and the skill to reward any woman who was tempted to play with him and play he did. Gibus held the same belief that most men of a certain age did; if he stuck his dick in the holes of younger women then he could be restored a fraction of his youth.

Sadly that wasn't his only attempt at youth.

Scyra wanted nothing to do with this man, past or present, but there he was, in her thoughts once again. So in- grained into her mind were his teachings that she could never be free of him.

Forever his victim.

Forever carrying his guilt.

There isn't always a shorter path. Sometimes you must take a longer trek to reach your destination.

She closed her eyes and took a deep breath. She want- ed to clear her mind, erase anything she had seen previously. With a final moment to ready her senses and her mind, she opened her eyes.

The temple room was rectangle, not uncommon for

holy building in any polis' jurisdiction. It was a smaller building, but again not uncommon for a village of this size. She started with her left and started looking around the room. Small tables and shelves once held vases and busts, each representing some aspect of farm life. They had each been smashed or broken. Dozens of artefacts lay in pieces as clay and stone dust hovered in the air, slowly spinning in the breeze. In the centre of the room was a dias. Here, sacrifices and tributes would be placed as the people prayed for healthy crops and bountiful harvest. It too had been smashed.

The walls were decorated with carvings and paintings of Opato, their doctrines and depictions of his great farmer mythling. Many of these carvings and paintings had been slashed, smashed or punched in. One of these, on the right hand side, had revealed a compartment hidden behind the wall.

Scyra walked to the hole and instantly felt the faintest of breezes slipping in through the cracks. She hadn't felt it near the other walls.

She paused. What was she missing?

Scyra stood in the stuffy room and found herself getting internally angry. If Gibus was so great a teacher then why couldn't she have figured this out? And why did he need to appear - albeit fictionally - to her if he had no answers?

It's the breeze, you idiot.

Scyra's eyes popped open and her head snapped to her left. If the room had no air flow, except for the secret compartment, then where was the breeze to the left coming from?

"This is why," Nikka continued as her voice began to register to Scyra once more. "I think that Aidox is trying to punish the gods by desecrating as many temples as possible."

"There are a couple details that don't add up," Scyra

said suddenly. All eyes suddenly turned towards her. "If they wanted to anger the gods, then why not simply burn them down? No, they left the building untouched and ransacked its innards."

"You think you have the answers?" Nikka said with a raise of an eyebrow and a scowl in her voice.

"Of course I do," Scyra said, suddenly returning to her bravado. "Am I not the FireKissed Thief? Does my intellect not ripple throughout the land so hundreds flock to me for knowledge?"

"No, they do not," Stellia scowled. She glanced at the group. "Is she always like this?"

Perigoss rolled his eyes and nodded.

"I will speak slowly for those not as swift of thought," Scyra said while pointing at Stellia. The soldier scowled and took a step forward. Scyra halted her with a wave of her hand. "Save all questions for the end.

"The giants, and by extension the gigas, are on a campaign of destruction. They seem to carry with them such a grand level of anger that they level any village they come across. Yet, they decided to leave the temples alone. Instead, they go inside and desecrate them; why?"

"They hate the gods," Nikka repeated.

"I mean it certainly seems that way. The gigas came in here, smashed every artefact and smashed a hole in the wall. Everything is either looted or destroyed. This seems like the truth presented before our eyes but when a painting appears too pleasant, it is easy to miss the finer details. Let your eyes grasp everything before you and you will see the truth for what it is: the gigas are looking for something specific and they do not want us to know what it is.

"The best way to hide one crime isn't to pretend it

did not happen, instead you hide it amongst a different crime. The temple looks like the gigas are trying to strike back at the gods because that is what they want us to think. In truth, they were looking for a very specific item. They found it amongst the items hidden in that secret compartment."

"Couldn't they have just been looting the place?" Stellia asked. "What makes you think it was specifically hidden there?"

"Once again, the Oibaloxian mind is limited in how they think," Scyra said with a smile.

"She knows I can stab her, correct?" Stellia asked.

"I believe a line has formed for that very task," Perigoss said with a shake of his head and a small chuckle.

"The gigas were wise enough to find this secret compartment. If they were simply looting anything they could find," Scyra said as she dramatically danced from the right side of the room to the left. "Then why could they not find this one?"

She rapped her fist against the wall and let the hollow-thud be heard. As the rest glanced back and forth at each other, Scrya looked down at the painting of…of….actually she knew not of whom the painting was depicting. Scyra had a hard time picturing what a Harvest mythling would look like let alone being able to name any of them.

"What was so precious that not only did it need to be hidden," Nikka asked aloud, her words slow at first. "But that the gigas were desperate to find?"

Everybody turned to look at the priest. The holy man simply shook his head. "The answers you seek are not ones I can openly give."

"We are simply trying to help," Scyra said with a dramatic roll of her eyes. "There are limits to my genius, however hard to believe that may be."

"You misunderstand him," Boroca said. He had been quiet for a long time but now things were starting to make sense. "He physically cannot speak of it. I guess there was some spell or something that now prevents him from saying."

The priest simply stood there, neither confirming or denying. He just stood still.

"When I was a kid, there used to be a rumour about the priests," Boroca explained. "The old kids always spoke how the priest had their tongues cut out so they couldn't repeat the secrets we told them." He glanced over at the priest and let out a nostalgic chuckle. "It makes sense now. The temple was hiding something powerful and they had to make sure that the secret of which remained so."

"What was the painting of?" Stellia asked. "I mean, if it was an object of danger, they would have simply destroyed it. If it was important, but dangerous in the wrong hands, then they would keep it but perhaps they left hints on the painting in case it was ever needed in a time of emergency and the priests were gone."

Scrya rolled her eyes, mostly to keep up appearances. In truth, that was a brilliant bit of thinking but there was no way she would let the Oibaloxian know that.

"It was of Heklious and the Cerynodes Vineyards," Boroca said. "I stared at that drawing my entire childhood. His heroics are what guided my path to becoming a hero."

Heklious was one of the legendaries mythlings. He was a hero of minor renown until the day his wife died. Desperate to get her back from the underworld, Heklious underwent a single task for each of the twelve gods. These would forever be known as the twelve labours of Heklious.

His task for Opato was to travel the near-infinite

Cerynodes Vineyards. There he had to pick each and every grape. This was no simple task as each berry was so fine and delicate that a touch even slightly stronger than needed would cause the berry to burst.

"Could that be a hint of some sort?" Stellia asked. The rest simply shrugged. Once again they eyed the priest but the holy man said nothing.

"So what is hidden in the untouched compartment," Scrya asked. "Is there anything that could help us stop the gigas and retrieve whatever was stolen?"

The priest eyed the thief suspiciously but nodded. "Those who took the same oath as I have were given access to a few special items. They were to be used to help the people of the village, of the temple and, if needed, of this land."

"Then why do they remain hidden?" Stellia asked with an annoyed tone. "Where are your champions?"

"None had proven themselves worthy," the priest said as he turned towards Boroca. "Up until now. Boroca, Son of Biroca, you have come to the aid of our people, our village and our temple. You have shown us your skill, your honour and your righteousness. Would you please take up arms once more for our cause? Will you forever be one of the heroes of this village?"

"I…I would be h…honoured," Boroca replied, stumbling over his words.

The priest walked towards the hidden compartment, opening it with the press of a hidden switch. He reached in and withdrew a shield. He carefully handed it to their hometown hero.

"This is the Timeworn Aegis. It was once held by Laodameia the Woetorn."

Boroca knew the name, every person in Mikha did.

She was a mythling who fought during the cataclysmic hydras rampages. She had retired in the village and spent her golden years teaching the young how to fight while protecting the village from the occasional threat. She had passed away nearly a decade before Boroca was born but her stories were still being told to the children of today.

"We bestow the shield to you, child of Opato. May the magics that bind it, aid you in our salvation."

Boroca held the shield in awe. It was a round shield with a semicircle indentation on either side. It was made from bronze but was so light. Most shields were layers upon layers of leather with bronze on either side. Yet for some reason, this shield felt far thinner and lighter than the one he currently carried. On the face was the symbol of Opato: a trio of wheat strands with a vine of grapes before it. For a moment Boroca's breath seemed to catch and no words came out. He always wanted to be a hero worthy of his home village but to carry the shield of his hometown legend, that was beyond comprehension. Eventually, he remembered how to speak.

"I will do my best to make this village proud." Boroca paused for a second and leaned in closer to the priest. "Do I need to cut out my tongue?"

The priest just smirked.

"Why is her gear not in the Hall of Mythology?" Perigoss asked.

"Some leave specific items of their gear where they see fit," The priest said. "Especially if it can help others. The Woetorn was not the only one to leave something here. Others have as well in the past, in temples all across the world."

"Is there nothing else you can offer us in knowledge?" Stellia asked. The priest just sadly shook his head. The hoplite sighed but nodded. "We should be returning to the others anyways."

She nodded at the others before departing the temple. One by one, the others followed. It wasn't until Perigoss attempted to leave that the priest spoke once more.

"Son of Oibalox," his words brought Perigoss to a halt. Scyra paused with him. The priest stepped towards him. "Boroca spoke how you helped him devise a method to defend our home. You have our thanks."

"There is no need," Perigoss began.

"It is rude to say no, hero," Scyra interrupted. She looked at the priest. "He is happy to receive any blessing you wish to give him."

Perigoss rolled his eyes.

"Hidden compartments are crucial for any temple," the priest explained. "There are secrets amongst men that the gods wish hidden. It is our task to keep them so.

"There are so many things that can be kept in a compartment like such." One at a time, he removed the items and placed them upon the remains of a table. "A scroll of whispers, a vial of wisdom water and a robe of holy devotion but there is one object that should exist in a hidden compartment. It should exist in every hidden compartment."

The priest reached in and pulled free a small pendant. It was a silver coin, etched with the symbol of Athonea, bound to a golden borden by four separate brackets. It hung on a purple cord.

"I would be hard pressed to picture in my mind's eye a hidden compartment that did not at one time possess a magical pendant." He handed the pendant to Perigoss. "This is a minor object, with only a little magic for sight within it, but still many have found it useful. I give it to you so that when you finally have a need for a hidden compartment of your own, you will have a pendant to place in it."

The priest smiled.

Perigoss looked confused.

"What are you talking about?" Perigoss asked.

"It's a good thing you are exceptionally cute," Scyra said with a smirk. She stepped forward to the priest, took his hand into her, and spoke to the holy man. "As a woman of my aptitude, there is little more that I like than a good loophole. So thank you, for everything."

The priest nodded back as Scyra pulled Perigoss from the temple. With a smile he turned back to the remainder of the table and grabbed the scroll of whispers and the robe of devotion and carefully returned both to the hidden compartment before closing its door once more.

CHAPTER THIRTEEN

There are two forces in the world; the sword and the faith.
The sword will always fall to the dirt. Faith exists forever.
- Castlex Proverb

For the first time that day, a burning flame in the town of Mikha brought comfort instead of fear as a large campfire burned in a pit near Boroca's home. The hometown hero sat on a log and watched the flames flicker as the evening's last rays of light faded away. The rest of his rebellious six either sat beside him or were nearby.

"I've been doing some thinking," Perigoss said. He held his map up by a small torch and frowned. "Our original plan may need some adjustment."

"How so?" Rarus asked.

"Our phalanx is moving towards Aoryna and so to are the gigas. Our phalanx is marching around the fields."

"I asked around to the survivors and from what they saw so too are the gigas," Xali added.

"The phalanx said they were going to hustle," Perigoss continued. "Which means with the increased speed, along with the removal of our two slowest marchers, they will be far more forward then we originally calculated."

"Who do you think are our slowest marchers?" Boroca asked, a quizzical look upon his face. "I mean aside from

Rarus, obviously."

"I take no offense from facts," Rarus replied as he took a sip of his wine.

"You best not mean myself," Xali sternly added.

"Of course he does," Scyra chuckled. "I mean, Nikka is swift as a hare and Boroca is far too fit and gorgeous to be slow. Accept your sluggish nature and be happy in that lethargic lifestyle."

"The slowest marcher is by far Scyra," Perigoss said without hesitation. "Our thief does not have the will, limbs or boots to march alongside the rest of us."

The group let out a small chuckle as Scyra pouted in the darkness.

"Regardless, we need to catch up to them before the gigas do," Perigoss continued. "I wish not for the phalanx to fight without us."

"Neither do I," Xali agreed.

"You sound like a man with a plan," Rarus siad. "What do you propose, apprentice?"

"The Pharian Fields separates Aoryna and Mikha. Instead of marching around it, we cut right through it."

Silence.

"Are you mad?" Scyra asked, sitting up. As the light of the fire reached her face, the look of concern was clear.

"There are only seven of us," Perigoss began. "We will not damage the fields like an army would. It would also turn a three day march into a single day."

"Damage?" Xali muttered in confusion. "Wait, does the mythling's prodigy not know the legends?"

"Armies, be it ours or theirs, avoid the Pharian Fields not to avoid damaging the vast fields of wheat," Boroca said softly. "They avoid it because those who trespass onto the golden wheat fields die amongst their stalks."

"Murderous wheat, surely you jest?" Perigoss said, nervously chuckling like he was missing a funny joke but when nobody else joined him, his eyes narrowed.

"The surrounding farmers make tributes to the Pharian Beasts before each season. In return, they are rewarded with the ability to harvest the wheat and tasked with replanting it. Anybody else who dares step in it becomes the very compost used to strengthen the crop." Borica shook his head. "Some have even been given permission to cross only to have that revoked half way in."

"I dare not put our lives at risk," Perigoss said, "But we will not catch up if we do not cut through. So what is our consensus?"

"Could we try a tribute of our own?" Scrya proposed slowly, her mind racing. "Or...or....could we distract them with a tribute of our own. We have two casters in our midst and I have seen the old man null the feeling of pain using his magics. Between the two of them we could lace the tributes with arcanas. Perhaps we slow their minds or even put them to sleep. It would let us pass."

"You would poison the tribute before you even know if it works or not?" Perigoss asked, disgust rising up into his throat. "Why do you carry such dishonour?"

"Honour is a currency that only the living can brag about," Scyra said with a shake of her head. "Look at this village. How many died happy knowing that their honour was intact and how many cried, begging for their life? We are at war, Perigoss. You can spend a lifetime trying to repair your honour if it means that much to you but that is a choice you will have only if you survive."

"Spoken like the words of a coward,"

"A coward who will still be alive when this war is over," Scyra said with a shake of her head. "Can you say the same for yourself?"

Perigoss stared at the thief, fire in his eyes and a boil in his blood. Every word she spoke enraged him. She lived a life so vastly different then his and she cared for nobody but herself.

"I agree with Scyra," Rarus said suddenly. Perigoss' eyes snapped to his master. "It is imperative that we reunite with the phalanx before the next battle." Too many lives would be lost without his healing; too many sent below before their time was due. "Therefore we must ensure our survival above all else and deal with the consequences after the fact."

"But....I..."

"This is war, son," Rarus said. He spoke first to Perigoss but eventually moved his gaze to all others, making eye contact with each, one by one. "War is about making decisions that you wouldn't normally have to make. Each of you made the choice to put the wellbeing of this town over that of your phalanx and I could not have been prouder of each of you. However, that choice came with consequences. One of which is the choice of what you will do next. If failure is not an option, then you are left with only two options: do you slay the monster of Pherian Fields or do you trick it?

"None of you will make it out of this war with your psyche untouch. Each of you will have your morals challenged, your core fiber tested and your mind assaulted. The true test of a soldier is to make sure that when you bend, you do not break. That is how you will make it home."

Silence.

Rarus let his words hang for a moment. In the distance he could see Stellia leaning on the tree, watching from afar. He knew that she was listening. He was hoping for it.

"Tomorrow we cross through the Pherian Fields and we will be devious with our tribute," Rarus declared. "I suggest you all get some rest, it will be a trying day."

"This is insa–"

"Watch your tongue, boy," Rarus snapped, interrupting Perigoss' outcry. "Take a walk, son, and let your head cool down. The choice was taken from your hands and so too has the guilt. You best find a way to deal with what we have to do."

Perigoss glared at his master before storming off into the darkness. One by one, everybody else peeled away, leaving only Scyra and the priest. He handed her a water skin.

"I should have questions as to how you know what this is," Rarus began. Scyra opened the top and gave it a sniff. She instantly recoiled at the oil-scent. This was war fire. "Dozens of these were in the temple before the gigas raided it. They used the temple's own supply against their very village."

"Why does a temple have green flame?" she asked.

"Save us both time and do not think me a fool," Rarus scowled. "I am far too old, tired and lonely to be playing that game. Speak the truth if you still know how."

"They were hiding an amulet," she began, subtly pocketing the skin. "Something so powerful that they were magic bound not to speak of it. Not only that, they were so afraid of its power that they were willing to destroy it with green flame instead of letting it be taken."

"Which leaves us with the most important question," Rarus prompted.

"What kind of amulet was it?" Scyra finished.

Perigoss stormed away, furious. What was Rarus doing? These actions were wrong. They were deceitful and backstabbing. It was beyond dishonest and yet everybody was simply fine with the idea. How had Scyra's ways become that of the group?

Perigoss drew his dagger and angrily tossed it at the tree. The blade dug deep into the trunk, a toss thrown true.

"You do little to hide your anger," Stellia said calmly as she emerged from the shadows, an act that seemed far easier than before. She walked to the tree and tried to pull the dagger free. For a moment she was shocked when it couldn't be easily withdrawn but with a second tug it came out. "Forget not your teachings. Anger is powerful but it can also distract you."

"I did not undergo the same training as you did," Perigoss scowled. "I was never a hoplite."

"I find your past curious," Stellia said as she slowly paced. "You are born in Oibalox, are clearly of fit build and stature but still you did not enlist. Clearly you are not a coward, so why do you not fight for your polis?"

"I would if they would have me," Perigoss said, "but I hold too much contamination in my blood."

"And your impurity would make you a hindrance," Stellia finished. She knew the words; every person in Oibalox did. There were some that doubted the validity of those sacred words but there were always the extreme disbelievers. "So why do you not serve your polis as the rest of the half-breeds do?"

"I was not built to be a farmer or a tradesman," Perigoss spat. "I was born to fight."

"So you do so as a half-breed coinling?" She mocked. "Do you dishonour your family so much that you fight this war as a mercenary?"

She basically spat the last words, the syllables feeling akin to bile in her mouth. There was little else as dishonourable as being a mercenary. Fighting was sacred, an intimate act between them and Cydomea. It was not something to be sullied by greed and coin.

"You would do best to watch your words," Perigoss said. His face was firm and his lips were tight. Perigoss was angry and he was ready to take it out on anyone he could. "I am no mercenary, I fight as a hero. There is honour in being a hero and I will not hesitate to prove it."

"You think you have the strength to back up that statement, half-breed?" Stellia asked.

"Do not call me that," Perigoss growled. The term was accurate. He had heard it his entire life but his loathing for it was beyond comparison.

"You are a child of Oibalox yet you fight as a hero," Stellia said as she approached him with no hesitation or worry in her steps. "It is impossible to be both. One day soon you will have to choose which side means more to you."

"Obviously the polis comes first," he replied without pause. Those words had been seared into his brain from his early days as a child.

"Yet you act as a cunning hero," Stellia said, a mocking tone in her words. "A child of Oibalox either negotiates or fights. There is no magical trickery."

The anger in Perigoss began to bubble up again, fueling his discomfort.

"The thief….it's…" his voice trailed off as he looked for the words to explain his emotions. "She is changing them all. She is infecting their minds."

"She is a virus," Stellia said. "One that infects everybody's mind and thoughts. This leaves one final question. What do we do with a virus?"

"We destroy it," Perigoss answered.

The thief was a virus.

The words fit so firmly in his mind, like a sword sliding perfectly in its sheath. Yet like a stone hiding at the bottom, there seemed to be a small blockage.

Scyra.

"Let us discuss how we rid ourselves of this virus."

Nikka walked around the darkness until she found Xali. The archer was leaning by the side of a tiny tool shed, slowly removing the ceremonial sticks from her hair. As the last one was withdrawn, Xali's bouncy ginger hair fell free, frolicking as the locks travelled down her back.

Nikka smiled as her eyes fell upon those of her spouse but it faded when Xali did not respond in kind.

"Dare I ask why you hide here, alone in the darkness?" Nikka asked.

"I wanted some time with you, alone and away from the rest," Xali replied.

"I would normally think that to be a savoury invitation but your tone suggests otherwise." Nikka said as she stood before her wife.

Xali stood up straight and reached for Nikka's arms, putting her hands just south of Nikka's shoulder. She slowly moved her arms, pulling them along Nikka's firm, strong limbs. It was an act that caused Xali to gently bite her own lip, despite the seriousness of the topic. Xali's fingers gently travelled over Nikka's muscles as they traveled down her forearm, stopping only when Nikka's hands were firmly in her own.

"Petal," Xali began, using her intimate nickname for the warrior. "The happiest day of my life was when we faced each other in combat."

"When I bested you in combat you mean?"

"Hush, I'm talking," Xali said, cracking a smile for the first time of the conversation. There was always a bit of pride between the two of them over Nikka's win. "I know few others that are as strong, powerful and skilled with a shield as you are. Fewer still can do that and still cast magic the way you do. You were a gift to me from Venodite and one that I will forever cherish."

Nikka opened her mouth to return the affection but Xali silenced her with another hush. Nikka, one not always skilled at waiting her turn to speak, bit her tongue. This seemed important and she needed to let Xali speak.

"I am an archer. I exist in the battle's rear. You are my champion; my frontline amazon; my unbeatable paladin. You will always see more combat than I. So you must protect yourself. You must use your magic that you have to look after yourself, not me."

"My arcane shield saved you this very day," Nikka defended.

"And you nearly perished because of it," Xali said. The archer was normally firm and unwavering; her emotions solid. In that moment, however, vulnerability decorated the archer's face. "I cannot watch you die."

"Nor could I with you." Nikka shook her head. "Our lives together are just beginning. I do not want the song of our pairing to be abruptly cut off."

"Then you need to use your spells to protect yourself."

"I do not need them," Nikka said, her voice lowering as she morphed into a reassuring tone. "I have you always watching my back."

"I cannot always keep my eye on your backside."

"Really? My eyes never seem to stray too far from your backside," Nikka said with a lecherous grin. Xali gently slapped the warrior's chest before returning her hold on Nikka's hands.

"I'm serious. I will always protect you but you have to use the spells on yourself."

"And what of you?" Nikka said. "I feel confident without my spells because you have my back but who has yours? That's why I enchanted you instead of me."

"But it is my duty to protect you."

"And it is mine to protect you."

Both women just stared at each other. The world had countless songs of a soldier's and a civilian's wedding, where the soldier promises to protect their mate till the world's last verse was sung. However, in a world where two soldiers wed and had to fight side by side, who protected whom in that scenario? Xali was used to protecting her mates of days since passed. Most had been scholars or frail casters but standing before her, bound to her by the goddess of love, was one of the strongest women she'd ever seen. Nikka had more muscles than most men and a wisdom to match. Neither woman would dare ask the other not to fight, they would not insult the other like that, but neither knew how to protect the other.

Each woman in turn opened up their mouths to speak but nothing came out. Several times this occurred but silence still hung in the air. So much was needed to be said but nobody had the strength to do it.

Nikka found the solution.

The warrior's hands pulled away from the archer's grip but, before Xali could object, Nikka's right hand swiftly leapt to Xali's face. She cradled the archer's head in her hands and gently steered her with a thumb on her chin. With gentle guidance she tilted Xali's head, just slightly, and leaned in for a kiss.

In a bit of irony, Nikka's lips were always the softest, plump and full of life, whereas Xali's lips were firm and tough; the perfect match. Nikka kissed her wife repeatedly, gently at first but growing with passion with each subsequent encounter. By the fourth kiss, any pretense of talking was gone. No argument or discussion was going to be found that night. Instead, they would find solace in each other.

Xali kissed back with hunger and lust. Her tongue was insistent as it explored her wife's mouth. Her hands moved on their own, racing back up the muscle-filled arms she adored so greatly and down the chest, until they found the warm, voluptuous globes that resided on Nikka's chest.

Nikka was a woman obsessed with Xali's rear but the archer's interests were more situated on the front of her wife's body.

Neither wore armour, it lay on the ground by the fire, so only cloth separated flesh from flesh but still it seemed too much between them. Xali broke the kiss and - reluctantly - released her wife's breasts. Her hands traveled downwards until she reached the warrior's waist. She began the arduous task of undoing the knot that held the belt together, a task made all the more difficult as Nikka began to kiss up and down the side of the archer's neck. The lower the kiss, the more starved her desire was, but the higher up it went, the more gentle it became. When Nikka's lips reached the archer's ear, it was no longer a kiss at all. It was simply a velvety tongue, tracing over every ridge of her ear, inside and out.

It was maddening.

That was Xali's weakness, the one act that turned a rugged, battle-tested archer into a pile of mush and mush was never very effective as undoing knots.

Nikka's actions were no mistake. In the short time since they had been wed, the warrior made it her duty to learn each and every sensitive area on her wife's body. She knew how she melted with attention to her ear, how she quivered with a few kisses down her chest and she knew what combination of fingers made for a louder squeal upon insertion. Nikka had learned them all and was looking forward to a lifetime of learning new ones.

Xali let out a victorious gasp as the knot came undone. A few seconds later, the warrior's chiton lay on the grass. Now nothing would stand between her and her wife's luscious breasts.

Nikka, however, had other ideas.

The warrior's hands were swift once more. Just as Xali was about to make contact, Nikka grabbed both arms, held them together in one hand, and raised them above Xali's head, pushing her back against the shed wall.

Xali whimpered. She had been so close.

She tried to lean in to kiss her wife but Nikka pulled away, denying her the contact. Instead, the warrior leaned in and let her tongue play quill once more. This time tracing the ridges of Xali's face. Her tongue running up and down the side of the archer's jaw at a slow pace, a maddeningly slow pace. Xali leaned in again for a kiss but was denied for a third time. She tried to squirm free of Nikka's grasp but failed.

Damn her wife's impressive strength.

Desperate for a kiss, she whimpered yet again.

Nikka ignored her.

Instead, Nikka's tongue began to move south, sensually tickling the neck and moving towards the chest. Nikka alternated from licks to kisses on the archer's chest, pridefully drinking in each and every quiver that Xali made.

Then Nikka stopped.

Xali twisted her body in an attempt to free herself, the hunger in her body was becoming overwhelming, but once again she fell victim to her wife's impressive strength.

Nikka leaned in and began to whisper in her wife's ears. Xali tried to focus on what was being said but the words seemed nonsense. Suddenly, realization hit the archer. She had heard those words before. They were incantations for a spell, a spell Xali knew all too well.

While she held the archer firmly in her left hand, Nikka's right dropped down to Xali's leg. She slowly ran the right hand up from Xali's knee, under her chiton and towards her groin. At the halfway mark, Nikka finished her incantations and the fingers on her right hand began to glow. Her fingers would now alternate from warm to cold. Every couple of heartbeats they would switch again. By the time Nikka's fingers had reached the archer's mound, Xali was already wet and waiting.

For a moment Xali's sinister side took hold. If she kept her legs together, perhaps she could use that as a way to wrestle control back to her side. Then she could turn the tides on her sexy juggernaut of a wife but again, she was too slow. Nikka's fingers swiftly entered the archer. Xali was hot and tight and any attention felt amazing. She instantly let out a brief squeal but was silenced when Nikka hushed her - an act that Nikka thought almost felt better than what they were currently doing.

Xali was forbidden to make a sound. This was for them and them alone.

Nikka's fingers were thick and sturdy. They moved like a battering ram, eager to break down the gate. Xali squeezed herself on the digits, wanting to feel every inch of what was inside of her. Nikka's strong fingers thrusted in and out while the spell kept alternating sensations. One moment the battering ram was warm and pulsating only to switch a few seconds later to cold and tingling. Xali's copious wetness allowed for deeper and more rapid plunges. To make matters worse, Nikka's thumb quickly found her nub and began to play with that. It wasn't long before the battering ram succeeded and the gate fell.

Xali bit into Nikka's shoulder, desperate to mute her scream, as ecstasy washed over her. The archer twitched and convulsed. Between her ear, her neck, her nub and her canal, there was no one single origin of pleasure. It was like a complete release of bliss.

Nikka released her grip and watched as Xali collapsed atop of her. The warrior held her firmly as her spasms began to fade, releasing the archer only when she had returned to normal.

But Xali was not done.

She grabbed her wife and spun her around, the two women switching sides. Nikka smirked as she felt the touch of wood on her back. Xali had not the time for such pleasantries for she was no longer incharge of her own body. The hunger had taken control.

Xali did not focus on kisses or teasing. The hunger needed to be fed and now. Xali dove for Nikka's breasts.

They were works of godly art. Far too large for any

one hand, they were perfectly rounded, teardrop-shaped breasts and sat high and firm on Nikka's chest. Stiff and hard as could be, her nipples provided perfect summits to the heavy globes. Summits Xali was eager to conquer.

She first conquered them with her hands, eagerly caressing them. She gripped them as best she could, enjoying the excess that spilled over the side of her hands. They were soft and pillowy and would instantly bounce back into place once released. She grabbed them again, cupping and squeezing them, bringing forth a moan from the warrior.

Eventually the hunger took control and her lips darted toward her wife's peaks. Normally Xali would kiss in circles, teasing her warrior in a method similar to how she had been teased, but with the gate being breached, Xali was eager for more.

She alternated between flicks of her tongue and gentle bites of her teeth. She would suck one while groping the other, switching back and forth. Eventually she stopped and began kissing down Nikka's chest. She greedily kissed every ab, every muscle and every inch of available skin before dropping to her knees before the naked woman. Xali grabbed one of Nikka's legs and placed it on her shoulder. Then she leaned forward and began to feast.

Hands, lips and tongue began to work in unison. Where Nikka had been like a battering ram, Xali was like a musician. Each movement of her fingers was delicate and precise. Like a harp player flicking the right string, in the right fashion at just the right moment in order to get the best sound possible.

That night, and every night, Xali did her best to play her instrument in a fashion worthy of its greatness and Nikka was one legendary instrument. Xali played as best she could until Nikka muffled a loud noise. If Xali's bliss was like a massive release, then Nikka's was like an exploding volcano. It erupted hard and the whole world felt it. The warrior tightened and began spasming, desperate to feel every drop of ecstasy before it faded.

The two women descended to the ground, entangled in each other's arms. They just lay there, waiting for their hearts to calm.

"We should get dressed and return to the fire," Xali muttered.

"Perhaps in a bit," Nikka said, blissfully content that her hand was finally resting on her wife's ass. "Perhaps in a bit."

The two lay in blissful silence.

Neither of them were aware of the eyes that watched from the shadows.

Rarus silently stared at the burning flame, the tongue flickering in the darkness. Most of the troupe had returned to the fire and bunked down for the night. The priest had yet to turn in.

He knew that they were not alone.

A faint snapping sound caught the old man's attention. He scowled. The only reason that sound was made was because the man making it was being polite. Rarus did not bother to look up. He knew who it was.

"I thought myself to never to be in your presence ever again," Rarus said quietly. "Yet here you are. Lecherously leering upon my allies and sneaking up on my camp."

"I have done no such sneaking," the hollowed voice said. "I practically sang out loud of my approach."

The tall human emerged from the shadows. His black hair, black clothing and black cloth mask all made for a frightening sight but one that Rarus was used to. He walked through the camp, carefully stepping around the sleeping soldiers. Shadows seemed to dissipate from him with each step, falling off of him and fading into the darkness.

"The King of Assassins stands before me," Rarus dictated aloud. "Surely you could have sent a lesser member to kill me."

"A lesser to cut the life thread of the Deathkin? Do you think me mad or improper?" The tall man shook his head as he took a seat on the other side of the fire. "I may be a killer but I have standards. No one in our organization would end your thread but I. It is my duty as King and my right as your lover."

"Past lover," Rarus quickly corrected. "And I am no longer the Deathkin. I renounced that title eons ago."

"But no other has stepped up for it. None have even tried."

"Good," Rarus snapped. No other Deathkin would be named as long as he lived and if he was successful, the title would die with him. "If you are here to kill me, Zagreus, then make it swift."

"You know I cannot. If I kill you, I take your title and no man can hold two. I would have to vacate your title first and I am not ready to do that just yet." He chuckled, the unsettling hollow laugh echoing endlessly until it became just another unnerving sound in the midnight sky. Some child would have nightmares that night and it would be Zagreus' doing. "The King and the Deathkin; so sweet those names sound together."

"And the power they bring you is no doubt a factor."

"No doubt."

"If you are not here to kill me," Rarus snarled. "Then why do you sit before me?"

Zagreus reached up and removed his mask. Rarus bit his lip slightly. Zagreus was a stunning man. There was no mystery as to why they got together in the first place but after all these years apart, the sight of him was still enough to rob Rarus of his breath.

"A war is about to begin," he began.

"It has already begun," Rarus snapped.

"The real war is about to begin," Zagreus smugly corrected. "I need all of my thieves and assassins at the ready. I need my army in order to fight."

"I am no longer in your army," Rarus reminded him.

"All of your age and wisdom and still you think the world revolves around you," Zagreus scoffed. "No, you march with a child of the shadows and I have come to collect."

"You cannot have her," Rarus scowled. "They are under my protection. You cannot have any child, assassin or thief this night."

Rarus glared with firm eyes and a stone-like demeanor. He was unwavering in his decision. He would not back down.

Zagreus just yawned.

"This is but a formality, Deathkin. My army will be ready when the battle begins," Zagreus said as he stood up. "Look after them during your petty squabbles with the gigas. I need them alive to fight in an actual war."

He walked away from the fire, retracing his steps as he exited the camp. He paused by the sleeping forms of Nikka and Xali and let out a lecherous grin. "Let the ladies know I enjoyed their show."

Shadows swirled around Zagreus, consuming him, before dissipating. As swiftly as he arrived, he vanished, taken by the darkness.

Rarus growled to himself. Zagreus was such a lecherous, pervert but he was the King of the Assassins. He was never to be taken lightly.

Rarus walked to his cot and got ready to bed down. He paused.

Shit.

He had to piss again.

CHAPTER FOURTEEN

Fight against the wilds and you will lose. Fight alongside them and no foe can stop you.
- Yascura Proverb

Stellia ran across the battlefield. Rage filled her blood and fueled her legs. Her vision blurred as tears filled her eyes and sorrow swamped her mind. There was nothing that existed in this world or the next except Aidox. He was her target and she would kill him.

She leapt into the air, spear in hand, ready to strike.

But she never made it.

Aidox pivoted around, slapped her spear to the side and stabbed with his own. It ripped through her armour and dug into her chest.

Pain.

There was nothing but pain.

"Whomever you are," Aidox malevolently whispered, "know that with my victory I have taken your honour and that of Oibalox."

Pain and regret.

Stellia bolted up from her sleep, her body covered in sweat. Her heart raced and herhand twitched. She looked down and found the broken spear in her hand. She hadn't even remembered drawing it.

Victory outlasts truth.

It was an Oibalox commandment and one she found comfort in. She could look at the truth of her failure, of how her body had changed but none of that mattered. As long as she killed Aidox, as long as she was victorious, then none of the truth mattered.

Victory outlasts truth.

Aidox sat by the burning fire pit, one of many scattered across the clearing. The gigas were camping down for the night. It was a well deserved rest after a long day's march. His army was still three days away from Aoryna. He was gleefully looking forward to razing that human settlement; it would be the final step before he invaded Hakros. A warm up for the main event. They had assaulted smaller populations along the way, the harpies were unruly flesh-eaters who bored easily, but those villages - if they could be called that - were little more than a distraction.

His gigas needed real battle and soon he would give them that.

Aidox looked to his left and saw the two weapons that rested beside him. One was a spear and the second was a wooden staff.

Aidox looked at his stolen spear. He was not one for human craftsmanship. It was often flimsy and tiny, without heft or durability. Their weapons often felt like a twig in his hands, one he could accidentally snap by pressing down too firmly with his thumb. This spear was different. It seemed larger than most - still running as a small weapon for him -

and the caculis blood that held the spear together made it as durable as a giant. Aidox had retrieved the spear from the fiery remains of a burned platoon. He now claimed the weapon as his own. He would return the blood of the legendary Tiahoka back to his people.

The wooden staff was different. He had looted it from the temple in Pylomia village. Despite knowing its true power, he sensed no magic within it. It would lay dormant until the final ingredient was added.

"I have your reports, Commander," A voice said. Aidox looked up to see the familiar sight of Foricu. She handed him a scroll that he reluctantly took. Foricu paused for a moment as she eyed the spear. "Why do you still carry a human weapon?"

"I find some ironic glee in this spear," he said with a sinister smirk. "It is a weapon made by humans with the express purpose to slay humans. Yet the only thing that makes it greater than any other weapon is the touch of giantkin that flows within it."

"What do you plan to do with it?"

"I plan to use it in the method of its creation. I plan to slay each and every human on this world and let their blood water the seeds for our new reign." He cocked his head slightly as he eyed her. "Is this not the world you wish for?"

Foricu frowned for a moment as she looked for the right words. Aidox was a fanatic. He believed in the cause so greatly that none could move him from this path. The problem with fanatics was any who did not match their enthusiasm were at risk.

"I think not at such grand levels," she began, speaking cautiously. "I am a simple warrior who revels in battle. I care not the reason for the fight, simply that I am included in it. I care not if the blood of our enemies will change the world, simply that I will be able to bathe in it."

Aidox let out a small chuckle and nodded in approval. As long as Foricu fought, he didn't care much for motivation. He dismissed her with a wave. From the corner of his eye he watched as the woman walked away. She paused at the first fire she came across, one by one eyed each of the random soldiers that surrounded it before picking one. She approached one of the males, slugged him across the face with a powerful punch before grabbing him and dragging him off to the nearest tent.

Seeing such tenderness made the gigas commander feel a moment of longing for his home and his wife. He knew that there would be other males to satisfy her needs - or at least attempt to - just as there were women here to fulfill his, but with her it was different. One did not have seven kids with the same mate if there was no special spark.

Aidox pushed the thoughts from his head. They were not helping. He missed her and his kids but he was doing this for them. He was changing the world so they did not have to live in the same torment that he did.

A sudden pulse of magic rocked his chest. It felt like someone had called out to him but he could not hear the words.

He was being summoned by magic.

Aidox held up his hand and began his incantation. Ashen swirls of magic began to emerge from the night sky. They swirled into his palm as they took the shape of a circle. With each word Aidox chanted, the swirls grew in number, morphing in shape until he was looking at the face of Blaze General Vulcos.

"Blaze General," Aidox growled. "What do you

want?"

"Commander Aidox," Vulcos began, snarling at the gigas' arrogance. "My reports show that your attacks have been successful."

"As if there was any doubt of my success," Aidox snarled.

"You will meet up with minotaur herds upon arriving at Aoryna," Vulcos said. "Use them to raze Aoryna before you make your way to Hakros."

"I do not need their assistance."

"You have it none the less," Vulcos scowled. He shook his head slightly before speaking again. "You will also meet our contact in Aoryna. Coordinate with them. They will have the missing third piece."

Perigoss stood in the back of the group as they prepared the trap. He eyed the thief. She was directing Rarus and Nikka as they worked their magic. The thief had gone around to what was left of the town folk and collected mead, honey, dates, flowers and bread to present as an offering.

They had so little and somehow she convinced them to give it to them.

Scyra was really good with people.

Perigoss winced.

She was a thief and a thief was nothing more than a virus on the people. A thief would only do what is best for them. He couldn't let himself get distracted from that fact.

"Okay," Rarus called out. "The tributes are ready."

The priest watched as Perigoss approached. He

frowned. The kid had become attached to Stellia, a fact that he was not pleased with. Stellia was a strong, capable warrior but her mind was so firmly planted in Oibalox thinking that she was undoing all the work he had done with the kid.

"Are we set?" Xali asked.

"I think we are," Nikka replied.

"When we approach the Pharian Fields," Rarus said, "we will let Boroca do the talking."

"Why me? Does the thief not have a more cunning tongue?" the hometown hero asked.

"Not as cunning as Xali," Nikka whispered, instantly receiving a playful elbow in her gut.

"The thief talks like one. She cannot be trusted," Perigoss spat. Scyra glanced up and internally winced. She felt the venom in his words and for some reason it hurt. The pain was surprising. She normally cared so little about others feelings, so why did his words hurt so much?

"I would have chosen different words," Rarus said with a scowl, "but essentially that is correct. We do not need cunning, we need sincerity in our lie."

Boroca nodded.

"The rest of us will keep our blades sheathed and weapons held back," Rarus said, eyeing Stellia. "We need not start a fight when we do not have to."

"And if they choose to fight?" Stellia asked, challenging the mythling with her query.

"Then we fight," he snapped back, a sense of dominance in his voice. "None of us will die this day, I will not allow it, but I will not be the one to start a fight."

"And yet we trap them," Perigoss muttered. Rarus glared at his apprentice once more.

"Let us grab our gear and move out," Boroca said as

he hoisted his shield.

Rarus walked towards Perigoss and pushed him back, away from the group and away from Stellia.

"Do you have words you wish to say to me?" Rarus asked. Perigoss eyes darted over first to Stellia and then moved to the thief.

"I do not like this," Perigoss said. "I made that clear last night and nothing has changed."

"I need you all to survive this," Rarus repeated.

"I know that but there has to be more than just surviving," Perigoss snapped. "I need to be able to live with myself and my actions after this war is done. This…this foolery is not who I am. This is the actions of the thief and her infectious selfishness. All she cares about is surviving. She cares not for the person beside her."

"Her name is Scyra," Rarus corrected. He let out a small chuckle. One that caught the kid off-guard. He was expecting a fight but got a jest instead. "You two are the sword and the shield, opposite ends of the spectrum. A soldier who fights with only swords cares not for their life and the one who fights with only a shield cares not for the fight they are in. A perfect soldier needs to carry both. What good is a soldier that only fights one battle and what good is a soldier who fights none? Our job today is to make sure you can fight in the next battle."

Perigoss couldn't believe it. Rarus' words had found a cord yet again. His anger hadn't faded, it was still the dark clouds that covered the sky, but somehow the priest's words were like glimmers of light piercing through. What had the Deathkin seen that granted his words so much wisdom?

"So where does a staff fall in this analogy of yours?" Perigoss asked, feeling clever.

"I have fought for too long with just a shield and even longer with just a sword," Rarus said. "A staff means I care not for victory or my own survival. I care only that all of you survive this war and the next."

"The next?"

"Do your best to survive this war but always fear the next," Rarus said. A fact more frighteningly true if Zagerus was involved.

As they approached the Pharian Fields, Perigoss found a hitch in his step, one brought on by the sight of the legendary fields. The Pharian Fields were a massive farmer's field that seemed to endlessly echo outwards. He knew there was an end, he'd seen it on the map, but while standing on the edge, the other opposite end seemed beyond his sight. Perigoss was no stranger to wheat, any of Oibalox's impure spent time working farms, but this was beyond that. Each stalk of wheat was perfect, glistening in the sun with a honey-golden colour that was beyond what any mortal man could grow. The stalks were higher than anything he'd ever seen, coming up past his waist and nearly up to his chest. All of the stalks seemed to weave back and forth, dancing on the wind, like waves on the ocean. He could see swirls of air, crests of waves and even what could be best described as a current that rippled through the wheat.

Scyra paused beside Perigoss, her amazement mimicking his own. She had heard of the fields, she made it her duty to know of anything that would kill her, but she yet to see them in person.

Stellia didn't stop. She simply walked past. Like most of the others, she had never seen the fields before. The only difference, she did not care.

Perigoss looked over at Scrya and for a moment he smiled. A second later it vanished. He scowled at the thief and pushed forward.

Boroca pulled out a small bundle, wrapped in a cloth, and quickly opened it. He carefully placed the items, one by one, at the edge of the wheat before stepping backwards.

"I am Boroca, Son of Biroca and hero of Mikha," he said loudly. "I bid your permission, in this dire time of need, to pass through your fields. I have come with offerings."

A ripple in the wheat suddenly appeared. It started further in and suddenly weaved towards the edge. Perigoss found his grip on his spear to be tightening and his right leg sliding backwards. Every urge in his body told him to raise his shields and level his spear. He glanced first at Stellia. She had her shield up and at the ready. He then glanced at Rarus. The priest stood without worry, leaning on his staff with almost a bored look upon his face. Perigoss took a deep breath and tried to relax himself.

The ripple grew closer with each passing heartbeat until suddenly it stopped. A female form suddenly emerged. She had merigold coloured skin and hair that shared a look and colour of the wheat. As the sunling flickered across her hair, it seemed to glisten a canary yellow. She walked around nearly nude, a fact that Perigoss couldn't look away from, and had a lithe body that was undeniable dripping with lust and sensuality. She walked across the grass with such grace it was like she was walking on water. Each step she took she did so knowing all eyes were on her.

"Your jaw is on the floor," Xali scolded her wife in a hushed whisper. "Pick it up, now."

"I will when you do," Nikka replied.

They silently reached out to each other and delicately held hands as they each contently drooled at the supple woman before them.

The wheat began to ripple as she stepped, like the stalks missed her presence, and suddenly Rarus understood what nature of beast stood before him.

She was an alseid.

Nymphs were a varied species. They had variants for nearly every type of environment. Nereids lived in the sea, oceanids lived in the oceans, oreads stuck to the mountains and dryads resided in trees. There even existed a variant that lived in the underworld. The Alseids, however, lived amongst groves and grains. These ones lived amongst the large, sun filled wheat fields. Suddenly it made sense why they grew so strong; the alseids' sheer presence was enough to make the grain grow stronger.

"Who would be so kind to present me with gifts?" the alseid said as she stepped closer to Boroca. She delicately ran her fingers up his muscle-filled arm and let out a little giggle that he found bewitching. "Biroca, is that you? It has been so long since I've felt your touch."

Boroca's eyes went wide. Her words had placed an image in his mind that he had to immediately eject.

"N…no," he said with a loud gulp. "Biroca is my father. I am his son, Boroca."

"I lose track of mortal time so easily," she said with a surprised giggle. "My name is Creusa and I used to play in these very fields with him. He was such a tender man with great vigor and stamina. Do you share these traits?"

Boroca gulped again. Standing this close to her, he could feel his body react in inappropriate ways. Nymphs were known for their sensuality and legendary for the skills in that endeavour. These were the fantasies that most men had and it was now that very thing was being offered to him.

Boroca, at the moment, struggled to remember just what this war was all about and why it was at all important.

A gentle hand on his shoulder suddenly snapped Boroca's attention back to the present. He looked over his shoulder to see Rarus standing there, nodding at him.

"I..um…we brought you gifts in order to ask you for a favour?" he stammered.

"You ask for a favour of me?" she asked with a coo. "What can I do for you?"

"As I said earlier," he swallowed. "We would like permission to cross your fields. There are people in danger and we need to save them. Passing through your fields would be the fastest way."

"So many people suddenly want to cross our home," she said, her voice sounding like a faint song. "But none have been as kind or offering as you."

"Who else has tried to cross?" Boroca asked.

"Those brutal gigas came stomping over my brothers and sisters," she said, her displeasure suddenly coming through. "We were not pleased."

"We promise not to damage any of your family or friends," Boroca said.

"Well, son of Biroca, perhaps I can let you pass," she said, leaning in and brushing his ear with her lips. "If you promise to stay a while with me."

Once again, his body reacted.

"Creusa, you are stunning and beautiful. I would be honoured to stay with you but I cannot." Internally, Boroca was kicking himself over and over. Why was he saying no? "There are too many people being hurt. I need to stop them…..for some reason. I can't really remember why at the moment….but what if I make you a promise?"

"I like promises."

"When this is over, I will return and you and I can spend some time together."

Creusa paused for a moment and frowned. She did not like waiting to play. Waiting took all the fun out of it, however this was the son of Biroca. There were not many mortals she remembered so fondly — or at all – but Biroca was one of them. Perhaps waiting would be worth it.

Creusa nodded and stepped towards the wheat. She leaned in and began to whisper to the stalks. A few moments later, ten ripples suddenly appeared in the wheat and began to weave towards them. Suddenly more alseids emerged. One by one, another alseid stepped from the wheat. Some were women, some were men and some seemed to happily ride the line in between. Scyra found her gaze locked on one of the males as he emerged. He lacked the sheer number of muscles that Boroca had but this alseid's body was firm, cut and every ab was clearly visible. Much like the women, the men walked out nude and Scyra suddenly found her gaze locked on one of the male's very generous organ.

"Um…hi there," Scyra said, suddenly becoming bashful. The male alseid didn't say a word. He just approached her, reached out with two hands and gently cradled her head in both hands. His thumbs started at her cheeks and slowly pulled downwards, catching her lips and gently pulling apart her lips. Then, he wordlessly leaned forward and kissed her. Scyra's eyes wide wide for a moment before falling into bliss. The kiss was warm like freshly baked bread, but sweet like honey. As the kiss ended, he gently ran his hands down her chest, and across her armor. He pulled away and walked towards the tributes. Lost for words, Scyra just stammered and swooned.

The swarm of alseid made their way through the group, their intoxicating fingers touching and dragging across the bodies of the seven, as they made towards the offerings. One by one they started to nibble on the bread, taste the honey and smell the flowers.

"The offerings have been accepted," Creusa said. "You may go now but do not damage the wheat."

The seven slowly stepped into the wheat fields and began to carefully walk through. Rarus grabbed Nikka and pulled her close. "Hold off on the spell for as long as you can."

She nodded.

Perigoss walked carefully through the stalks, watching his step as he tried to find the swiftest path. His foot suddenly bumped into something and Perigoss stumbled backwards. He stopped himself, just barely, before he fell onto the wheat. He glanced at what he had tripped on and let out a startled yelp. Lying on the ground was the body of a dead gigas. The roots and dirt had already begun their consumption of the body. The body could only be a few days old but somehow the earth had begun to reclaim it.

Perigoss looked back at the alseid. How powerful were these creatures?

For several long minutes the group walked. They did their best to be careful but the inevitable happened. Stellia lost her footing and accidently stepped on a stalk. The cracking sound that filled the air seemed deafening. The alseids suddenly stood up, their gaze suddenly snapping towards them. One of them pointed and let out a screech while four more dove into wheat. Four ripples sped towards them.

"Now," Rarus called out. Both him and Nikka turned to face the tribute. With a sudden burst of energy, they released their magic. Arcane sleep filled the lungs of any who ate the tribute bread. Three of the ripples suddenly stopped, crashing into the dirt with a loud thud.

"Run!" Stellia yelled and the group took off running.

They stuck to the dirt path between the rows as they moved as swiftly as they could. More ripples appeared in the wheat, darting towards the group. A female alseid leapt out of the wheat and attacked Stellia. The hoplite was able to get her shield up just in time to protect herself. Stellia dropped to one knee and flung the fey over her head, tossing the alseid back into the wheat.

Boroca gripped his shield tightly as he ran, but even he was not fast enough. A pair of hands suddenly darted out from the wheat and grabbed his legs. Boroca fell hard into the dirt and suddenly found himself being dragged across the dirt and into the wheat.

Rarus was the next to fall. A male alseid dove out of the wheat in a flying tackle. He collided with the priest and sent both to the ground.

"We have to save them," Perigoss yelled. Nikka and Xali nodded. Perigoss looked for Scyra but the thief was already gone. He swore out loud and looked back. "Save Boroca. I'll get the priest."

The two nodded and bolted. Perigoss looked for Stellia but spotted her fighting off an alseid of her own.

Damn, he could really use the thief to even the numbers had she not succumbed to her cowardice. Perigoss pushed his disappointment from his mind and bolted for the priest. The sudden sound of rustling wheat caught his attention. He had just enough time to get his shield up when a female alseid leapt at him. His shield rocked with her impact and sent him stumbling backwards. Perigoss twisted his spear and leveled it to strike but as his arm pulled back, reading to thrust, a pang of regret filled him. Every inch of his body suddenly felt a sense of wrong. He couldn't stab this alseid; he couldn't stab any of them, but why?

Left with no choice, Perigoss raised his shield once more as a pair of claws swiped at him. The ear-piercing sound of claws on metal filled the air and caused him to wince. Perigoss retreated a few steps more. He tried again to ready his spear but the pangs of regret filled him once more. Left without any option, he spun his spear around and struck with that. The butt end slammed against the alseid and this time she was the one forced to retreat. Perigoss rushed her and struck again, thrusting twice with speed using the butt of the weapon once again but neither strike landed. The alseid dodged, swaying and moving like the wind as she twisted. Her sudden burst of speed came also with her attack. Her claw strikes were suddenly different from the ones before. They moved and swayed like her dodges, as if her limbs weren't moving on their own power but instead were at the whim of the wind. An errant attack suddenly shifted and caught him by surprise. The attack was strong, far stronger than he expected from a woman of her stature, and sent flying off his feet. He fell onto his back, colliding into the soil with a thud. Perigoss tried to stand up but was shocked when he couldn't. Roots had suddenly shot up from the soil and wrapped around his hands and feet. The alseid leapt atop of Perigoss and straddled him. She let out a cackle as she gently dragged her claws across his neck. Pulling her arm back as she readied a strke.

"Wait, what are you?" she asked suddenly. Her movements were frozen and her face stunned "You are one of—"

She never finished her words. A flying kick connected with her chin and knocked her off of Perigoss. Surprised, he looked up to see Scyra standing over him. Two quick slashes cut the roots on his hands. Perigoss quickly sat up, drew his own gladius and cut his legs free. He scrambled to his feet, taking a stance beside his saviour.

"This is beginning to be a trend, me saving you," she teased. "Soon the topic on every tongue will be you and I."

Perigoss found himself chuckling.

"This is two on one," she said. "We cut her down swiftly and save the others."

"I…I can't hurt them," Perigoss admitted. "There is something preventing it."

"Now is not the time to grow a sense of humour." She looked up at his face and frowned. He was serious. "And now is definitely not the time to grow a conscience."

A loud screech filled the air and all combat seemed to halt. The female alseid walked slowly towards them. Both Scyra and Perigoss raised their swords.

"Who are you?" the female called out. "You attack us but you are one of us? What is this insanity?"

Scyra and Perigoss looked at each other. Who was she talking to?

"Trilleia," a voice called out. "Why do you call for a halt? These humans damaged our wheat and trapped our offerings?"

"He is one of us," she replied. Perigoss stared at the alseid that had been straddling him, Trilleia, and shook his head.

"I…I….do not know what you mean?" he stammered.

Trilleia approached once more, her claws since retracted into her hand, and gently pressed her hand against his face. For a moment neither moved but eventually she nodded, slowly at first but quickly with more enthusiasm.

"I am certain. He carries nymph blood within him," she explained. "He is human, of that there is no doubt, but he has our magic flowing through his blood. My guess is either his mother or father was a nymph."

"My….mother?" Perigoss stammered, unable to speak in any other method. "I…I did not know."

One by one, several alseid walked over and did as Trilleia once had. They put their hand on his face and after a few moments, each came to the same conclusion as she had.

He was family.

Perigoss didn't know what to do. He didn't know what to say or to ask. Instead, he just stayed quiet. Scyra, however, did the talking for him. Her tongue was sharp and her wit was swift. Quickly she negotiated the release of their friends and passage through the field. One by one, their tackled or downed allies returned to them. All except for Rarus. They waited for several moments but he did not arrive. After a few moments more they decided to look for him.

They found him on the ground, still pinned by a male alseid. Both were eagerly kissing one another. Scrya let out a loud cough. Startled back to reality, Rarus broke the kiss and sheepishly looked up at all the familiar faces.

"Did we survive? That sounds like the second most pleasant thing to happen to me today."

CHAPTER FIFTEEN

The heroes pray for peace for it is the heroes that carry the
weight of war.
- Hakros Proverb

The town of Aoryna was unlike the ones before it.
Mikha and Pylomia were farming towns. There was little else
in the way of industry but the town of Aoryna was something
different. Aoryna was a walled city with various farms located
outside of the barrier. Those farmers were the ones who dealt
with the alseids and their side of the Pharian Fields but inside those walls, Aoryna was unlike any small town within the
reach of any of the poleis.

While many cities held forges and blacksmiths, but
Aoryna was one of the few to have mageforges. If a regular
forge would be used to craft a mundane weapon, a mageforge
was used to enchant it. A skilled blesser could take a finely
made sword and give it the properties of fire, lightning or various other magical blessings. Nowhere else in the world - not
Oibalox, not Athonea and not Hakros - had as skilled blessers
as Aoryna. Heroes the world over came to Aoryna to get their
equipment.

As Scyra stepped past the walled threshold and entered the town, she cared not for an enchantment or equipment. All she wanted was a bunk to sleep in.

The seven of them entered the town and each were as exhausted as Scyra. Even with the blessing of the alseids, the run across the Pharian Fields was not an easy one. Scyra's legs felt like mush and standing seemed all but impossible. She leaned on the nearest building and let out a loud wince.

"I hear you," Rarus said. His exhaustion was well past his limits. Even the staff could do little to keep him going. "There is a hero barracks over there. Let me get us each a cot."

Scyra let out another wince. A barrack cot was better than the dirt and the bedrolls she had been sleeping upon lately but it was still far beyond what a woman of her stature and delicacy required.

"You do that," Scrya said. "I will find an inn and rent me a room of leisure."

"Dare I ask how you intend to pay for something of the sort?" Boroca asked.

"You may not," she replied, sternly. "But play your cards correctly and you may benefit from it."

With a wink she sauntered away. Perigoss watched her depart, her hand darting to the waist of a random man she passed and quickly stealing his purse. Perigoss shook his head. Time and time again the thief proved why she was a blight; committing crimes before the eyes of his allies and yet none of them even batted an eyebrow. Yet despite that, Scyra continued to come to his aid. Thrice she had saved him.

Perigoss was conflicted.

"Is Diomestor here yet?" Xali asked. Rarus just shook his head.

"No, not yet," he replied while leading the way to the barracks. "This town looks too tranquil. I suspect that they will arrive early tomorrow."

"Should we warn the town or something?" Nikka asked.

"I…I don't know," Rarus said. He paused and turned to face the others. "Diomestor is in command. We have deviated from his plan enough already. I fear to think what would happen if we alter his defense plans."

"You wish us to take the evening and simply do nothing?" Boroca asked. "But this town will be under siege in two days time."

"We have one of the greatest mythlings leading us," Rarus said. "We trust him with our lives. We must trust his plan."

Bliss. It was the only thing Scyra felt as she woke up. Finding herself sleeping in a bed instead of on the dirt was such a relief. After departing the six others, she made her way to the nicest inn she could afford with stolen coin. There, she took a much needed bath, sated her thirst with wine and then collapsed on the finest of beds. In truth, the bed was average at best but as long as there wasn't dirt beneath her back and she was not using a stone as a pillow, it was more than enough for her.

Scyra quickly dressed. A glance outside the window showed her that she had slept the day away and the evening light began to descend on the town. Scyra did not mind. She had work to do and she always preferred to do so after nightfall.

As she left the inn, she made her way to a dark alley and moved through it. Scyra was no stranger to Aoryna.

She had been here many times and, more surprisingly, was not wanted by the guards. There were few towns where that was still true. One dark alley became two and suddenly Scyra found herself in a different part of the town. Aoryna was not so large a city that it had numerous sectors or divisions, but it did have a workers' part of town and a uppermens' part of town. She was now clearly in the former.

She stopped at a large wooden building with a red sign clumsily hanging from a post. It read Raven's Roost. She pushed open the doors and walked in. The Roost looked like a dirty inn, with well worn furniture and an uneasy feeling that seemed to permeate from the walls.

All of this was intentional.

The Roost did not want the average worker or citizen to enter here. They wanted to be left alone. Everybody who entered the Roost did so for a reason that often fell below the line of morality.

The Raven's Roost was the home of a powerful thieves guild and this was the worst kept secret in all of Aoryna.

So why did the guards not stop them? Because the guild helped whenever possible. Aoryna was a town always in need of weapons and arcane supplies for their mageforges, many of which were not easy to obtain. When legal methods dried up, the town turned to the guild. They approached the problem with different solutions, all to keep the mageforges running.

Scyra approached the bar and smiled at the satyr tending it. He raised an eyebrow at her.

"I heard you got pinched," he declared. "Heard you got sent to war."

"Niah, please," she said to him with a scoff. "You

think me the type to get caught? Please, if I were to have been caught, it would only be that because I allowed it to happen."

"If a truthful word were to ever escape your lips," Niah said with a shake of his head, "I doubt as to whether or not you would be even able to recognize it."

"If a truthful word passed through my lips, then the end of my days is upon me," Scyra playfully shrugged. She nodded to the back. "Is the big lady in?"

Niah shrugged and nodded to the side door. Scyra gave him thanks and moved towards it. As she pulled open the door she heard the faint sound of a tiny bell in the distance. Niah had signaled the boss about her approach.

Scyra walked down a long hallway. It was an unnerving long passageway and narrow enough to instill a sense of unease. This was yet another example of intentional design.

She reached the door at the end and gave it a gentle rap of her knuckles. Silence. After a few moments she knocked again. Silence. Scyra leaned forward to knock a third time but just as she was about to rap, a voice asked her to enter.

How did she always know?

Scyra entered the room. There was a large desk in the center and a middle-aged woman sitting at it. She looked up from her work and suspiciously eyed Scyra.

"I heard that you had been arrested and sent to war," she said sternly.

"I've been hearing that alot," Scyra said with a chuckle. "But please, Foivi, have some respect for my skills."

Foivi stared at Scyra with a firm gaze that screamed disbelief. Eventually the older woman just gave a disappointed sigh and stood up. Foivi was a shorter lady but her lack of height did nothing to lessen her danger. She had curly, walnut brown hair that was losing an invasion to the colour grey. She kept her hair in a bun atop her head. She wore a long flowing robe with spider-black sashes draped across her. From her initial glance, Scyra could not spot a single weapon on her but that only meant that there were at least three.

"What brings you to my door, Scyronna?" she asked. Scyra instantly winced. There were few people who could call her by her full name. It was a symbol of a time past, so when it fell upon her ears it had an instant reaction. Scyra went from being the confident thief that she was to a scared squire, desperately seeking the attention of her betters. "Do you come to make good for the Bramble Blade? I lost a great many coin on that job."

"I have come to warn you," Scyra said, quickly brushing past her recent failure. "The gigas invasion army is only a few days away."

"This war was always going to come my way," Foivi said, unimpressed. "You think me unprepared?"

"I do," Scyra said quickly. "I think Hakros is unprepared. The gigas alone have already destroyed so much. Nobody was prepared for their skill or viciousness, let alone that of the giants. You need to flee while you have the chance."

"You wish that I would flee and you want me to take you with me?" Foivi said with a chuckle. "Is that it?"

"I...I...." Scyra paused for a second. She wanted to run. Every urge in her body said to, but she couldn't. She had to stay. "No, I will be staying. You need to flee without me."

Foivi walked towards the thief and stopped a few paces away. She studied every aspect of Scyra's face, not believing what she just heard.

"Why are you staying?" Foivi asked.

Scyra did not know. She tried to lie to herself and say it was the coin that Diomestor had offered but she knew that was not true.

Whatever it was, she could not admit it, to Foivi or herself.

"Have you taken to the path of Hakros?" Foivi said with a chuckle, turning away. "Have you embraced the moniker of the FireKissed Thief? I have tried for years to lure you into the Corrupt Cluster but instead you take the path of a hero."

The Corrupt Cluster was a terrible nickname for the unnamed hierarchy of thieves. Guilds like the Roost existed across the world. Each operated independently but all answered to the Cluster. At the top of the Cluster was Zagreus, the King of Assassins. The criminal world had its own champions, heroes and titles and each answered to the King. Scyra had no problem dipping in and out of any guild for as long as it suited her but she was not a joiner, not anymore.

"I mean no allegiance to either side. I care–"

"Stop," Foivi ordered. Scyra instantly sealed her lips. Foivi spoke as she walked to a small cupboard. "You bounced from village to village, hiding from everybody and nobody, and eventually you ended up at my door. I was warned against you. You were too flighty; you were too untrustworthy; you would never join the cause. I should have listened to each of them but I did not. Instead I saw a young woman who mirrored me in my youth.

"I took you in, protected you and helped you find whatever footing you needed. I did not ask of your past, I cared not. Instead, I guided you to a path, as a mother does her daughter."

"The carnal pleasure you and I once shared makes that analogy a little weird."

"Quiet. You are ruining this," Foivi scolded. She

withdrew a wrapped weapon and returned to the desk. Carefully placing the weapon upon the desk, she turned back to Scyra. "I know not what is keeping you here but I know it is not duty, but if you intend to fight you need to have this."

Scrya stepped forward and gently unwrapped the blade. It was a gladius but the blade was both longer and thinner and the metal was stained wine red.

"When word reached me of the FireKissed Thief," she explained. "I thought it necessary that a named hero have an enchanted blade to match."

Scyra ran her hand over the metal before pulling it back. It was warm to the touch. She raised an eyebrow.

"It will forever keep the heat of a flame within its edge," Foivi explained. "And if it comes in contact with new flame, it will carry that on the blade as well."

"W…w…why?" Scyra stammered.

"I had you figured out from the moment you showed up at my door," Foivi chuckled. "You think yourself a charismatic enigma but in truth you are but a bad mystery play where the ending was easily deciphered."

"The offense you throw at me cut far deeper than any blade," Scyra scoffed.

"You are not meant for my world. You have simply been hiding in it," Foivi explained. "You've changed, Scyronna. You have found motivation where none once existed."

"It's not like that," Scyra defended. "There is simply coin to be made in my actions."

"Lie to me all you want," Foivi said with a chuckle. "But do not lie to yourself."

"Fine, I will speak the truth," Scyra said sternly. "I need you to leave. People are going to die when they attack and I can not have one of them be you."

Silence.

Foivi stepped forward, took Scyra's hand into her own and suddenly pulled the thief into a hug. She reached up and around and held her close.

"If it means that much to you, I will go." Foivi whispered. "But listen closely. Years ago I built a precaution in case the uppermen wrongfully thought that they no longer needed our kind. The precaution still stands to this day.

"If the gigas breach the wall, lure them into the uppermens' section. Find the black lamp, the unlit lamp, and light it. Whatever you do, do not get caught in the blast."

"Thank you, Foivi, for everything," Scyra said.

"Take this blade and go," she whispered. "Whatever has brought about this change in you, whatever that has given you this motivation, go to it."

Scyra nodded. She grabbed the blade and made for the door. She paused, looked back and locked eyes once more with Foivi. The guild leader just nodded and whispered the words once more.

Go to it.

Sycra repeated the words over and over in her mind until they morphed into their true meaning.

Go to him.

And with that, Scyra vanished.

Perigoss walked through the village of Aoryna. He was unsure of exactly what he was looking for but that didn't stop him, he just kept walking. It had been a few hours since they arrived and since then he had been able to sleep, eat and even get some of his clothes washed. Now he was walking through the town, admiring the weightlessness of his body.

At that moment he wore no armour, carried no shield, and held no spear. There was not even a sword hanging from his waist. There was, of course, a dagger. He was not a foolish man. Aoryna has guards on patrol which meant that here he did not need to look over his shoulder; he did not need to worry about any attackers. His body could relax. It could heal. Even back in Hakros, during training, he was constantly on guard and pushing his body to the limit. He didn't need to do that here.

For the first time in nearly two months he was at ease, even for just one night.

The sound of stone on metal caught his attention and snapped Perigoss out of his content mental wanderings. He looked around, not sure of where he was, and shrugged it off. Aoryna was not so large that he couldn't find his way if needed. The moment of unknowing felt nice. Instead, he decided to follow the sound. He sauntered passed two corners before realizing he was near the barracks. There he saw a familiar face.

Stellia sat on a bench, with a new shield leaned up against her legs and a bucket of water at her feet. Beside her was a new set of matching armour. She had a sharpening stone in one hand and was slowly, and methodically, passing the stone back march forth over the edge of the shield.

"Dare I ask what it is you are doing?" Perigoss asked as he approached. Stellia looked up with focused eyes before returning to her task.

"I thought you an Oibalox raised child. Do you not know the task of a sharpening stone?"

"I am quite familiar with its design," he said, sitting

down next to her. "What I am confused about is why you would sharpen a shield?"

Stellia rotated the shield and held it upright. It looked like a round shield but the edges of the bottom half were rigid instead of smooth. Only upon a closer look did he notice the addition of small blades.

"The gigas stand above us," Stellia said sternly before mimicking a horizontal slash with her shield. "I mean to use my sharpened shield to take them out at the knees. Then, when we face them eye to eye, I will introduce them to my spear."

"Have you rested yet?"

"I will rest when I have completed my preparations," she snapped. "Not a moment before."

Perigoss eyed the hoplite for a moment, until a look of concern crossed his face.

"Stellia, what is wrong?" he asked. His voice suddenly lowered and became softer. Stellia shook her head. Perigoss continued. "I know we have known each other for only a few days but you can confide in me."

"I...I..." Her words trailed off. A small shake began to form. Few outside of the polis knew the struggles of an Oibaloxian Hoplite but perhaps Perigoss could. "Something happened to me at Pylomia. My body changed and I am plagued with nightmares." She took a deep breath. "My memory is filled with holes but my brain is not. I think....I think I died."

"Nightmares be damned. They cannot hurt you here," Perigoss said as reached over and gently put his hand atop of hers. He continued to speak with a soft tone. "If you did die, it did not take. You are here, in the land of the living, with me. The underworld cannot hurt you and neither can the dreams. You are Stellia, Daughter of Stellios. You are here, in this moment, safe and without harm."

Stellia cracked a hint of a smile. Her shake began to lessen and she looked over at Perigoss. This was weakness; she did not show that others. So why did she show it to him? Why did she show to a half-breed of all people? He leaned in slightly, slowly closing the space as he provided comfort. For a moment it was like all the voices in her head, the ones that constantly assaulted her, had finally quieted. For the first time in a long time, there was silence.

It was relieving.

For too long voices had been assaulting her. She carried the voice of every brother or sister who died beside her and with them, their guilt. The voices would cry out, time and time again, assaulting her. Why did she live when others did not? Why was she capable of shrugging off death when so many of her brothers and sisters in arms could not? Why did she still live when everybody else died?

But now they were silent.

It was unnerving.

It was a silence she did not deserve.

Stellia shoved Perigoss away and the voices instantly assaulted once more. She stood up and walked away from the bench. Her breathing became shallow and rapid as she began to pace.

"Stellia," Perigoss said, keeping his calm as he stood up. "You need to slow down for a moment. We are okay, we are safe and you are unharmed."

"How dare you speak to me as such?" She snapped. Anger flowed throughout her body and was moving swiftly. She did not know what she was angry at but the emotions were far easier to deal with than the undeserved silence. "How would a half-breed know anything about an Oibalox hoplite?"

Half-breed.

Those words came from her tongue and struck harder than a blade. He had heard those words his entire life. Perigoss had spent his entire life training and fighting and still he was not good enough for Oibalox. No matter what he did, that was how they would always see him; how she would see him.

"I will leave you be," Perigoss said. The softness in his voice vanishing with each passing heartbeat. "If you need someone to talk to, find someone else."

"I forgot, you refuse to help unless coin is involved," Stellia lashed out, hating herself the moment she said the words.

"I came to you because you needed help," he said. "I want to help you and you spit it back at my face. I care so little for coin. All I want is to fight for my home and its people, be it on the fields of battle or the warscape that is your mind." He shook his head and turned away. "I just want to be worthy of my home."

"Are you strong enough to be worthy?" she called out. Stellia approached Perigoss, grabbed him by the shoulder and spun him around. "Oibalox needs the strongest. Are you that?"

She shoved him backwards. Perigoss stumbled back a few paces. He contemplated turning away again but never got the chance. Stellia tried to shove him once more, only this time he slapped the hand away.

"Stop that," he sternly ordered.

Stellia did not listen.

Instead, she fired a punch at him. It was slow and clunky, not even a real punch by her standards, but the message was clear. Perigoss had to prove his strength. He quickly blocked the strike and stepped back as Stellia fired another.

This one passed before his eyes, leaving him untouched.

"Stellia, don't," Perigoss said.

"Prove your strength," she snapped back. When she was confused or scared, she turned to battle. Combat brought physical pain and great honour; both were far easier to deal with then what was occuring in her mind.

The third strike connected. It was a knee shot to his gut, one that caused him to double over. She prepared a kick to his face but this time he was ready. He grabbed her foot and pulled her off balance. She tumbled forward and collided with his extended arm. The closeline knocked her to the ground, hard. Stellia cursed, drew her dagger and she spun back to her feet.

"Stellia, this has gone far eno–"

Stellia lunged with her dagger. Perigoss swiftly drew his, bringing it up to block with barely enough time to protect his face. Stellia struck again and again, her attacks gaining speed with each strike. Perigoss blocked or dodged each but with less and less time to spare after each one. By the last attack, her arms seemed to echo; a spectral shadow that lingered in the air.

"Where is it?" Stellia called out. "Where is the strength you showed me at the temple?"

Stellia struck again, this time her blade catching his cheek. Anger flowed through Perigoss and the water bucket began to shake. Suddenly his stance shifted and his movements changed. Perigoss' motions became fluid and his speed increased. As the light from a burning torch flickered across his hair, it appeared as if it had turned into a cerulean blue. Perigoss was no longer just barely avoiding her blade, he was blocking her strikes with enough time left over to strike with his open hand.

The two continued, blade versus blade. Spectral strike versus a water stance. For a moment Perigoss flashed back to their fight at the Mikha temple but this duel felt different. At the temple they were two warriors, fighting as equals. There was honour and pride in that fight. This was something different. The knife fight felt tainted, like bile was residing in his heart and mind.

Stellia pulled away and readied for another attack. A faint shimmer started to form around her body and Perigoss fought to hide a smile. He knew what was coming, he had seen it at the temple. He stepped forward and over extended a slash. This left his back completely vulnerable. That's when Stellia vanished. A heartbeat later she reappeared, this time standing behind Perigoss. Only this time he was ready for her. In the middle of this blink, Perigoss fired a powerful rear kick. When Stellia reformed, the foot collided with her and sent her flying backwards. She slammed against the side of the barracks. Stellia tried to peel herself off the wall to re-enter the fight but Perigoss was on her, his knife pressed against her neck.

"This is over," he snarled.

"You won," she admitted. A sultry look crossed her eyes. If she couldn't hide in anger, then she would have to hide in lust. "Claim your prize."

Perigoss stared at her for a moment. He took the blade from her neck and pressed it underneath her chin. Using the knife, he slowly guided her chin upwards until her lips were at the perfect level. Then he kissed her.

It wasn't a gentle kiss or a romantic one. It was a dominant action that staked claim to his property. He kissed her, over and over. Stellia attempted to kiss back, to gain control of the half-breed in their carnal pleasure, but Perigoss didn't allow it. When she stepped away from the wall, he slammed her back against it. The painful impact caused a moan to slip from her lips and she allowed a look of lascivious hunger to cross her face. Perigoss withdrew the blade as he grabbed Stellia's shoulder and spun her around. The hoplite had barely enough time to raise her arms before she got slammed face first into the wall. Perigoss brought his knife to the back of her chiton and started cutting downwards.

"That's my only chiton!"

"I fail to see how that is my problem," Perigoss growled.

He continued to cut downwards, tearing apart the cloth that covered her body. A few seconds later, it fell off of Stellia's body and fluttered to the ground. He turned her around again, returning her to face him. For the first time since he first met Stellia, he saw modesty and shyness in her. She crossed her arms over her chest, using them to cover her small but athletic breasts and the scar that ran between them. The scar she feared the most.

Perigoss let her stand helpless and nude in the night air, gleefully watching her shiver in the evening breeze. Her timidness was like a victory in his dominance. He let her stand for a moment longer before giving her relief. He flicked his dagger into the dirt and stepped forward. Stellia stared at him, a defiant smirk on her lips and a look in her eyes that begged for more. Perigoss grabbed her by the neck and started to squeeze.

"Harder." The words were barely able to slip past her lips but the taunt was unmistakable and one that could not go unpunished. With one hand around her neck, he used the other to slap her hard across her breasts. He started with her right breast, calling her degrading names with each strike, before switching to the left. The sound of each slap seemed to echo throughout the empty courtyard but the words he muttered to her were secrets meant simply for her ears. Secrets she quivered the moment they reached her ears.

"You dirty quean," he growled; giving one of her nipples a sudden and fierce twist. "You are mine to use as I please."

Perigoss released his grip upon her neck and placed a hand on her shoulder.

"Knees," he commanded as he gave her a firm push. Stellia eagerly obeyed. The moment her knees touched dirt, she stared up with pleading eyes. For a long moment, he didn't respond. She just kneeled on the dirt, degradingly sitting on her heels, waiting for approval.

Eventually, after what felt like an eternity, Perigoss nodded. Stellia reached up and began to untie the knot that held his belt together. She opened up his chiton and stared with a hungry lust at what she found inside. His phallus was engorged, eager to be touched and pleasured and she was more than happy to do it.

She parted her lips and took him in her mouth.

There was no teasing or playfulness in her actions. There was simply determination. She would remind him what an Oibalox partner could do and what a thief could not.

"You filthy slattern," he growled. His anger at her earlier words came out more and more with each passing moment. He grabbed the back of her head, gripping her sunset hair between each of his fingers, and aided her efforts with several pushes of her skull.

As abruptly as he allowed her to start, he stopped her in the same fashion. He pulled her off of his organ. With a firm yank of her hair, he pulled her to her feet.

"You will respect me," he growled. His fingers reached down and swiftly entered her. There was no need for preparation or teasing. She was already wet and ready. His thrusts were not gentle or kind. They were fierce and brutal, caring more about his dominance than her pleasure. "Never again will you challenge my strength. Never again will you challenge my worthiness."

He withdrew his fingers and gripped her waist with both hands. He hoisted her into the air and slammed her back onto the ground. Once again she let out a loud moan. Perigoss grabbed her by the legs and folded them back until her legs were pressed against her chest. Stellia reached for his arms, a defiant final act to regain control, but he shoved them aside. Properly pinned, he thrust inside of her, his final conquering of her body.

"Punish me," she moaned between thrusts. "Punish me like you should punish your thief."

Perigoss growled, his pelvic assaults increasing in intensity. He tried to focus on his actions but her words crept into his mind once more.

"Your thief couldn't do this," Stellia moaned, her words boring deep into his mind. "No woman but an Oibalox woman could withstand your assault."

Perigoss' hand gripped her neck and once again started to squeeze. He was tired of her words and would not hear anymore of them.

"No...blight," she said as she struggled for air. "Could....feel....this....good."

Their releases were simultaneous. Hers was like an explosion, deafening the voices in her mind. His was like a victory, planting seed deep inside of her.

He removed himself from within her and fell to the

ground beside her. Side by side, they lay in the dirt. Each panting as their chests heavily heaved. Stellia looked over and gave him a sultry smile.

"I knew you would eventually act like Oibaloxian," she said with a chuckle.

Scyra walked through the streets of Aoryna. She nervously fidgeted as she walked, randomly speaking aloud to herself. Foivi had told her to go to what motivated her and that was what she was doing.

She couldn't lie to herself anymore. In truth she probably could. She was very, very good at it, but she no longer wanted to. She knew what had motivated her and what had changed her.

Perigoss.

She was drawn to him, from the moment she first saw him, and it was affecting her. She thought of him often and felt pain when she disappointed him. She was a coward who would normally flee but time and time again she was rushing into battle to save him. If that wasn't love then what was?

Scyra slid to a halt.

What had she just said? Had she just used the dreaded L-word?

A warm calm flowed over her, pulsing stronger the more she accepted it.

She was in love with Perigoss.

A smile crossed her lips; a genuine smile. It wasn't a greedy smile or a fake one. It was a real, honest smile and she hadn't had one of those in a long, long time.

Scyra took off into a run. She needed to find Perigoss and she needed to find him now. Boroca told her to check the barracks' courtyard, having seen him heading in that direction.

Scyra bolted around the street corner and slid to a halt. Her eyes went wide as she stared at the scene before her.

There, lying on the dirt, was Stellia as Perigoss repeatedly thrusted into her. Wordlessly, Scyra turned around and walked away. She didn't know what to feel but she needed to get away. She turned the corner and prepared to take off into a run when the sound of marching reached her ears. Her eyes went wide as she spotted Diomestor and the phalanx marching towards the barracks.

They had arrived, and earlier than expected.

Diomestor spotted her and peeled away from the group. He walked over, stopping only when their noses were basically touching.

"I was wondering where you got off to. Did you get your hero side out of your system?" Diomestor said, his charismatic vale eyes consuming her with glee. "Are you ready to get back to work?"

Scyra eyed the ground. Who was she kidding? A thief was who she was and who she would always be. She might as well make as much coin as possible in the process.

"Yes," she whispered. "Yes I am."

Diomestor reached down, hooked his finger under her chin and slowly guided her head upward until Scyra had no option but to look him in the eyes. Diomestor flashed a crooked smile.

"Good girl."

CHAPTER SIXTEEN

Fight against the wilds and you will lose. Fight alongside them and no foe can stop you.
- Yascura Proverb

The six of them stood in a line, each staring directly ahead of them. To the side stood Stellia, wearing a newly purchased chiton, watching as the mythling known as Diomestor paced back and forth. The phalanx arrived late in the evening, taking to the barracks like a swarm. Diomestor was letting most of the soldiers sleep-in but not these six. He dragged them out at first light and had proceeded to yell at them well into the morning.

It was not Stellia's form of leadership but what was she to expect from Hakros' attempt at discipline. She shook her head in objection. No wonder Hakros was so pathetic. The polis had long since overstayed their welcome.

"Did you rid this insanity from your blood?" Diomestor yelled. He shook his head. "Each of you disobeyed orders, abandoned the phalanx and needlessly risked your life. None of that is acceptable. Need I remind each of you that none of you are heroes at this moment. You are each a soldier of Hakros and you are fighting a war."

Diomestor sighed. He pinched the bridge of his nose and growled.

"I hope you had a relaxing day and got plenty of sleep because each of you are on double duty and patrols for the rest of our stay." Diomestor pointed to the barracks. "Each of you is dismissed. Go, now."

One by one, they peeled off and ran away. Just as Rarus was about to break into a jog, Diomestor called out to him.

"I expected more from you, Rarus."

"And I hadn't expected you to fall so far from the hero's path." The priest turned away and jogged off.

Diomestor shook his head. He looked up and saw Stellia watching him.

"And who the hell are you?" Diomestor reluctantly asked.

"I am Stellia, daughter of Stellios. I am a hoplite from Oibalox," she said as she stepped forward. "You and I need to talk."

"Here they come, our returning champions," Lypos called out as the seven entered the mess hall. Cheers rippled throughout the hall. Even Domos came and gave Scyra a hearty clap on her back and an acknowledging grunt. The triton waved them over and offered each of them a chair. "So how vicious was the old man?"

"I am not vicious whatsoever," Rarus said with a chuckle. He sat into the chair with a series of grunts and noises reserved for men with children.

"He yelled quite a bit," Xali said. "But all truth, he was fair with his punishment."

"I still do not regret a thing," Boroca said. "We helped

a great many people and I feel pride for my actions."

"As you should," Lypos said with a smile.

"So what did we miss?" Perigoss asked.

"Very little," Tik replied. The myrmidon clicked as he tried to recall. "We came across some eidolons but they were little in the way of challenge or a threat. We also laid several traps and ambushes to slow the gigas."

"I have seen more eidolons in the past few days than ever before," Lypos said, thinking out loud. He eventually shrugged it off. "So who is the new girl?"

"That is Stellia," Perigoss said quickly. "She joined up with us at Mikha."

"Careful with your words," Scyra warned. "She is from Oibalox and prefers to speak with her blade."

"Oh great, another one," a random voice said and the group devolved into chuckles.

"I have little time at my disposal," Perigoss explained. "I have just enough time to eat before I am put on patrol but when you see the kid, tell him I need a word."

Diomestor drummed the table with his finger as he leaned back in his chair. Ashen swirls of magic rolled along his knuckles, dancing like an illusionist's coin, as he resided deep into thought. The gigas would be upon them soon. While others thought the eventual battle for Hakros to be more crucial, in truth this meant more to him. Hakros sent him here, knowing Aoryna to be the best chance to make a final dent in the gigas forces before their descent on the polis. Regardless of how this played out, the war would forever change.

Domos entered Diomestor's makeshift office and let out a small growl. A few seconds later, Scyra entered. Diomestor sat up, his ashen swirls dissipating.

"Thank you both for joining me," he said as he sat upright, offering each a chair. "I need both of your minds at the ready. The odds are against us in the battle and we need to find ways of overcoming our deficit.

"Our scouts have located several herds of minotaurs making camp on the outskirts. We believe they are here to join Aidox." He glanced at Domos. "They are being led by Goremaster Jakus."

Domos let out a deep guttural growl.

"I know of Jakus. I am bloodsworn to slay him and he has labeled me a traitor to the herd. I look forward to ending his life on the battlefield."

"Be not too eager," Diomestor said. "We know not how the battle will play out but I mean to avoid combat as much as possible."

"Why do you say such a thing?" Domos growled.

"We are outnumbered and out muscled. They have gigas, harpies and now minotaurs united as one. They will not fight as we do nor do they cherish honour like we do," Diomestor explained. "If we expect them to fight like us, we will lose. We need to think with a mind unlike that of any of our heroes or soldiers."

Domos grumbled as once again he found his eyes falling upon Scyra. Minotaurs valued strength. Only the strongest could lead and the rest were either slain or fell in line. There was no strength in trickery.

Domos scolded himself. He was past that line of thinking. His people were limited in their way of thought. That was why he had left them and why they had forever labeled him a traitor.

"This is Aoryna," Diomestor said while unraveling a map. He slid it before Scyra. "You can fly, you can gore and you have the strength of giants. What do you do?"

"What are our defenses?" Scyra asked.

"I have spoken with Guard Captain Larittany. He has shown me where they can put archers atop the wall and how the gates will close," he explained. "What I need to do is look at this and see what I cannot."

Scyra's mind fell into deep calculation. There were secrets she could reveal, traps within the city place by the Roost, but she decided against it. Roost secrets were just that, their own. They would provide little in the aid of a wall defense.

"If I was Aidox, I would start with the fliers," she began. "We know that the gigas may have green flame at their disposal. Send harpies over and drop the flames along the wall. It would cut off our archers and if luck be on their side, the flame could spread and create new entrances.

"Next would be the minotaurs. Their strength is frightening. If they charge our shield wall, we will crumble. Our obvious counter is to spear them or arrow them before they get close. However, if they charge with shields of their own, we cannot stop them."

"No minotaur would ever do such an act. There is strength in our charge, not fear." The minotaur's charge was a show of strength. Wearing a helm or holding a shield was simply a form of cowardice and weakness.

"Hold your anger, Domos," Diomestor said. "We need to think of the unexpected. I can guarantee that is what Aidox is doing."

"It does not mean I have to enjoy it," Domos grumbled.

"What else do you have, Scyra?" Diomestor said. "This is where you truly earn your pay."

Commander Aidox brought his troops to a halt. Across the large grass plain he could see the walled city of Aoryna. A bitter growl slipped past his lips. He would have been here sooner if it weren't for those blasted alseids. After he had wiped the humans from the face of the land, the fey would perish shortly after.

A cautionary voice pointed forward. Aidox watched as a large herd of minotaurs approached. Aidox turned to his second-in-command.

"Foricu, break march and set up camp," he gruffly ordered. "Double our usual watch and keep them alert at all times."

Foricu nodded and broke away from the group. Her words were loud, brutal and not a single soul dared question her orders.

Aidox waved down the harpies as he walked forward. Xarica landed beside him. Aidox greeted the minotaurs. Their leader was a red-furred beast with glimmering jewelry hanging from his horns. He barked, speaking in a tongue only their kind knew. Several others grunted back. They joined the gigas in setting up camp, putting their tents on the opposite side of the giant-kin.

"Warwing Xarica, may I introduce Goremaster Jakus," Aidox growled. The Goremaster let out a loud howl before performing a slight bow. Xarica simply screeched in return.

"My father spoke of you, Commander Aidox," Jakus spoke carefully. "He warned me to be weary around you."

"Old distrusts do not die easily," Aidox replied. The minotaur and gigas had their own history of conflict. In the rocky landscapes, where little grew, the two cultures fought for what little they could salvage. "If memory serves, neither did he."

Jakus snarled. This gigas was so cavalier about his attempt to kill his father. Every urge in the Goremaster's being was screaming to live up to his title, to run his horns through the Commander that stood before him. But he didn't. There would be plenty of time when the humans were slain. Until then they were allies, reluctant as they may be.

"My united herds are here, ready for the battle," The Goremaster said. "We fight alongside you at the behest of the Blaze General."

A familiar pulse of magic rocked Aidox's chest. He was being summoned once more by magic.

"Rest your troops, Goremaster," Aidox said. "We plan our attack shortly."

Aidox stepped away and started walking to a quiet place. A sinister smile crossed his lips. This was the summons he had been waiting for.

Scyra rubbed her eyes as she exited Diomestor's make-shift office. She was tired and night was already falling upon them. An entire day was spent with her being devious and sinister. Every selfish, crooked and sneaky instinct she kept within her was being fanned and fueled. The flame that was her duplicitous nature had been stoked to a full bonfire and frankly, she was happy for it. It reminded her who she truly was.

She was no hero, she was a thief and finally someone appreciated her for it.

"Scyra," a voice called out. She lazily turned her head to see Nyreus approaching. Pausing, she allowed him to catch up. "Have you seen Perigoss?"

She shook her head. She had been inside all day. She quickly waved over Tik and asked them.

"Perigoss is upon the top of the wall," Tik clicked. "His punishment for heroics has resulted in double watches. He is beginning his second rotation."

"Oh, thanks. I have the tales he needed," Nyreus said, to no one in particular before bolting off. Scyra watched, envious of the speed and energy of youth. She was not so old as to be exhausted by exercise but over the last few months she had been brutally awoken by the difference of age.

Wait, what tales did Perigoss need to know about and why would he go to the kid? The kid knew nothing about anything, with the only exception being tales of mythlings.

The amulet.

Scyra let out a loud, exasperated sigh before running after Nyreus.

Several minutes later, after climbing a large ladder, Scyra found herself panting atop the Aoryna wall. She looked up and saw Nyreus unbothered.

Scyra loudly cursed the young.

"Are you to survive?" Rarus chuckled as he approached the pair. He had been stationed atop the wall. Scyra dismissed him with a wave. He walked over and gently put a hand onto Scyra's back. A small pulse of lilac-coloured magic rippled through her, rejuvenating her stamina. "Why are you two here?"

"Perigoss wished to speak with me," Nyreus said cheerfully. Rarus stared for a second and shrugged. He escorted them towards a perch where a clearly tired Perigoss stood, leaning on his spear.

Perigoss nodded a greeting to the kid before glancing at Scyra. She simply scowled and looked away. Perigoss frowned. Stellia was right, why was he ever bothering with the thief? She would choose coin over them each and every time. She did not belong with heroes.

"So what can I do for you?" Nyreus asked.

"I need to know if any connections exist between Heklious and a magical amulet?" Perigoss asked.

"Of course there is. The first would be his amulet of wind and the other would be one part of the Sanguine Trinity."

The three of them simply stared at Nyreus in confusion.

"From the Labours of Heklious?" Nyreus offered.

The three stared even more.

"What do you know about the Twelve Labours of Heklious?" Nyreus asked with a sigh.

"Heklious' wife died," Rarus explained. "Desperate to get her back, he made a deal with the twelve gods. If he performed a labour for each, they would return her to the land of the living."

"The gods know how I hate the bard version," Nyreus said. Again he was met with confused stares. "Most of the mythling tales are performed as plays. That is how most of the public knows of them. The problem is these plays are rarely complete. I blame not the bards, it is their duty to make an interesting play that people pay coin to see. That means they want a happy ending, an easy to digest plot and nothing off-putting.

"Take the story of Heruca the Kingloved. Everybody knows the story of her and Diomestor, how they stopped a war and their love conquered all. What nobody talks about is her endless war with the demons. Heruca has slain so many demons that they put a bounty on her head. Demons hunted her, endlessly, until they eventually took her life. When a demon puts a bounty on a mortal life, the bounty does not end with death."

Rarus frowned, Perigoss stared in silence and Scyra let out a low, somber whistle. None of that was in the plays she ever saw.

"What have the bard left out of the Heklious tale?" Perigoss asked.

"After the twelve labours, the gods did not simply return his wife to him," Nyreus explained. "They sent him on one final quest. The labours granted him three magical items. One was a wooden staff carved from the divine trees, the second was a large, circular gold amulet with a hollow middle and the third was a clear gem. The gem fit into the amulet which is then attached to the end of the wooden staff. This was the Sanguin Trinity. Once joined by scornblood, Heklious would travel to the underworld and use the staff to open a portal. This allowed his wife to bypass the ferryman and return to the land of the living."

"So why do they not tell this side of the story?" Perigoss asked.

"Because of scornblood," Scyra quickly answered. The scorn were those who once held the blessing of a god but no longer did. They had been forsaken by the pantheon and because of such, their blood had become special. Every drop of blood held the touching of one god or another. Scornblood made up for the lacking with a magical essence, one that had become a powerful element in dark rituals.

"Draining the blood of a downtrodden soul does not make for good plays," Rarus said. "It would give a child or two nightmares."

"Why do you suddenly care about this?" Nyreus asked.

"We think the gigas are collecting the parts of the trinity," Scyra said quickly. "They got an amulet from Mikha and looted something just as important from Pylomia. If they are connected as we suspect, then they only need one more item. The one question remains is why?"

"To free Typhaon, King of the Giants," Nyreus whispered.

Silence.

Nobody had to say anything. They all knew the stories. When King Typhaon failed in his war with the gods, he was cast down to the underworld to be punished. A living soul, forever trapped in the land of the dead. He was a giant of enormous power before the war, now he was fueled by hate and revenge. If he was freed it would be catastrophic.

"They would force open a gate to land of the dead," Rarus said. "That would allow eidolons and adeiazo to escape in the thousands. It could even allow the demons to cross to the surface in uncontrollable waves."

"We have to stop the gigas," Scyra said, shocking herself. She internally scolded her scandalous behaviour. She was not a hero.

"How do you know all of this?" Perigoss asked the kid.

"It is the duty of my family," Nyreus revealed. "My great-grandfather was a scribe, as was my grandfather, my father, my siblings and I. It was our job to record the tales, in detail, and write them down. It was our job preserving them. I have been studying the tales since I was a child."

"Then why are you here?" Rarus asked. "You have a dynasty already set for you."

"A scribe's name is never mentioned. My father spent his life recording the deeds of others but nobody will remember his name," Nyreus said. "But if I become a hero then one day Nyreus, son of Dyrellio will be scribed and then it can never be taken away. My father's name will forever be a part of mythling legend."

"That is a noble pursuit," Perigoss said.

"It truly be nothing of note," the kid defended. "You would do the same for your father, would you not?"

"The tale of my father and I," Perigoss said with a wince, "it is anything but a pleasant song."

Rarus ignored the awkward exchange between the two kids and looked over at Scyra. She seemed distant, like her mind was a world away and not somewhere pleasant. "Are you okay, Scyra?"

The words seemed to abruptly return her to the present.

"What? Oh, yes of course. I was just thinking of the bard's omission of history." Scyra said, lying as fast as she could. Her true mental self flagellations were not what she wanted to talk about. "This is why I know so little about Diomestor. None of the plays ever mention his magic ability."

"His what?" Nyreus asked, suddenly cutting of Perigoss mid-word. "Diomestor does not have spells."

"Yes he does," she defended. "I saw him using magic

not a week ago."

"Diomestor is one of the ungifted," Nyreus said. The ungifted were a small percentage of the population that could not learn mortal magic. The talent was simply not in their blood. "He was famously known for being unable to cast a single cantrip or spell."

"There are more magics than just mortal kind." Rarus tapped his staff to make his point. "There is divine magic, there is necrotic magic and of course, there is also giant magic."

Two long days had passed since Diomestor's arrival in Aoryna. They were spent preparing the guards, the troops and the soldiers for the attack to come. On the dawn of the third day the horn sounded.

The gigas were readying to attack.

One by one, each member of Diomestor's phalanx quickly donned their armour, weapons and shields and ran to the city gates. Every member stood in line, nervously waiting. Stellia stood at the front. Nowhere else would give her direct access to Aidox. Perigoss stood beside her, envious as she put on her helm. A sudden calling of his name caused Perigoss to look behind him.

It was Scyra.

"Take this," she said, offering him a water skin.

"I already have one," he explained.

"Take it regardless," Scyra admitted. "I know not how it works but you seem to fight better the more water you are near."

Perigoss opened his mouth to argue but no words came out. He did not fully understand what she meant but she seemed sincere enough. Perigoss thanked her and attached the second skin to his belt.

"Domos and Scyra: front," Diomestor said. Both the thief and minotaur broke ranks and walked towards him. "Troop status report."

"We have archers on the wall and troops at the gate. Guards are moving civilians out of harm's way as we speak," Domos growled. "The gigas commander is waiting for you in the center of the field. He stands with a harpy and Goremaster Jakus."

"Good, let us meet him face to face," Diomestor sternly said. "You two will be joining me."

"What good would we provide?" Scyra asked, suddenly worried.

"I need you by my side to think like a thief. I trust not the gigas," Diomestor explained. He looked at Domos. "I bring you so we can parade their so-called traitor before Jakus' eyes and show him what true strength looks like."

Domos let a content growl.

Diomestor led the pair to the gate. He ordered it pushed open and left that way until his return. The soldiers nodded. Confidently, Diomestor walked out onto the field. Halfway between the Aoryna and the gigas horde stood Commander Aidox, Goremaster Jakus and Warwing Xarica. Diomestor smirked as he approached.

"I have heard tales of your strength and brutality, Commander Aidox," Diomestor said loudly as he walked. "The armies of Hakros shiver at your name and the destruction you cause." Diomestor stopped a few yards away from the gigas. "But as I stand here, looking up at you, I wonder what it was that scared them in the first place."

"Your words are like that of a morning bird," Aidox laughed. "Some find it cute but most simply find it irritating." Diomestor looked over at the minotaur. "Goremaster Jakus, may I present Domos?"

"I know of the traitor," Jakus snarled. "By herd law you must hand me over to him to be executed."

"If you want me," Domos growled. "Come and get me."

"Rumours say you are collecting the pieces of Trinity," Diomestor asked, looking back to Aidox. Scyra's eyes went wide and she snapped her head towards them. He knew what the giants were planning? Why had he not said anything? Why had he not warned Hakros?

"Rumours are true," Aidox replied.

"Do you dare ignore me?" Warwing Xarica screeched. "Am I so beneath your human arrogance that you think not to acknowledge me like you do the others?"

Diomestor just chuckled as he glanced in her direction. "I have not a clue of who you even are."

Xarica screeched again.

Every hair of Scyra's body stood on end. Her body was telling her to run, to flee. Something was wrong. Her chest began to heave and her heart began to race as she desperately scanned the battlefield. Something was about to go bad but she had to figure out what.

Perhaps it was an ambush?

She eyed the troops in the distance. They were too far away to do anything of the sort.

Perhaps the commanders would attack?

Aidox and Jarkus were simply standing there. Aidox was insulting Diomestor in the giant tongue and the mythling seemed to be replying in kind.

Xarica agitatedly paced back and forth, clearly insulted by the slight but taking no motion to attack.

Were her own troops about to attack? She looked back but none had moved. They simply stood there with their shields at the ready.

What was wrong? What was missing?

It felt like a word just out of reach. That feeling when you couldn't remember a single phrase no matter how hard you wracked your brain. That word was forever stuck on the end of your……

"When did you learn to speak giant?" Scyra suddenly asked, her words cutting through all others.

"That?" Diomestor let out a small chuckle. "I learned that when I allied myself with Queen Porphyria."

"The giant queen?" Domos asked. "Why would you ally with h—"

Diomestor's arm moved in a blur. In one swift motion he drew his mythling dagger from his belt and plunged it deep into Domos' neck. Scyra let out a shocked shriek, one that echoed across the battlefield.

Diomestor looked at gigas and spoke once more.

"All hail King Typhaon."

CHAPTER SEVENTEEN

You can make a throne of blades but you cannot sit upon it for long
- Castlex Proverb

Scyra had seen swift strikes before, she was no slouch in speed herself, but Diomestor was on a completely different level. Scyra's eyes were barely able to track the strike's speed. One moment Diomestor was standing firm and then, with a blink of her eyes, suddenly there was a dagger in Domos' neck.

Scyra let out a shriek. She didn't intend to cry out like such, it was an involuntary reaction.

Diomestor drew his emerald-stained blade and swiftly spun. The gladius cut through Domos' neck with one swift slash. A second later, Domos' head tumbled off the shoulders and bounced to the ground below.

"The traitor, as requested," Diomestor said. He kicked the bleeding head towards the Goremaster. Jaruk roared in victory. Diomestor knelt by the minotaur's body and wiped his blade clean before returning it back to its sheath. Digging into his pouch, Diomestor pulled free a clear gem. He returned to a stand and held it up before Aidox's gaze. "The gem is present."

"Very good," Aidox chuckled.

"What is happening?" Scyra asked. Diomestor turned towards her and stepped close.

"We are making the change that this world needs," Diomestor said, a sinister tone entering his voice. It was an inflection that had always been hiding just beneath the surface of his voice and now had finally been set free. "You and I are joining the gigas now."

"What of the phalanx? What of Aoryna?"

"Do you truly care about their fate?" Diomestor asked. "These are the people that despise you. They banished you from the Ithoma Seminary and expelled you from your home. Oibalox thinks you an abomination and Hakros sent you to your death by drafting you into this war. I kept you from a pointless death. They do not care about you. Do not lose yourself in whatever reminisce of morality that echoes within yourself. You are a thief; that is your true self. Embrace it and come with me. I will look after you."

Scyra's mind raced. He had the trinity; he had the ability to open the gate and free Typhaon. All he needed was one remaining component.

"You care not for me," Scyra snapped. "You simply want my blood."

"Does that truly matter?" Diomestor asked. He gently placed his hand on her shoulder. "I promised you more coin then you could ever imagine and the offer still stands. Stay with me and you will be both safe and rich."

Scyra's body froze. She wanted to twist away from his touch but didn't. She was terrified. Safety; her body screamed for it. Aidox was about to ransack Aoryna. The safety that the village once held was quickly evaporating. That left Diomestor. As long as he needed her, she would be safe. Eventually the well of her value would run dry and she would be discarded but until then she was the safest under his watch.

And she would be rich.

With enough coin she could flee. She could start over somewhere else, heal the wounds that ran deep and maybe even be the person she truly wanted to be.

All she had to do was accept his offer.

All she had to do was be who they thought she was.

All she had to do was be happy with her lot in life.

All she had to do was be a thief.

"N…n…no," she whispered. The words surprised him and herself. Apparently, deep down, she had a conscience. "No. I will not."

"Pity. I could have used your mind in the underworld," Diomestor calmly said. "Your blood will have to suffice."

Diomestor thrust his dagger deep into her gut. The blade tore through her skin with no hesitation or resistance. She gasped; shocked into silence. Diomestor gave the blade a twist and she finally screamed. As swiftly as he stabbed it in, he removed it.

Scrya dropped to her knees and clamped both of hands over the wound. Blood seeped through her fingers and dripped onto the ground. Diomestor walked over and placed the clear gem underneath her wound. As blood trickled down upon the gem, it quickly got absorbed. Diomestor yanked Scyra's hand away, allowing the blood to flow more swiftly. He watched the gem absorb the blood until it became completely red.

Aidox handed him the staff and the amulet. The amulet was a golden circular piece with a hollow center. Diomestor placed the gem inside the center and it instantly locked into place. Then he attached the amulet to the top of the staff.

The Sanguine Trinity was complete.

"Y….you are going to doom us all," Scyra said between gasps of pain. Diomestor simply looked away.

"Thank you for your patience, Commander Aidox," Diomestor calmly said. "But you do not have to wait any longer. Raze Aoryna to the ground."

"With pleasure," Aidox said as he started to walk back to his troops. "Jaruk, do me a favour and crush this woman."

"Finally," The Goremaster growled. He stepped forward and gave Scyra a swift kick to the chest. The blow slammed against her and instantly made her cry out. Blood gushed out quicker. She tried to squirm away but he kicked her again.

Why was she doing this? She had it all, everything she had ever wanted had just been offered to her. So why hadn't she taken it? What hadn't she just behaved?

"Look at you, squirming away," Jaruk menacingly gloated. "Acting like the worm you are. What a pitiful sight. Do you have no strength, thief?"

Minotaurs always stood a head taller than most men but in the moment, Jaruk looked as tall as a giant. He towered over her and Scyra felt smaller than ever. Desperate to escape, Scyra continued to try and squirm away. Jaruk placed his hoof on her ankle, trapping her where she lay.

"Nowhere to go and no god to pray to," Jaruk cackled. "This is how you die."

Scyra's hand dropped to her waist. She grabbed a water skin and quickly popped the cork. She pointed it at the Goremast and gave it a squeeze. Its contents swiftly expelled and drenched the minotaur.

"You spray me with water?" Jaruk scoffed. His nose recoiled at the oil-scent. "Is there no strength left in you, weakling thief?"

"T...t...that was not water and I am no mere thief,"

Scyra said as she drew her blade. "I am the FireKissed Thief."

Her red-blade began to glow as Scyra willed every ounce of strength she had into it. She tapped Jaruk with the edge and instantly the oil ignited. Green flame exploded across the Goremaster's body. The minotaur screamed, backstepping off of Scyra's leg, as he tried to extinguish the flame by slapping them. The action provided no solace, it simply caused his hands to burn as well.

Scyra climbed to her feet and started running towards Aoryna. She knew not where the strength came from but she was not denying it. Behind her, the smell of burning flesh filled the air while the curdling screams filled her ears.

Scyra tried to push both out of her mind as she ran forward.

You should have just taken what you were given.

You should have been happy with what he offered you.

Scrya tried to push her own doubts out of her mind as she ran forward.

Pain assaulted her legs, her chest and her heart, but she kept running.

Her foot stumbled and she dropped to one knee. Scyra pushed herself up and kept running forward. She could not stop and she could not fall. If she fell, she would not be getting back up. If she stopped; she died.

A harpy screech filled the air as Warwing Xarica took to the air. She dove for Scyra, her talons slashing across the thief's back.

Suddenly everything slowed down.

All of her strength abandoned her legs and her feet gave way. Without solid footing, her entire body fell forwards. There was no avoiding it and there was nothing to save her.

She was going to fall.

She was going to stop.

She was going to die.

Scyra closed her eyes. She did not want to see her final moments. She was going to die, on a battlefield, alone. She had no god to pray to and nobody to comfort her. It would end with heavy thud of the ground and the vicious talons of the harpies.

All that remained was the thud.

The thud never came.

Instead she felt the grip and warmth of a strong pair of arms catching her.

"I got you," a voice said. The voice was soft, soothing and comforting but held a level of strength that she dared not argue with. Scrya opened her eyes.

Perigoss was holding her.

There he was, with cerulean hair, holding her in the middle of the battlefield. He held her tight; protecting her. As long as he drew breath, her body would not touch the dirt that day.

Xarica circled in the air and tried to slash once again but this time Perigoss was ready. He grabbed the Flamekissed Blade from the ground, the blade instantly becoming a cerulean colour, and slashed twice. The first blocked the attacking talons and the second slashed at her legs. Xarica screeched in pain as she frantically flapped her wings, climbing higher into the air. Suddenly, fired from atop the roof, Xali's arrow ripped across the sky and dove into the Warwing's side. She screeched again as she crashed into the ground.

"Let us flee," Perigoss said as he hoisted Scyra up in both arms. He started running, moving with blinding speed as he carryed her back to safety.

Commander Aidox simply shook his head. Not moments ago he had two additional commanders at his side. Now one had just painfully burned alive while the other screeched in agony. This was why he no longer trusted the other races. They were not worth his time.

Diomestor turned back and raised his hand. Ashen-coloured wisps of magic began to swirl around his palm. They formed into an orb and quickly grew in size until it matched the size of his head. Then Diomestor slammed his palm into the dirt.

Perigoss ran through the city gates.

"Close the gate," he yelled. "Close them now!"

"We can't."

Perigoss spun around. Each side of the gate was suddenly held open by a series of magical, ashen coloured chains. The gates were stuck open.

"Over here, boy," Rarus called out. He was standing at the far end of the phalanx, near a makeshift cot. "Place her upon here, carefully."

"Y…y…you saved me?" Scyra asked. Perigoss just smiled and he carefully laid her down. "Why?"

"You're one of us," he said.

He was as surprised at his actions. Stellia had told him not to go but the moment his eyes lay upon her, choosing the path of heroes instead of the path of greed, he knew that she was one of them. He knew that she had some honour inside of her. He knew that she was special.

He had always known it. He had simply lost sight of it.

Perigoss stepped aside as Rarus approached. The priest gripped his staff tightly as he summoned forth the lilac-coloured magic and willed it into Scyra. She cried out as her wounds began to knit together. The healing hurt nearly as much as the wounds had. The priest did not have time to dull the pain.

"What happened out there?" Lypos asked.

"Diomestor betrayed us. He killed Domos," Scyra said between cries of pain. She pushed Rarus away and tried to sit up. Her body instantly objected but she did not care. "He has completed the Trinity and is trying to free Typhaon."

"If you will not lie still," Rarus ordered, "I will make you."

Scyra lay back as Rarus resumed his healing.

"Diomestor is gone, as is Domos," Nikka said. Everybody looked around. Everybody was thinking the same thing but nobody wanted to say it.

"We need to run," Boroca said, breaking the silence. "We cannot defend this without them. Most of us can count the amount of shield wall we've been a part of on one hand. The gigas are bred for this. They have countless more battles beneath their belts."

"Stellia," Perigoss called out. She quickly ran over. "Line us up and take command. You have more phalanx experience than all of us combined. You said fate put you on this path. Now it is time to embrace it. Be our lokhagos and lead us to victory."

All around her, several heads nodded in agreement. Stellia took in a deep breath and slowly exhaled. She could do this. She had to do it.

"I want a line-up at the ready," Stellia barked. "Spears at the front. We are holding this gate."

One by one they all formed up. They were the heroes of Hakros. She was a hoplite of Oibalox. Together, they would not fail.

"Stellia," Rarus called. She looked over at the priest. "It is only a victory if we survive."

Stellia nodded at the priest. There was no mistaking his message. She just nodded. She turned and began to walk up the line.

"Boroca, have you deciphered that shield?" she asked.

"I think so, yeah."

"Good. You will stand by me at the front," she ordered. "Perigoss, I want you there as well."

He nodded and grabbed his shield. Stellia looked at Xali.

"Take your archers and set them on the wall. Keep the air clear and stop anything that comes close."

"You have my word." Xali said. She glanced at her wife. Nikka kept her hand behind her back but still the archer saw the glow. "Not this day. Look after yourself."

"Petal…" Nikka tried to dispute the argument but Xali shook her head. Reluctantly, Nikka pressed the spell to her own chest. The magic rippled through her. Xali leaned in and gave her wife a passionate kiss.

"Regardless of what happens on this day, the fates cannot keep us separated for eternity," Xali said. "No man, beast, giant or god will keep us separated. I found you at the tournament and I found you on the battlefield. No matter what, I will always find you again."

"I love you, Petal," Nikka said.

"And I love you." Xali kissed her wife once more before grabbing her bow and climbing up the ladder.

Stellia reached the phalanx's front and turned back. She looked upon all of the eyes that stared back at her. Guard, soldier and hero stared up at her. They were scared. She understood. So too was she.

"Many of the citizens are still trying to flee this town," Stellia began. "They will not make it to safety unless we slow the enemy. I know that this was not what all of you expected. I know that fear and doubt has taken root in your mind. Fear has also taken root in my thoughts as well. Doubt, however, has no place in my brain.

"You are soldiers, you are heroes and you are the defenders of the weak. The gigas are going to come down that hill and assault us but we will hold this gate. We will be victorious and of that, I have no doubt.

"Hold your shield with honour, wave your spear with pride and stand firm, warriors, for on this day our names will reach the stars."

CHAPTER EIGHTEEN

It doesn't take a hero to order men in combat. It takes
a hero to lead them into battle.
- Hakros Proverb

Silence hung in the air for several long minutes. Not
a bird, beast or man dared speak. It was as if a single whisper
would summon the gigas. Perhaps, they irrationally thought,
if we remained perfectly silent then we would also remain
unharmed. Yet as unnerving as the thought of battle was, the
silence was doubly so.

The sound of marching feet was ironically a relief.
The gigas crossed the field, shield and weapons in their hands.
A low, guttural noise began to crawl with them. It was music,
a gigas war song. It held long, deep low notes and chest heavy
growls. Every few minutes, the gigas army would each slap
metal across their shield and the clang would be heard for
eons, like a frightening sound that rippled across the threads
of time. There would be children born, far into the future, that
had never heard the clang but would still instinctively know
to fear it.

Nyreus watched, trying to keep his nerves at bay. The
sand giant had been bad enough. He still woke up in sweats
after nearly dying to Kruzza, but this was something different.
Despite being smaller than other of their kin, the gigas felt

like a far greater threat. Storm giants and the caculis seemed like impossible threats conquered by impossible heroes. The gigas, however, seemed relatively no different than him. They were simply brutal warriors fighting a war.

Somehow that was far more unsettling.

Yoo-hay-ohh
Doom Harra-nay

The voice started from the back. It was discordant singing but somehow it resonated with each of them. It was filled with hope and strength. Several faces turned around to see the music coming from Lypos. It was a Triton song and even though they knew not the words, somehow each member began to sing. The longer he sang, the more the words took form in their minds. One by one they all joined in, until their song drowned out that of the gigas.

Yoo-hay-ohh
Doom Harra-nay
Warriors alway fight
For their home and their heart.
Yoo-hay-ohh
Kala Harra-tai
We swim the river long
So the current may guide the way
Yoo-hay-ohh
Torno Harra-zul
We fight so others mustn't
And so peace may lead the way

"Ephodos!" Stellia yelled. The singing came to a halt. "Shields!"

Shields snapped up with a uniformed rattle. The gigas would charge next and slam their shields against that of the heroes but Stellia's phalanx would hold firm.

Aidox smirked as his troops approached. They walked firmly but had not gone into a run. He knew that the humans would be unnerved, unsure as to what he was thinking. That was not enough. He wanted them scared.

"Foricu," he called out. "First wave."

A horn blew and four bodies peeled off the gigas horde. They quickly moved from a trot into a full run. The jewels that hung from their horns glistened in the sun as they ran.

The minotaurs were charging.

Xali spotted them first; her keen eyes rarely missed much. She notched an arrow and swiftly drew back. Xali took only a heartbeat to aim, she seldom needed more than that. She let loose the arrow and watched it fly. It tore across the sky, diving towards the lead minotaur's face.

The arrow never hit its target.

Part way through their run, each minotaur suddenly raised a small shield and held it before their eyes. The arrow instead collided with that. Xali and her archers fired again, hoping to sneak one past the shield before they collided with the phalanx.

No arrow found a home in flesh.

"Krousis!"

The heroes braced for impact as the minotaurs slammed against them. The impact was powerful and devastating; unlike anything they had ever witnessed. The gigas were far stronger than any human but a charging minotaur was nearly impossible to stop. As the first minotaur collided, the shieldman was sent flying backward. The minotaur roared at his success and began swinging his shield around like a club. Nikka rushed up, sword drawn, and started stabbing at its gut. The minotaur was strong but it had little place to move within the formation. The blades quickly cut deep until the minotaur fell over.

The second and third minotaurs were next. Their collisions were just as powerful but now Stellia knew what to expect. In the brief moments between the lead and his followers, Stellia closed the gap and tightened the wall. More shields meant more people holding them, which meant the wall would not fall. The impact sent shocks through each heroes' arms, like striking a metal pole with a metal weapon. It reverberated throughout each of their bodies.

The wall still stood.

Small gaps opened as spears began to stab out. Wild and rapid thrusts emerged from within. Some tore through a leg while the other ran through an arm. Eventually one tore through a chest while the other feasted up a neck. Both the minotaurs fell.

Stellia peeked between the shields as she spotted the third minotaur. It was charging directly towards her. The hoplite smirked; she was waiting for this. She loosened her shield from the other and waited. Her timing had to be just right.

Just as the minotaur was about to connect, Stellia pulled her shield away. Expecting an impact when none was to be found, the minotaur suddenly began to stumble forward. Stellia dropped to one knee and slashed its leg with her shield. The sharpened edge ripped across her leg and forced the minotaur to crash into the dirt. Three heroes were already upon him stabbing him as he lay there.

"Get rid of the corpse and check the wounded," Stellia cried out as she replaced her shield in the wall. "The next wave is coming.

Aidox deviously smirked as he watched the second wave of minotaurs rush in. Their attacks were already pushing the limits of the humans' strength and their will. Each attack was like a battering ram slamming against a wooden gate. Eventually the shield wall would crack and crumble, but until then, each clang would be a blow against their sanity.

"Foricu, tell the Warwing to take flight" Aidox said calmly. He turned to the rest of the gigas and waved them forward. "Onwards we march."

With a roar the gigas marched forward.

Scyra winced as she sat up. She reached down to her stab wound. The priest's magic had closed the wound but the area was still tender, bruised and still in pain. It was evident that the kicks had caused more lasting pain then she had realized. She looked over and saw several guards pulling both injured heroes and minotaur corpses out from the shield wall. The town guards were not trained enough to be in the shield wall but they could still help and when the wall fell, they would be forced to fight alongside everybody else.

"What is happening?" Scrya winced as she stood up. She spotted the priest kneeling over an injured woman, his lilac magic doing its best to restore her.

"I warned you about standing up," Rarus snapped

without looking up.

"What has happened?" Scrya asked again.

"Minotaurs are smashing against the wall," Rarus explained.

Scyra's eyes went wide. She bolted towards him, her body crying out in protest with every step. She grabbed Rarus and pulled him away from his patient.

"Were they charging with shields?" she frantically asked. Rarus just nodded, a quizzical look upon his face. Scrya cursed.

Diomestor was using her ideas.

He had baited her for ways the gigas could win this battle under the guise of preparing to counter them. Now he was using them against her, against the phalanx.

Scyra ran to the wall, as fast as her pain riddled body would allow, yelling with every step.

"Get off the wall!" She saw the harpies approaching, flying through the air with small vases in their talons. Scyra yelled louder, repeating her instructions over and over, but her voice was not enough. Vases dropped from the air, crashing into the wall in balls of green flames.

Xali watched as the second wave of minotaurs began their charge. She let out a frustrated grunt as she notched another arrow. Normally the only way to stop a charge was to fill their eyes and skulls with arrows. Their use of shields robbed her of that option.

Xali notched another arrow and pulled back on the string. She shifted her aim, lowering it just slightly, before releasing. The arrow shot forward and dove into one of the chargers' legs. The arrow was not enough to stop the charging beast, a minotaur's legs were famously strong, but it did slow it slightly. A slower minotaur meant a lighter collision for Nikka.

"Harpies," an archer called. Xali nodded.

"Arrows up," Xali ordered. "Clear the skies."

Xali held her drawstring longer than normal. Harpies were notoriously difficult to hit. They could move like a leaf and could suddenly turn on just as much notice. The first wave of arrows ripped into the air but few found their mark. The harpies zigged, twisted and dropped; each movement sudden and unpredictable.

The pained yell of a voice barely reached Xali's ear. Yet try as she might, the archer couldn't make out the words. She turned her head.

It was Scyra.

The thief was somehow upright and running, yelling with every step. She looked frantic and was desperately yelling. Xali cocked her head slightly, with the hopes of hearing her better. Suddenly the words started to become clearer in her mind.

Get off the wall.

Xali snapped her head back to the approaching harpies. Only then did she notice the vases in each of their talons.

Xali notched another arrow and drew back. She let loose and drew another, and another and another. A trio of arrows flew towards the approaching harpies, each desperate to stop the harpies before they got closer, before they flew over the wall. The third arrow tore through the Warwing's shoulder and sent her spinning downwards but not before she dropped what she carried.

"Flee!" Xali yelled.

The vase dropped down to the wall and shattered on

contact. The oil ignited with an explosive burst of green flame. As each vase crashed, they exploded as well. The explosive force was massive and Xali was pitched off the edge. She tried to twist her body as she fell off the wall, attempting to grab something - anything - to save herself. But when nothing was available, Xali crashed into the roof of a cart, her body bouncing off and slamming into the dirt below.

Air swiftly evacuated from her lungs. She tried to breathe and tried to call out but the shock wouldn't allow it. Instead she lay there helpless, gasping for air as panic took hold. From the ground she could see the second wave of harpies. Like the wave before it, they each dropped a vase of their own. They shattered on impact and exploded. A storm of green-flame and massive stones rained down upon the archer. Air returned to Xali's lungs just in time for her to scream.

Commander Aidox led his troops as they slammed against the human phalanx. Shield crashed against shield as othismos began. The part of combat when everything devolved into a shoving match. With each push, Aidox and his troops forced the humans back a couple paces. With each shove, the gigas got closer to either breaking the shield wall or pushing them back beyond the gate. Either way, it was only a matter of time before the breach occurred.

Human spears popped out from behind the shields, each desperate to rip into gigas flesh. Aidox decided to respond in kind. With his stolen spear, he thrust. The flaming weapon collided with the force of a hammer and the crimson flame hungrily burned whatever was nearby.

"The end of day is inevitable," Aidox menacingly roared. "Accept your fate."

The sound of the first explosion filled the air. A second one a few moments later. The Warwing's aerial assault removed the archers from the battle and rained debris down on the phalanx below.

With a thundering roar, the gigas gave one final shove.

A few of the front line heroes fell backward, their shields dropping from the wall. Seeing an opening, Aidox thrust his burning spear into the gap. He felt his weapon collide with flesh, heard the blood curdling scream and smelled the unmistakable scent of burning skin. A few more shields fell and Aidox pushed his way through.

The shield wall had fallen.

Now it was time to massacre them all.

CHAPTER NINETEEN

It is better to die standing firm and holding your
shield than to live on your knees.t takes
- Oibalox Commandment

Guard Captain Larittany was no stranger to war. He was seen battles in his youth, before he stepped away and became a guardsman. He had fought against other humans and even defended against various monsters but what he had never before witnessed was the might, viciousness and savagery of the gigas. Where a man fought to win a battle, a gigas fought to obliterate their foe. A man could show mercy. The only clemency a gigas could ever show was death; crushing their foes into dust beneath the heels of their feet. Larittany thought himself a man of stone, unwavering in a moment of urgency, but at the sight of the gigas he found himself frozen in fear.

A pair of insectile hands grabbed him and yanked him to the side. Larittany returned to focus as his eyes fell upon the myrmidon.

"Your attention is very much needed on the present situation, Guard Captain," Tik said with a series of clicks. "Please return to the back and escort all non essential souls out beyond the town's limits."

Larittany nodded.

Tik turned back to the battle and drew his blade. He ran a free hand over his bandolier and quietly clicked to himself.

"We fight for our queen and she will fight for us." Tik hoisted his shield and dashed into combat.

The myrmidon were not known for their fear. They often fought without hesitation or trepidation but as he squared off against one of the giant-kin, he couldn't help but get worried. It wasn't that his kind lacked fear, they were sentient kin, but what fear they did feel was often quelled by the presence of their queen. Her aura was powerful as was her charisma. She was dynamic but most importantly, she provided a sense of belonging. When the myrmidon were first created, they did so for war. After the battle ended they were without direction. They were lost in a sea of possibilities. From within, a queen arose. She gave them each motivation, she drew a path for their species and more importantly, gave them a sense of belonging. Their queen was their absolute and few ever questioned her. Tik had been away from his queen for nearly five years and still he was learning to adjust to fights without her.

He was still learning to adjust to the fear.

Tik ducked beneath the axe of a gigas and lunged in with his sword. His strikes were fanciful flourishes, like a paintbrush across a canvas, but they were also deadly. Like a dynamic stroke, his sword made a curving slash across the gigas' chest.

Fear would not hold him back.

Tik pivoted around the gigas, his thin frame granting him speed as his love of dance gave him a sense of grace. Tik painted his canvas again and again, not stopping until his art was perfect. Tik withdrew his blade and stepped back, admiring his work as the gigas collapsed to the dirt below.

Fear would never stop him.

Lypos' spear rose up as he blocked the minotaur's hammer strike. The triton backpedaled as he began to swiftly spin his weapon as his mind suddenly fought off the woe of longing.

Sometimes he despised his mind. It never seemed to stay on topic. Even as he fought for his life, defending the innocents, his mind would still wander. As he deflected yet another attack, his mind replayed his memories of the sea. When he was a younger man his wandering mind would focus during battle, harnessing the thrill of combat to super-charge his thoughts, but now they no longer did. Now it just reminded him of a man long since past. Perhaps this was a sign. Perhaps, when this war was over, it would be time to hang up the spear.

The minotaur roared and lunged forward, trying to gore Lypos with his horns but the triton was not allowing it. He sidestepped, and thrust once more. His triton spear diving deep into the beast's neck.

When this war was over, it was time to return home. It was time to feel the currents of his sea once more.

Perigoss was furious. He kept trying to run for the gigas threat, to end Commander Aidox, but everything kept stopping him. First the minotaurs charged him, then the harpies descended upon him. He knew not why they thought him such a threat but he cared not. He would slice and kill each and every soul that stood between him and victory.

A harpy dove for him and Perigoss raised his shield. He braced himself as the flying screecher slammed against it. Perigoss shifted his weight, altered the angle of his shield and suddenly pushed downward. The harpy slammed against the ground and suddenly found herself pinned to the ground. She frantically screeched as she tried to escape. Perigoss silenced her with a pull of his gladius across her neck.

Diomestor. He needed to be stopped. That wasn't going to happen as long as the gigas were attacking.

Perigoss dropped his sword as he picked up a javelin. He took a quick aim before flinging it forward. It dove into a minotaur's neck. The beast roared as it frantically twisted, looking for its attacker. At the last second he spotted him. Perigoss was leaping in the air, sword back in his hand, for a diving slash. The minotaur never got a chance to react.

If he killed them all, he would get to Diomestor.

Foricu pulled her axe from the frail human body and kicked them away. A second woman lunged towards her, a sword in both hands. Foricu easily deflected the attack and struck the human with an elbow to the face. The women fell to the ground, a little stunned from the blow. Foricu brought her axe down, felling her in one swipe.

These humans were pathetic. Time and time again they were found lacking.

A third rushed in with a spear but Foricu reached out and fearlessly grabbed the spear. She used her gigas strength to push back against the charging hoplite, bringing the rush to an abrupt halt. Foricu brought her axe down and snapped the spear in two. She brought it back up and slammed the blunt end of her weapon across the human's face. It was a glancing blow but enough to knock the human to the ground. Foricu approached, ready to strike again but with the proper side of the axe.

A shield suddenly slammed into her side and caused

her to buckle slightly. She pivoted around to see yet another human attacking her.

"I've got you," Boroca said, holding his magic shield aloft. "Back away, quickly."

Foricu spun and swiftly attacked. Her axe slammed down against the shield but neither it or Boroca budged. Boroca slashed with his sword, catching her by the arm. The wound infuriated Foricu and her rage began to fuel her. She slammed down with her axe, over and over, but again Boroca didn't move. Instead, his shield began to glow. The images of wheat etched on the front began to sway as the magic within the Timeword Aegis activated. Suddenly, the animated stalks began to grow all across the shield. Suddenly, Foricu's attacks were no longer connecting with the shield, they were struggling to make it through the magically formed wheat.

Opato's blessing was upon Boroca.

A blast of lilac magic slammed against her side and dropped her to one knee. Foricu looked up and spotted Rarus. His staff glowed as he prepared a second blast.

Foricu allowed the rage to lessen as she looked back and forth between the warrior with the magical shield and the priest with the glowing staff.

Two on one was a losing battle that only a fanatic would fight.

She would never be a fanatic.

Foricu slowly backed away.

Scyra's blade burned brightly as she fought. She had not her usual dervish style of fencing, her wounded body would not allow it. Nor did she have her usual tricks. She was running dangerously low on cunning. Instead she had a blade that burned brightly and she was swinging it at anyone who got close.

The battle, however, was going just as pooly.

The heroes were doing their best to hold their own, allowing what was left of the city to flee, but they were losing souls all around her. The gigas were strong, the minotaur were brutal and the harpies were viciously ripping apart any they could get their talons on. The archers were scattered, the wall had been breached and the gigas commander was mercilessly ripping apart any who he came into contact with.

They needed to flee.

Scyra looked around, desperate to find Stellia. She spotted the woman in the midst of battle, frantically fighting while trying to organize what was left of her troops. Scyra bolted - hobbled if she was being accurate - towards the Oibalox soldiers.

The longer the fight went on, the longer Stellia struggled. With each person that fell, a little bit more of her died. Why them and not her? Worst still, she was in command. It was her duty to protect them all.

"On me," Stellia barked, calling as many to her as possible. She stabbed with her spear at the nearest harpy, catching it mid-dive before violently flinging it to the ground. If she could grouped up then they could push back and force the gigas out. She could turn the battle. She could be victorious.

"We need to flee," Scyra said suddenly, running towards her. Stellia scowled.

"Of course you say that," Stellia barked. "The thief wishes not to fight."

"We cannot fight," Scyra defended, "because we have already lost. The battle is over. We need to save as many as possible."

"No," Stellia snapped. "Aidox slew my phalanx. He has decimated several towns and killed countless innocents. I will not stop until Aidox is dead. I will keep fighting until it is either him or I who lies still."

"Are you so fanatical that you cannot see the truth before you?" Scyra asked.

"If he does not die, then every soldier today, yesterday and the days before that who died by his hand will have died for nothing." Stellia shook her head. "I cannot let their lives be for naught."

"And what of those who die in this lost battle? What will they have died for?"

Stellia paused. Rarus' words suddenly echoed in her brain. They were faint at first, barely able to be registered, but with repetition they became louder until they were all she could hear.

It is only a victory if we survive.

Stellia cringed, ashamed by her own actions. She had lost herself to revenge. Worst still, she had allowed it to stain the glory of battle. She needed to retreat.

"I know that your dislike of me is beyond compare," Scrya said, cunning sliding back into her voice as a plan began to formulate. "I suspect it is because of my looks. I have a stunning posterior."

"It has nothing to do with your looks," Stellia muttered, her annoyance at the thief returning.

"But at this moment, you need to trust me," Scyra said. "I have a plan."

The horn sounded across the air. Every soldier and guard paused for a brief second. The battle was lost. It was time to flee. One by one, they peeled off and started running away. As they took off running, they spotted Scyra. She was pointing everybody to the north, to the uppermen's section. One by one they exited the north and the gigas followed. The uppermen's section was filled with nicer buildings. They were constructed with finer materials and assembled with better care. The wealthy lived in this section of Aoryna and it clearly showed.

The gigas circled a corner and found themselves gathering in the town square. A stone fountain sat in the center, in front of the town square. Spread throughout the square were several lamps. All but one burned, the flames needlessly flickering in the afternoon light. Their bronze postings were always well kept, well maintained and well cleaned. Not a speck of dust or dirt resided on them.

Then there was the unlit lamp.

It was made from blackened metal and stood alone on a corner. It had not been cleaned as webs draped down from its edges. Nobody touched this lamp. It was not because they feared it but mostly because they did not notice it. Distortion magic rippled throughout its makeup, making the lamp hard to see. Even Scyra, who knew of its existence and location, struggled to lay eyes on it. It was as if the lamp sat in the corner of her eye, just always out of sight, and when she turned towards it the lamp would shift again. Foivi had commissioned a lamp that could not be seen. Even at that moment, despite having seen and touched the lamp, Scyra had to actively remind herself that it existed lest she lose it again.

Scyra and Stellia stood by the lamp with Guard Captain Larittany standing nearby. He constantly looked to the right of the women, his eyes struggling to focus on something that just wasn't there.

Commander Aidox eyed the women suspiciously as he turned the corner. They were just standing there. In the distance, he could see the remainder of the humans fleeing. Did these two human women believe that they could make a difference? That they could slow him down enough for the rest to flee?

"Are the houses all empty?" Stellia asked calmly.

"The wealthy are always the first to flee," Larittany said.

"Good," Scyra said. "It's time for the pair of you to mimic their actions."

Larittany nodded as he departed.

Stellia glanced at Scyra. The thief smiled. "It is time for you to follow."

"I'm not leaving without you," Stellia said, pulling off her helm. "A lokhagos does not leave the battlefield until each of their soldiers have."

"Let honesty pass between us and accept the fact that I was never your soldier," Scyra said with a smirk. "If I do not make it, look after him for me. He tends to need saving every once in a while."

"Wh…what? Wh..who?" Stellia stammered.

Scyra stepped close, and gently grabbed Stellia by the head. Two fingers rested beneath Stellia's ear and two above. The thief's dexterous thumb gently stroked the hoplite's cheek. Stellia opened her mouth to speak but Scyra did not allow it. Scyra leaned in and tenderly pressed her lip against Stellia's. For a brief moment, Stellia stood there stunned as Scyra kissed her. A moment later she returned the affection. The two women kissed for what seemed like forever before

Scyra broke the connection.

"I needed to know," Scyra quietly said. "I needed to know why it was not me."

Scyra pushed the hoplite away. She turned towards the gigas and stepped forward.

"Aidox," Scyra called out. "I think you and I have a mutual friend."

"I doubt that," Aidox laughed as he approached.

"I swear it be true. You and I are friends with Leonidax."

"Son of Anaxious?" Aidox said, surprised.

"Of course."

"I slew him in battle," Aidox laughed as he continued to approach. "Just as I will slay you."

"Slay me if you wish but I give to you the same warning I give each of my sexual conquests," Scyra said as she reignited her blade. "Let us both see if you can survive me first."

Scyra brought her burning blade around and pressed it against the torch. A few heartbeats later the unlit torch finally ignited with flame. The fire burned not the mix of red and orange that most were used to, instead, it burned with green flame.

Scyra was not an expert in green flame. It was not a widely known substance. Foivi, however, made it her duty to know everything about everything. The Queen Raven was fascinated with green flame and made it duty to secretly brew as much as she could get her hands on. Whenever any temples, cities or alchemists needed green flame, they came to her. Foivi held more green flame than anybody else in Hakros' reach. Most of her supply, however, was stored in the town square. Hoarded in specially crafted magical containers, each hidden all across the uppermens' section, were gallons of the oil. All it would take to detonate was the ignition of one specific, magical torch.

As the fire atop the black torch brightly burned, the distortion spell began to dissipate. Suddenly everybody was able to see the torch. Magical sparks began to erupt from the torch but instead of harmlessly falling to the ground, each floated to a different building.

Aidox's eyes went wide as he turned around and ran away.

Scyra turned the opposite direction and ran, chasing after Stellia.

As each spark collided with the building, it suddenly caused one of the hidden containers to detonate, exploding in a burst of green flame.

Foivi was a woman who knew to be prepared. She understood that her power in Aoryna existed because she was of use. She also knew that the wealthy had short attention spans. Eventually the uppermen would try to kill her. Either she would gain too much leverage or they would forget her usefulness. Regardless, they would try to remove her in the most permanent of methods.

The unlit torch was built to prevent that.

If they came for her, she would burn the entirety of the uppermens' section to the ground. The lowermens' section would remain unharmed and the town balance would forever be changed.

Instead, the gigas, minotaurs and harpies were the unlucky ones to feel the wrath.

Building after building exploded as green flame rained from above, consuming anything in its path. Gigas soldiers screamed as the hungry war fire began to burn them alive. Minotaurs ran amok, slamming into the nearest wall as they desperately tried to extinguish the searing flames. Harpies let out bloodcurdling screeches that shattered the nearest ear.

The smell of scalding flesh, searing wings and burning hair filled the air. It was a smell that would stain the stone of the surviving buildings. In the years that came, when Syceux brought rain down upon them, the smell would rise once more and remind them of the battle that once was.

CHAPTER TWENTY

War does not determine who is right, simply who left alive
- Athonea Proverb

Scyra ran as fast as her broken body would allow but when her legs proved not enough she was forced to adjust. Green flames were raining down from above. She could not stay out in the open. With no other choice, she dove beneath a balcony. Green flame rained down upon the building and already the thief could hear the walls and supports whining as they struggled to stay upright. A pillar was the first to crack and the building began to collapse. Scyra tried to move but debris fell, suddenly blocking her path. The balcony began to creak again before collapsing entirely. Scyra dove for a corner and tried to make herself small as the building fell all around her.

Scyra just lay where she was, pinned under debris and unable to move. She knew not how long she was there but each heartbeat felt so far apart. Song and sonnets could be recited between one beat of her fading heart and the next. Every attempt to move her arms or body resulted in failure. Scyra found her breathing quickening but with each gasp she felt the air weaken around her and somehow, the walls seemed even closer. Scyra, the nimblest of thieves, was finally stuck completely still. She had nowhere else to run.

Stones and beams suddenly shifted as several hands began to pull debris off the piles. A beam of light cracked through the darkness as stones were moved. A gasp of fresh air - albeit one that smelled like burning flesh - filled her lungs. A few moments later, two pairs of hands pulled her free.

Scyra stood, happy and relieved, and looked up at the grinning faces of Perigoss and Stellia.

"How many times must I save you this day?" Perigoss asked with a smile.

"Are you sure that it was I who you saved?" Scyra replied in her usual banter, masking the relief in her voice. "For my greatness would never require rescuing. Perhaps it was Stellia who needed your grace?"

Stellia stepped forward, grabbed Scyra by the neck and hoisted her into the air, slamming her against the wall.

"If you ever dare to kiss me again," Stellia growled. "You best mean it."

She released the thief and turned around to face the small collection of soldiers that had followed her back into the town.

"We are missing some of our own," Stellia barked. "Your orders are to find them and flee." She took in another long breath. "I will not be joining you. It does not end for me until Aidox lies forever still."

"Stelli—"

"You have your order," Stellia barked, cutting off the objection before it even started. "Any questions?"

Perigoss sheepishly raised his hand. Stellia nodded at him.

"What was this about a kiss?"

Pain.

It was all she felt when her eyes open. She was surprised that her eyes had opened at all but still the pain was unbreakable.

Pain.

She could feel it in her arm. It had broken in the fall.

Pain.

She could feel it in her back. It had been crushed by rubble.

Pain.

She could feel it in her ribs. They had been cracked in the explosion.

Pain.

Xali was quickly tiring of it.

The archer tried to climb to her feet, a task that seemed all but impossible and yet somehow she had barely accomplished it. Xali leaned on a pile of random rubble as she tried to find strength in her legs. Satisfied they would hold her, albeit unsure for how long, she began to look for her supplies. Amongst the rubble and burning fires she looked for her bow, her blade or dagger. In truth her bow was useless to her. With only one functional arm, there was little she could do with it. Her sword was just futile. With her injured back and ribs, swinging a blade was beyond ineffective. She would have no strength in which to use it. Xali needed a dagger. No, what she needed was to find Nikka. She had promised her wife that she would find her, no matter what.

She would not break her promise.

Xali limped forward, carefully stepping over a pile of rubble slowly being consumed by a fire of green flames.

"You!" The harpy screech hit her ears and forced its way into her mind. Xali froze. She could feel the sounds throughout her body, from the tip of her hair, down her battered spine and towards the tip of her toes. "You must die!"

Xali looked up and saw Warwing Xarica hovering above her. The harpy leader screeched once more.

"I have fought battles high above your worthless humans. I have battled the arctic winds and the hurricane cyclones and did so unscathed." A scowl crossed Xarica's face. "How is it you have wounded me not once but several times?"

Xali wished she was as swift and clever as Scyra. The thief would know just the proper retort, a witty saying that would stun her foe long enough to outsmart them. Xali wasn't that woman. She said the only words her mind could conjure. "I…made…a….promise."

Xarica dove for Xali and slammed both feet into the archer's chest. The blow sent Xali flying backwards. The archer crashed into the nearest wall and slumped to the ground. She winced as she tried to get up but Xarica was already upon her. She slashed with her talons but Xali twisted her body to use her left arm as a shield. It was already broken, there was no sense protecting it. The claws tore at the flesh, ripping it as viciously as one did with bread. Xali screamed as she looked for something, anything she could use as a weapon. Her right hand grabbed a rock, picked it up and used it to strike Xarica's face. Both harpy and archer screamed in pain. As Xarica took to the air, Xali struggled to breathe. She gasped for air but found none. Breathing was hard with her injured chest and the armour was only making it worse. Xali awkwardly undid the straps and let it fall to the ground. She gasped for air but only got little amounts.

"Nikka," she winced between gasps. "I….promised."

"Again you injure me!" Xarica screeched as she circled. "I am beauty. I am perfection. You have spoiled it!"

Xarica dove again. Xali tried to find her stone once more but could not grab it in time. Xarica's talon dove into her chest, ripping through the flesh with ease and sending agonizing pain throughout an already injured soldier. Xarica did not twist or withdraw her talons, instead she squeezed the wound to better her grip and began to drag her across the dirt.

"You think yourself more beautiful than I?" Xarica taunted. "You think yourself better because you are mated?"

Xali's head bounced off of the dirt as she was dragged towards a green burning pile. With her free talon, she grabbed Xali's skull and pressed it into the green flame.

"Will she love when your beauty is gone?" Xarica taunted. "Will you be worthy of any love when you are impossible to look at?"

Xali tried to fight against the shove but still the left side of her face approached the flame. Xali could feel the heat and her skin burning. The skin began to bubble and pop and her left eye suddenly went dark. Xali cried out in pain.

Xarica pulled her away and tossed the archer into the ground. "You will never be worthy of love again. You will never be worthy of anybody's attention or care. You will forever be a burden!"

Blood poured from her chest, her face was burned and her strength was quickly fading but she still had a promise to keep.

She still had to find Nikka.

Xali grabbed a burning stick and, using the last of her strength, swung it at the harpy. The green flame collided with Xarica's face and she screeched in pain.

"Nooo," She wailed. "I will kill you."

Xarica's talons slashed across Xali's neck.

The archer froze, her body quivering for a moment

before she dropped to the ground. She tried to breathe but got nothing. She tried to move but got nothing. She tried to do anything but got nothing.

She was about to die.

She had failed.

She had broken her promise.

She had left Nikka alone.

Two torches burned side by side, forever shining light upon the darkness, until one was extinguished, making the world a far darker place.

A far lonelier place.

An arrow shot across the air and slammed into Xarica. The harpy snapped her head around and spotted a muscle-filled woman approaching.

Nikka was never good with a bow but somehow, in this moment as she wielded Xali's bow, she was a perfect shot. She drew another arrow and shot again, and again and again. Three arrows slammed into the harpy leader and dropped her to the ground. Nikka dropped Xali's bow, drew her sword and charged in. Xarica waited until the warrioress was close before slashing with her talons. They slashed across Nikka's neck.

Xarica cackled in victory. None in this realm could dodge that slash. Yet as she turned to her victim, her eyes went wide. Nikka was unharmed.

Nikka smirked as the last of her protection spell faded. Xarica tried to flee but Nikka grabbed her by the leg and slammed her against the dirt. Nikka slammed her foot into the harpy's chest, pinning her to the ground. With a single slash, Nikka viciously separated Xarica's head from her neck.

Wingwing Xarica was dead.

Nikka dropped her blade and ran toward Xali, sliding

in beside her. Pink magic began to form in each of her hands. She pressed one onto Xali's neck and one onto her chest. The magic began to flow into the archer. Slowly both the bleeding chest wound and the gash in her neck began to knit together.

"I….I failed…." Xali muttered, finally able to breathe again.

"I found you," Nikka cried, holding her wife close to her chest. "It was my turn and I found you, Petal. You will always find me and I will always find you and damn them to the underworld anybody who dares to separate us."

Foricu approached Aidox. The commander sat on a stone, quickly tending to his wounds. Foricu frowned. The Commander was furious. She could see it as he hastily attempted to bandage a burn wound. He had barely escaped the burning rain where many others did not.

"Commander," she said. "We need to retreat."

"Victory is at hand and you wish to flee?" Aidox roared. "You coward."

"Aoryna is in ruin," Foricu explained. "We are already victorious."

"We are not until every human is crushed beneath my boot," he ranted. "We will be the avatars of their extinction. We will rewrite this world in our image."

"We've lost over half of our gigas forces," Foricu reported. "The harpies have fled with the Warwing's death and the minotaurs herds are nearly wiped out."

"We are at the precipice of glory," he roared. "And if none of them are willing to grasp it, then I will slay the humans all on my own."

With his axe in one hand his flaming spear in the other, Aidox marched toward the humans. Foricu just shook her head. Fanatics were never to be trusted.

Stellia spotted Aidox and her vision narrowed. Her breathing became shallow and her temper quickly began to rise. A sudden hand on her shoulder snapped her back to the present.

"You cannot do this alone," Perigoss said from one side of her.

"He is far too strong," Scyra said from behind.

"I cannot let him live," Stellia painfully said.

"Then he dies today," Nyreus said from behind. Stellia looked behind to see nearly a dozen of the phalanx standing by.

"The boy is right," Lypos said. "You led us into battle. You are one of us now."

"We will work together and end him this day," Scyra said.

"When did the thief become so brave?" Lypos said suddenly.

"Are we sure it be the same thief?" Nyreus added.

Everybody let out a small chuckle.

"I dislike his new version of myself as much as all of you do. I blame Stellia for this transformation." Scyra looked over at Stellia and gave a small smile. "She is a bad influence on all of us."

Stellia smiled back before looking back at Aidox.

"Let us end his life so badly that not even Charon will accept him."

Rage bubbled up from within Aidox. These decrepit humans had just crippled his army and now they had the gall to stand before him, to challenge him. They would be punished for such arrogance. They would witness his rage; they would feel his wrath; they would suffer at his vengeance.

He roared as his pace quickened, transforming into a full fledged run.

Stellia and Aidox were the first to meet. Gigas strength versus the sheer determination of an Oibalox hoplite. Gigas slammed against her shield but Stellia did not fly backwards. She held her ground, giving up not but a few inches. Aidox let out a vicious roar as he slashed with his axe. Stellia blocked with the shield and brought up her sword, knocking aside the burning spear that dove at her. She thrust with her own gladius but to no avail. Aidox's assault was unrelenting. There was no opening.

At least not for Stellia.

Lypos attacked from Aidox's flank. His spear tore at the gigas' side. As Aidox turned to strike, so too did Nyreus. The kid slashed the gigas' back with his blade. The metal caused the commander to stagger. The heroes relentlessly assaulted that opening.

Scyra showed up from behind and stabbed her burning blade deep into his leg.

Perigoss assaulted from Stellia's side and tore at the other leg.

Stellia stepped in and thrust her blade deep into his gut.

Aidox screamed as he fell to his knees.

Who did these insolent humans think they were? He was the gigas commander. He was the avatar of their extinction. He was the tool of fate meant to restructure the world. He would not be beaten by pathetic humans who were no better than insects.

Aidox gripped his spear and willed the magic to activate. The caculis blood deep in the spear began to flow into him and began to merge with his own. Every drop of giant-kin blood held magic; giants were a magical race. Yet gigas blood was unique. They had not the fire of caculis or the magic sand of the sand giants. Instead, they could meld their blood with that of another and create something stronger, faster and deadlier.

As caculis blood began to merge with his own, Aidox's body began to shift. His slate-grey skin began to glow flame orange as his eyes became a furious red. The magic did little to heal his wounds, instead it just nullified the pain. Aidox roared as he stood up, unleashing a burst of magic that shot everybody backwards.

"I will slay all of you," Aidox yelled. "I will ascend the mountain, force my way into the heavens and conquer the gods. I will burn this world to the ground and rebuild anew."

Scyra winced as she scrambled to her feet. She was getting really vexxed with the amount of pain she had suffered today. She sighed. Life was far easier when she was a coward.

"On an unpleasant note," she said aloud. "Our foe seems to have gotten far stronger. How does this affect our plan of attack?"

"It doesn't," Stellia said as she scrambled to her feet. "The plan still remains to attack."

"Perhaps," Perigoss suggested. "We listen to Scyra and we flee?"

Stellia shook her head, hoisted her shield and charged in.

"So much for that idea." Perigoss rushed in.

Aidox spotted Stellia as she charged. He swung his axe and Stellia ducked beneath it but only barely.

Aidox was faster now.

He thrust with his spear but Stellia raised her shield. Spear collided with metal and instead of a loud clang, the shield suddenly started to get very warm. Stellia pulled away and glanced at her defenses. The spear had begun to burn so brightly that it was burning a hole through her shield

Aidox's spear burned hotter.

He fired a forward kick into Stellia's shield. The blow sent her flying backwards. She skipped across the ground like a stone on a lake until she collided with a building.

Aidox was stronger now.

Perigoss and Scyra ran into battle together. They wordlessly nodded and split up. Perigoss assaulted with his gladius, doing his best to hold the gigas' attention as Scyra took to the rear. Aidox assaulted with furious speed and Perigoss struggled to block and dodge. Seeing an opening, Scyra lunged in and thrust her burning blade into his back. Yet as the flames touched his skin, they seemed to leap from her blade and into his spear, strengthening the rest of the fire at his control.

Aidox was now immune to fire.

His axe caught Perigoss in the side and dropped him to the ground. He screamed in pain and quickly rolled away. Another hoplite ran in, desperate to save the thief. Aidox spun around and thrust with his spear. It dove through the chest armour and into the warrior's chest. Aidox gave a sinister smirk and gave the magic a flare. Suddenly the spear's flames rapidly ignited. The warrior died, his soul burned out from the inside.

Nyreus and a female hoplite charged next. Aidox

spun around and kicked. The blow caught the kid and sent him flying backwards. The female hoplite thrust with her spear but with no success. Aidox's axe slapped it aside before striking at her neck. A single strike was all it took to separate head from shoulder and for her to fall to the ground, dead.

"Is that the best you have to offer?" Aidox roared.

"Not to side with the villain of this tale," Scyra winced. "But is he correct? Do we have much left?"

"I've died once to this beast," Stellia said. She looked at her hand and started to focus. She allowed the rage and anxiety inside of her to rapidly well up and grow. Then she willed it throughout her body. Her hand began to become translucent. "It did not keep. So until he himself no longer moves, I will always have more to give."

Stellia charged in once more. Perigoss stood up to join her but Scyra grabbed his arm.

"Wait," she ordered. "Hold back and find the water."

"What are you speaking of?" he asked, confused by her words.

"I know not what it is, but you have great strength and speed inside of you," Scyra explained. "I have seen you battle, ascending to a new level. You become a vastly different warrior, a far greater one and somehow you absorb the water to do it."

Perigoss opened his mouth to speak but no words came out.

"I feel we need that ascended warrior," Scyra said. She pointed to the stone fountain. "You have plenty of water to draw from, so figure it out."

"What of you?" Perigoss asked. "What will the FireKissed Thief do without fire by her side?"

"I will find a new flame." Scyra walked over to the

green flame and held her blade over it. The usual flames that danced along her blade suddenly took an emerald hue. Foivi had mentioned that when the blade came into contact with new fire, it could hold that flame. Now it was time to put it to use.

Stellia attacked Aidox once more. With each slash of her gladius, her limbs seemed to echo. She struck faster and harder with her blade as she deflected with her shield. Aidox's superior strength was no longer a defining issue. She could counter his strength with her spectral form. When he slammed down with his axe, her arms no longer buckled. When he kicked her, she no longer flew backwards.

Her gladius phased through his guard as it ripped through his flesh. First on his left then across his chest.

But Aidox did not fall.

She slashed at his neck and cut down his back.

But Aidox did not fall.

Instead, he simply got faster. The fire inside of him grew and his speed increased. Stellia continued to fight, looking for any opening she could, but it was proving fruitless. The speed of the gigas commander had grown too vast. Even when she knocked away the axe, ridding him of one of his weapons, he still adapted. Suddenly his massive hands grabbed her and slammed her against the ground. He pinned her to the dirt with his foot as he raised his spear up high, readying for a final blow.

A javelin slammed into his eye and Aidox roared in fury as he clutched his face.

Nyreus ran in and struck with his spear, aiming for Aidox's leg. The wound was enough to break the stance and for Stellia to roll away. Aidox swung with his free limb, hoping to backhand the kid but Nyreus was able to duck.

"The spectral warrior was not enough to fell me," Aidox cried out in disgust. "So they think a child will best me?"

"I will best you and I will live in history for it!" Nyreus retorted.

Lypos screamed from the back, urging the kid to flee. Nyreus did not listen. He continued his assault. A flurry of thrusts and stabs came from the kid but few connected. Nyreus was not deterred.

"I will be scribed for my deeds. I will be remembered for my success here," he called out. "I will not be forgotten and neither will my family. I am Nyreus, son of Dyrellio and I will be written into the books of history, forever trapped in history."

Nyreus stabbed with his spear once more. Aidox suddenly caught the weapon with his free hand and snapped it in two. He spun the spear head and slammed it into Nyreus's leg. The kid's youthful endurance came to a screeching halt as pain - true pain - rippled through his body. The kid dropped to his knees before the commander, shocked into stillness.

"You will be nothing but a footnote to the dirt on my boot," Aidox viciously laughed as he thrust with his flaming spear.

Nyreus closed his eyes. He did not want to see his end. He wouldn't cry or beg. He would be brave like the myth in his stories.

But the blow never came.

Nyreus opened his eyes to see Lypos standing before him, the burning spear having run right through his chest.

Lypos tried to speak but his body wouldn't allow it. The fire began to pulse within him. He could feel it burning him from the inside. His last thought, before the fire consumed, was regret.

He never got to feel the currents of the sea one more time.

Lypos, Triton Hero, was dead.

Scyra's blade slashed across Aidox's back. The green flame ripped through the flesh and heinously feasted on his back. Scyra sighed in relief. She knew green flame was unlike regular fire but she hoped his newfound immunity didn't extend to the alchemical fire. As he spun around, Scyra also moved. She pivoted around him, grabbed Nyreus and dragged him away as Stellia ran back into battle.

Perigoss stood on his own, desperately trying to discover this power Scyra was speaking of. If he closed his eyes and focused, he could sense a weave of magic nearby. The closer he was to the fountain, the stronger it became. It was like the magic moved in a path and he was standing beside it and try as he might, nothing he could do would force the magic towards him.

It was frustrating. He needed this magic; his friends were counting on him. They needed him to harness the power. But he couldn't tap into it. It wasn't obeying. It reminded him of a time as a kid, when he and his father were rowing up a river. He remembered the feeling of endlessly rowing, putting all of his strength into each pass of the paddle and getting little to no progress. The currents of that river were so strong, they couldn't fight against it.

He couldn't fight against the current.

He was an idiot.

The power came from water. Water flowed in a current and no man could change the path of a river. No man could change a current. Success was only found when you went with the current, not against it.

He couldn't bend the magic to his path, he had to change to match its path.

Perigoss took a deep breath as he stepped forward, entering the weave. Suddenly he felt it, the magic flowing through him. Every part of him suddenly felt different. His limbs could move faster and more fluidly. His mind suddenly was open to new thoughts he never had before.

Perigoss opened his eyes. His eyes, his hair and his blade were all cerulean blue.

He bolted towards the fight. Just as Stellia found herself once more on the ground, Perigoss arrived. His blade blocked the spear and knocked it aside. His body twisted as he dodge the flurry of strikes, cutting back whenever he found an opening. It needed not to be big, the water granted him such grace that he could make do with the tiniest of slivers of an opening.

Stellia winced as she, yet again, climbed back to her feet. She was tired of tasting dirt and she was tired of seeing Aidox still alive. How were they going to slay Aidox? How did they slay something with such speed and strength? How did one stop a beast that did not feel pain?

A heartbeat pulse suddenly rippled through her body.

Stellia froze for a second, unsure of what had just happened. What was that pulse and why had it seemed so familiar? She knew it. She had felt it before but where? Memories of pain and confusion kicked in. Anxiety suddenly overtook her. It was how she felt every time she had a dream of her death but why now? What was she missing?

The pulse happened again, this time from her waist.

She glanced down and suddenly found her eyes focusing on Mericoi's broken spearhead. As she grabbed the weapon a realization suddenly took form. She recognized the talon that acted as the spearhead. She had seen it a lot lately.

It was a harpy's talon.

Stellia drew the weapon. It was bigger than a dagger but smaller than a shortsword. Yet as he hands gripped it, she could feel the magic flowing through her. It began to glow a faint ember-coloured magic. Stellia tried to split her focus. She needed both her spectral form and the magic of the dagger.

It was the only way to win.

Perigoss dodged another attack but found no opening of his own. With each strike he landed, Aidox suddenly became faster. Perigoss knew not the limit of this new weave, this river of magic he possessed, but he knew he was nearing his limit. He could feel in his bones.

"Move!"

Perigoss didn't need to be told twice. He pivoted away as Stellia stepped in. Her spearhead glowed ember as the rest of her body appeared translucent. Her first strike was a blur, slamming into Aidox's arm, and with each strike of the talon her speed only grew.

Aidox was shocked. Suddenly he was on the defensive. This woman moved like an eidolon but struck like a zephyr wind. It was only a matter of a few seconds before her speed matched his own. Aidox tried to rely on his strength but once again, his giant-strength was nullified by her spectral form.

Echoes of each strike filled the air. It was all anybody

could see. Aidox swung with a backhand but Stellia ducked underneath. She pulled the sharpened edge of her shield across his leg and watched him buckle.

Desperate to regain control, Aidox flared the magic in his spear. A pulse of fire emitted, forcing Stellia back. She stumbled back a few paces and Aidox thrusted.

"Move!"

Stellia didn't need to be told twice. She pivoted to the side as Perigoss stepped in. He moved with the current, bringing all the magic of the weave to his hands. Then he grabbed the flaming spear. He held it tightly with both hands. The flame did not harm him but the aquatic magic that protected him was not going to last. He was already feeling the heat in his hands.

"Now!"

Scyra didn't need to be told twice. She leapt in and struck. With Perigoss holding the spear and Aidox unwilling to let it go, his arms were unable to move. This left a very vulnerable limb for a very opportunistic strike. She thought herself many things but above them all, she was a very opportunistic woman. Scyra struck with her green flame blade and carved into Aidox's arm.

Finally the magic broke, the pain returned and the gigas commander screamed in agony. His grip weakened and Perigoss pulled the spear free.

Stellia stepped in, her shield discarded, and struck. A flurry of blurring strikes assaulted Aidox. Stellia slashed at his chest, over and over, until she finished by stabbing him deep. The harpy talon tore into his chest. Stellia struck with her palm, slapping the butt of the spearhead and forcing it deeper in.

Aidox dropped to his knees and gasped.

"Spear!" Stellia called out. Perigoss tossed her the weapon. She grabbed the weapon and shoved it into Aidox's mouth.

"When you get to the underworld give Mericoi a massage," Stellia ordered. "Tell the Lokhagos that his job is done and he will never be forgotten."

Stellia flared the spear and watched as the fire consumed the gigas.

Commander Aidox was dead.

Foricu stood in the distance, the ashen swirls of magic in her palm formed the visage of Blaze General Vulcos.

"The Commander is dead," she reported.

"Good," Vulcos replied. "Take what's left of your forces and make your way to Hakros. It is time to prepare for the assault."

"I will comply," she replied.

"Very good, Commander Foricu," Vulcos said. "Just remember, there is no place in this war for fanatics."

Foricu smiled. She would never be a fanatic.

CHAPTER TWENTY-ONE

It is fatal to enter a war without the desire to
be victorious.

- Oibalox Commandment

Rarus plopped down on the nearest cot as exhaustion filled his body. It had been nearly a day since Aidox had fallen and he had spent the entirety of that healing whomever he could. His staff, much like his body, had run dry.

The phalanx had made a makeshift camp several hours walk away from Aoryna. They were tending to their wounded, of which there were many. There were losses, an unavoidable aspect, but hopefully he kept more alive than he had let pass. Nikka had provided help where she could, but the warrioress' attention was firmly on Xali. The archer had lost the use of her left eye and the left side of her face had been badly burned.

With an old man grunt, Rarus reluctantly pushed himself to his feet. He started wandering throughout his camp until she found her. Xali was hiding in nearby trees, alone and away from everybody else.

"I can still hear you, priest," Xali said as he approached. "You move as silently as a hound does when its owner throws a ball."

"I have been known to eagerly chase after a ball or

two in my youth," Rarus chuckled as he approached. He circled around to approach by her right side. "I have come to check on you."

"Save your magic for those more in need," she scolded.

"I have plenty of magic left for everyone," Rarus lied. He needed sleep and he needed it badly. He crouched down and began examining her, starting first with her broken arm. "Why are you here alone?"

"I'm doing everyone a favour," she said sharply. "They find it difficult to look at me and even more difficult to eat when I'm nearby."

"Interesting," he said, letting her vent. "And what of Nikka?"

"What of her?"

"You are avoiding her. You are hiding here alone, from even her."

"She did not sign up for this," Xali said, pointing at her deformed face. "She will not love me like this. How could anybody?"

The Warwing's words echoed in her head.

"Is that not a choice of Nikka's making?" Rarus asked.

"She will not make it," Xali said. "I'm making it for her."

"Trust in your love, child," Rarus said. "Love took a murderer like me and transformed him into a priest. Not a wise priest but a priest nonetheless. Do not be so quick to break up what Venodite brought together."

The two sat in silence for several moments while Rarus checked her arm. The silence was broken when Nikka appeared in the woods.

"Priest, you better check on your boy," she said. "He's packing some gear and readying a stolen horse."

Rarus nodded and climbed to his feet, swiftly jogging away. Nikka slowly approached her wife. She eyed the packed bag lying in the dirt beside her.

"Are you going somewhere?" Nikka asked.

"I'm leaving," Xali replied, unable to look at her.

"Fine. Allow me to fetch my things and we can leave together."

"I'm leaving without you," Xali clarified. "I'm leaving to be away from you."

"Fine, we can leave to be away from me, together." Nikka replied. She stepped closer and gently put her hands upon a safe place on Xali's body. She gently touched her chin and turned her head, forcing Xali to look at her. "If you think that a burn will make me love you less, then you sustained a powerful blow to the skull. You are my wife. I love you with everything I am and I will never let that go."

"But I am hideous," she cried.

"When we found each other on the battlefield, it was not your beauty that was revealed to me as we fought. It was your strength, your kindness, your caring soul and your wonderful mind. I am here, by your side, for the better parts and the worse ones. I am here because you are beautiful to me, even now. Nothing can change that."

"You promise?"

"I promise," Nikka smiled. Her arms wrapped around her wife and pulled her close. One hand subtly dropped down Xali's back until it reached her rear. Nikka gave it a firm squeeze. "Now if this posterior had been damaged in the fire we would be having a different discussion."

Xali let out a laugh, the first one in nearly two days,

and gently struck Nikka's chest before placing her head upon it and finally crying.

Rarus re-entered the camp and saw Perigoss feverishly packing a bag. Several people, including Stellia and Scyra stood around him. The priest walked over.

"Is someone brave enough to inform me as to what is going on?" He asked. Numerous heads turned towards him. Perigoss did not.

"Perhaps you can speak wisdom into him," Boroca said. "I feel my words have fallen on deaf ears."

"Are you going somewhere, apprentice?" Rarus asked.

"I am, Master," Perigoss confirmed. "I cannot have you trying to stop me."

"You have made your mind upon a choice but dare not tell me what it is," Rarus said calmly. "You are ashamed of this choice."

"I....I am," Perigoss answered. He stole a glance at Stellia but quickly looked away. "I am abandoning my phalanx yet again."

Stellia winced.

"I'm going after Diomestor," Perigoss explained. Despite his shame, there was no hesitation in his voice. "He needs to be stopped."

Rarus stepped forward and grabbed his apprentice by the shoulders. He turned the kid to face him. "Tell me why?"

"He has the completed Sanguine Trinity," he explained. "He will open a gate to the realms of the underworld and free King Typhaon. Worse still, if that gate opens, even for a moment, eidolons and demons will be freed onto our world.

"This is not revenge and nor is it some blind allegiance to heroism. This is a task that needs to be done. There are innocent lives that will be put at risk beyond that of the war. Why must people suffer when we can try and prevent it?"

Perigoss adjusted his stance so he stood between Rarus and Stellia. His gaze silently moved from one to the other before resting on the priest.

"I know you do not approve. You have told me to not run head first into death but here I am, running directly towards it. How can I walk away to protect the innocents of Mikha but not leave to stop Diomestor? To me, they feel like the same path." He turned his gaze to Stellia. "I know the shame I will bring to my name, my father's and more importantly to that of Oibalox but as difficult as it is for me to form these words, they are truthful. This feels more important than the polis."

"What is your plan?" Scyra asked.

"I will take this horse and track Diomestor. I know not where he's going but I will find him."

"He is heading to a small wooden shrine north of here," Nyreus said suddenly. "It is about a two days walk from here. With a swift horse or two, it could be done in just under a day. From there you can descend and find the river styx." A couple people opened their mouths to speak but the kid shook them off. "There is more to my family than I may have mentioned but that is not a discussion for today."

"If you go this route," Rarus warned. "There is no guarantee that you will be able to return. The path to the underworld is traditionally one way. Are you sure?"

"I am, Rarus," Perigoss said. "And I am sorry that I am such a disappointment and a failure to your teachings."

"Son, stop your words and open your ears," Rarus said calmly. He quickly removed his bracers and attached them to Perigoss' arms. The apprentice opened his mouth to protest but the priest quickly hushed him. A glow of lilac magic rippled through the pecan-brown leather, rejuvenating the once torn and cracked look. Suddenly a symbol of Haluta appeared upon them.

"Firstly: Where you go, Cydomea cannot reach. Her wars are over in the underworld. This is Haluta's realm. Go with her blessing.

"Secondly: If you find a man by the name of Neilo, let him know that he is still loved and never forgotten."

Rarus bit back his emotions as he tried to focus, but tears still managed to escape his grip.

"Thirdly, and most importantly: I have never been more proud of you. In such a short time I have seen a massive change in you. This is a far cry from the aimless coinling I met."

Perigoss choked back a well of his own emotion as he quickly looked away. He glanced at Stellia.

"You have my approval as well. This task is important and know that you go with honour." Reluctance crossed her face. "But I cannot join you on your journey."

"I can use your skills down there," Perigoss said, trying not to let too much pleading enter his voice.

"I…I travelled to the underworld once already. I am not strong enough to do it again so soon." Her face looked scared, her lips quivering as she struggled to maintain her composure. Perigoss reached out and took her hands into his own. He tried to comfort her, to relieve her of any guilt she had, but the moment their hands touched, her eyes suddenly turned black.

"Travel to the Asphodel Meadows and seek out your father. Draw not the water from the darkened rivers. Seek the ferryman's coins that were once lost and know that I love you, Dewdrop." Stellia blinked, her eyes returning to normal.

"What was that?" Perigoss asked.

"I….I know not," she whispered. Whatever feeling that had once kept her from Oibalox, that directed her to this moment, had now vanished. Whatever gave her that message and had bestowed upon her that duty, had obviously been sated. Stellia grabbed the flaming spear from her back and offered it to Perigoss. "I feel like you will need it."

Perigoss shook his head. "Keep it, you are far more skilled with a spear than I."

"I'm going with you," Scyra said suddenly. She started grabbing her stuff and packing it up. Perigoss tried to stop her but she shook him off. "This may be a noble pursuit for you but for me, this is revenge. Diomestor will pay for betraying me."

"I will join as well," Nyreus said. He drew the coral dagger from his belt and examined it. "I have a debt I need to pay."

"A group of three chose to enter the underworld," Rarus said. "Once you cross over, a guide will arrive. That is the last favour I can offer."

"You have done more than enough. Thank you, Rarus."   And with that, they hugged.

Rarus looked around as the three rode off. With a sigh he limped to the camp. He was the mythling. He now led this phalanx.

"Stellia: First thing in the morning we break camp and march for Hakros," Rarus said. "The war is coming and the MythKing will need every shield at its disposal."

"I will not be joining you," Stellia admitted. "I will be returning to Oibalox."

"You are staying with me," Rarus said with a shake of his head. "Now start spreading the word of our departure."

"I beg your pardon, priest?" Stellia said, her lips tightening as her back straightened. She glared at Rarus as he walked away. "Do you wish to tell me, once again, what I can and cannot do?"

Rarus sighed. He thrust his staff into the ground and walked away from it as he approached Stellia. He held out his hand, took a deep breath inwards before letting out a large exhale. It was the type of exhale that released not only the air within his chest but also the stress in his limbs and his restraints on his body. Whatever walls he had been holding up, Rarus had just released them.

Suddenly all the nearby shadows leapt from their host and darted towards him. They began to swirl around his legs before crawling up his body and descending down his arm. A heartbeat later, they formed a sinister looking weapon with an ebony blade that seemed to consume the light around it. Rarus' face seemed to shift as it took a more gaunt appearance.

The Deathkin had appeared.

Then, after another breath, the blade vanished, the shadows dissipated and everything returned to normal. Rarus walked back to his staff and plucked it from the ground.

The priest had returned.

"W...what was that?" Stellia asked.

"You may think yourself special with your eidolon blessings," Rarus said calmly. "However, you are just one of many in a deep, darker world that even the heroes and myths dare not tread.

"Without even looking at you, I can tell you are desperate to know more and I am the only one who can properly teach you. Now, you and I could do the dance of denial where you will play hard to get and I will do my best to woo you but I am an old man and wooing is the game only young lovers have patience for. So instead I say that first thing in the morning we break camp and march for Hakros."

Stellia stared at him for a long moment before looking back at her hand. She stared at it for a moment and watched as it took on a spectral form only to snap it back into place.

"What does that make me then?" She asked.

"With the boy gone," Rarus said with a pause. "I suppose you are my new apprentice."

"I will not call you master," she warned.

"Nor did I ever think you would," he said with a sigh. "And if you wish to approach me with such submissive behaviour then know that not only are you barking up the wrong tree, you are in the wrong orchard."

Stellia scoffed slightly.

"You can train me to be like you?"

Rarus paused his walk and looked at her.

"No. I will train you to be better," he said. "I will train you to not make the mistakes that I did."

Stellia was on a precipice. It was his job to stop her march from the furthest light. If he didn't, she would forever be lost to the darkness. There would never be another Deathkin, not as long as he drew breath.

"You have spent far too long as a soldier, Stellia," Rarus declared. "It is time you learn to be a hero."

Three horses rode as quickly as they could. They crossed the vast plains as they carried the humans north. When they reached the end of the woods, the three dismounted and continued inwards. At first the trees were nice and sparse but as they progressed inwards, the woods became thicker and thicker until each step was forced to be a carefully chosen one. Their arms became more scratches than skin and twigs and leaves hung in every part of their hair. A cold, eerie bleeze pushed through the trees causing an unnerving whistle to carry upon the air.

Scyra felt her nerves stand on edge. She was scared and not afraid to admit it. A quick glance in Perigoss' direction told her that he was as well. Yet somehow, Nyreus seemed unbothered. The kid walked with ease, unfettered by the forest.

"We are close," the kid said suddenly. He took another step and somehow found himself in a small clearing. Unlike the thicket of trees that surrounded it, the clearing had flowers, short grass and even a gap that allowed a large circle of light. In the center of the clearing was a small wooden shrine. It guarded a small door that somehow led downwards.

"Of all the souls I expected to show up yours was not one I could have predicted," a voice suddenly said. Scyra and Perigoss spun around to see a body approaching. It looked like a minotaur but with the features of a black ram instead of a bull. It had a more slender face, hornes that curved back around its face instead of jetting upwards, raven black fur and stood a head shorter. The creature was dressed in robes. "The Nyxidon Prince steps before me. How are you, young prince?"

"You know that is not who I am," Nyreus said.

"Your mother can relinquish any title she wants," the robbed ram said. "Your blood still holds the lineage."

Nyreus turned back to Scyra and Perigoss. "This is Gorunno. He is a minovato. They are the guardians of these shrines all across the land."

"If you are a guard then Diomestor must have gone another route," Scyra said.

"A human carrying a staff?" Gorunno asked. Nyreus nodded. "He passed through here."

"Why did you not stop him?" Scyra asked, aghast.

"My task is indeed to prevent those who wish to pass through this gate," Gorunno said with a gravelly voice. "However, I only care about those who wish to pass from the other side to ours. Everybody eventually passes by going one direction, few ever make the return."

"He is ahead of us," Perigoss said. "We need to go after him."

"I will not halt you but, young prince, be aware of this fact," Gorunno warned. "If you attempt to come back up, I will be forced to stop you. Not even your lineage can prevent me from performing my duties."

"I know, Gorunno," Nyreus said. "Thank you."

The descent downwards was long, a series of stone steps that seemed to endlessly cascade into darkness. Perigoss walked, unsure as to how long he had been walking for. With each step it became harder and harder to remember a time when he hadn't been walking. He paused for a moment, fog suddenly assaulting his mind.

How had he gotten here?

A hand on his shoulder suddenly jolted him. Nyreus looked at him with a smile.

"It is okay," he said calmly. "This place messes with your mind. Once we reach the bottom, your memory should return. We have just a few moments more of walking."

"Wh…who am I?" Perigoss muttered.

The bottom felt like a dark cave with a dirt base instead of stone. A smell of salt filled the moist air. Scyra let out a small shiver and exhaled, blinking in surprise as she suddenly could see her own breath. This cave was cold, very cold. She reached for her arms and started to rub them but with no relief. In the distance, they saw a familiar form of Diomestor the Battleband.

Diomester stood alone, holding the Sanguine Trinity before him. Ashen magic swirled all around his body as the staff began to summon forth blood-red threads of dark, ritualistic arcana.

"There he is!" Scyra bolted forward. Nyreus was close behind. Scyra drew her blade as she ran, igniting the edge with the remininates of the green flame. She struck quickly, using what speed that remained in her injured body to thrust with blinding speed.

It was still too slow.

Diomestor did not bother to draw his blade, he needed it not for the like of them. Instead he gripped the Trinity in one hand and used it to block. Scyra's accelerated strikes were pitiful in comparison to a mythling of his caliber. Using little effort, he swiftly brought the Trinity up to parry each thrust. The blade always seemed like it got close to his face, the burning green blade casting a sickly emerald flicker upon his face. Yet as close as it was, at his skill level in combat, a hair's width away from his face was essentially the same distance as a yard away.

Nyreus was next, his spear lunging in from the flank. He knew he had no chance one-on-one but hoped to catch the mythling off guard.

Diomestor was not so easily fooled. The mythling summoned an ashen ball of magic and used it to block the kid's spear while continuing to deflect the thief's attacks.

Scyra glanced at her opponent's face, desperate for some hint of his next move. What she saw stunned her. Diomestor did not smirk or grin like Aidox had. He was not some insane fanatic or some sinister villain. The look upon Diomestor was sorrow and suffering.

Scyra hesitated. Something was wrong. Something was not what it seemed.

Hesitation was an opening and Diomestor was too good a warrior to ignore it. He blasted Scyra with the ashen ball and sent her flying backwards. He then swung with the Trinity and slammed it across Nyreus' face. A second strike, one more powerful, pitched the kid into the air.

Both kid and thief slammed into the ground with a loud yelp. The cry of pain was enough to snap Perigoss back to the present. He spotted Diomestor and charged. Shield out and sword in hand, Perigoss struck. Diomestor brought the Trinity up to block but finally needed both hands in order to do so.

"Of all the souls that I expected to come and stop me, yours was not on the list," Diomestor said, generally surprised. "You are a nobody in our world and are just as unimportant in yours. So why do you stand against me?"

"If you open that gate countless lives will be lost," Perigoss yelled between strikes. "You need to be stopped."

"This world cared not for me or my wife," he calmly retorted. Blocking each of the half-breed's slashes. "They sent her to die. I am simply returning the sentiment."

Diomestor struck back, first with a couple staff smacks against Perigoss' shield. Then he went for a thrust with the Trinity. The attack was too high on the shield and simply a touch slower than normal. It was a trap and the half-breed fell for it. Eager to deflect the staff and to put the mythling off-balance, Perigoss used his shield to slap away the staff. The problem was his chest was now vulnerable. Diomestor blasted the opening with a ball of ashen magic and sent him flying backwards into the air. Perigoss crashed alongside the other two. Diomestor waved his hand as wisps of ashen magic suddenly pinned the three to the ground.

"This is over," Diomestor said calmly. "I have waited a very long time for this and I will not be denied any further."

Diomestor summoned forth a final wave of blood-red threads into the staff before slamming the base into the dirt. The Sanguine Trinity began to quiver as magic erupted from it. A tear in the air began to form as a gate appeared. Eidolons started to escape one by one. As the gate reached its full size, it revealed the imposing figure standing on the other side.

He stood well over thirty feet tall with grey, wind-worn skin and massive muscles. His wrists and ankles were locked with cuffs but the chain that once held them together had long since been shattered. The giant let out a deafening roar that shook the underworld and the land above it.

King Typhaon was free.

Typhaon stepped through the portal and let out a boisterous laugh, one as deafening to mortal ears as the roar was.

"My freedom is at hand," Typhaon boasted. He glanced at Diomestor. "You have done well, mortal."

Diomestor did not reply. He simply watched with keen eyes and an attentive gaze. From her trapped position, Scrya did her best to look around. She needed an exit. She needed a plan. She needed cleverness. Yet all she could see was ashen swirls of magic wherever she looked. She paused. There were a lot of ashen swirls; an absorbent amount of ashen swirls. What was Diomestor casting?

"Who are these mortals that lay so helplessly?"

"They opposed your return, your highness," Diomestor said.

"Then I will vanquish them." Typhaon raised his hand but nothing happened. He tried again but still nothing happened. He growled as he looked at his palm. "My magic has not returned."

"Nor will it for as long as the gate remains open," Diomestor said. "Your magic funnels the spell."

"Then close it and let us return to the surface. I have been gone for far too long."

"That will not occur," Diomestor said. Before Typhaon could question that statement, Diomestor pulled all of the ashen swirls together. Unified, they formed an orb twice as big as any human. He slammed it into the ground. A heartbeat later, countless ashen chains suddenly sprung up from the dirt. Each latched onto one of Typhaon's four cuffs. All of the chains yanked at once, pulling the storm giant to the ground, forcing him on his hands and knees.

"You traitor!" Typhaon roared. "You dare betray my Empire? You dare side with the humans for this war?"

"I care not for your futile invasion," Diomestor yelled, raising his voice for the first time since the fight began, "I allied with your wife simply to get the parts of the staff needed. I orchestrated this war to place myself and this staff in this exact position. I care little about the humans or the giants. I care only for my wife."

Diomestor walked to the staff, removed the gem and pocketed it. The gate never waivered. He turned his back on both parties as he walked towards the gate.

"Your wife is dead," Perigoss yelled. "Eidolons already pour free and soon the demons will as well. Do you mean to sacrifice so many lives just to save one?"

"My wife is dead. She died a hero, a myth, but does she reside in Elysium with the rest of the heroes?" Diomestor called out as he turned back around. Tears rolled down his face. "No, she is stuck in Tartarus being tortured by the vilest of demons. Hakros sent her to her death. They abandoned her in order to protect themselves. So as far as I am concerned, Hakros and the rest of world can burn. Let the fires of hatred consume it all. Let your pitiful war fill the underworld until it is overflowing with the souls of men and giants alike. I do not care. My wife deserves better in the underworld and I intend to save her, regardless of the cost."

Diomestor stepped through the portal and walked away. Many long minutes passed as the three of them watched even more eidolons cross through the gate and flee up the stairs. Eventually the ashen wisps that kept them pinned faded away and the three humans were able to climb to their feet.

"He took the gem," Nyreus said, confused. "Why hasn't the gate closed?"

"The gem was required to open it," Scyra said, cursing. "We will need it in order to close it again."

"And as long as it is open, the undead and demons can flee," Perigoss finished. He walked over and retrieved his sword and shield. With a final sigh he moved towards the gate.

"Are we really taking this step?" Nyreus asked. "Are we really stepping into the realms of the underworld in order to stop him?"

"Have we any choice?" Perigoss asked. "The world is in danger and it needs heroes to save it and aside from us, do you see anybody else?"

"What is the plan?" Nyreus asked.

"We find the gem, get it back or smash it," Scyra said. "Either way the gate closes."

"What of him?" Scyra asked, nodding towards the trapped king.

"The underworld guards will retrieve him," Nyreus said. "Or so it is written."

The three stared at the gate for a long moment. Then, wordlessly, each stepped over it.

"I was wondering how long it would take you to cross over," a joyous voice asked. The three turned around to see a red-haired man standing before them. "I have been waiting for you."

"Who are you?" Perigoss asked.

"I am your guide." The man looked at Scyra. "I am surprised, however, that you do not recognize me."

"Should I?" Sycra asked. She was fairly sure she had

never met this man before but her certainty of that was wavering with each beat of her heart.

"I mean, you have been claiming to be my friends for eons now," he laughed. Their guide offered his hand. "I am Leonidax."

"Son of Anaxious?" Scyra asked in disbelief.

"Obviously," he confirmed.

"What are the odds?"

EPILOGUE

Dozens of men and women silently walked towards the river. They walked without sound. Their footsteps were like those of a deer, moving gracefully without disturbing the ground beneath them. Each moved to the large boat that waited at the river's edge. Behind them was pain, suffering and the war. Ahead of them was peace and safety. All they had to do was cross the river on the ferryman's boat.

Commander Aidox looked around. Dozens of familiar gigas faces marched alongside him, as did those of harpies, minotaurs and even humans.

Aidox paused. Where was he?

He spotted Goremaster Jakus and Warwing Xarica standing by the dock. He approached. Xarcia growled. Her head was still attached to her shoulders, something that had not been true a moment ago. Jakus, on the other hand, still carried the horrific burns on his skin.

"You fell as well," Xarica laughed. "Your new world will happen without you."

"Wh…where are we?" Aidox stammered. "I…I was stabbed. I had a hole run through my chest. I….I…." His voice trailed off as realization set in.

He had died on the battlefield.

Memories flashed through his mind. The pain of the spearhead slamming through his chest and the agony of the flames that took his life. Each second played over and over in his mind.

"You were weak," Jakus laughed. "Your brain assaults your mind with the memories of your failure. They will do so eternally until you ride the ferry across."

Jakus pointed to a barge, floating towards the dock. A hooded man, dressed in long back robes gracefully steered it.

"It's time to go. Elysium awaits us." Jakus reached into his belt and withdrew a pair of coins. Aidox did the same. The barge pulled up alongside the docks and a hollow bell rang throughout the air. It was a deep sound that Aidox had never heard before yet somehow it sounded familiar and she instantly knew what it meant. It was time to board Charon's ferry.

Aidox heard a splash of water and blinked in surprise as two lampads emerged from the river Styx. Each woman carried a handheld lamp that, despite dripping with the water Styx, did not seem to extinguish. The lamp light flicked across the land, surprisingly strong for such a small lamp, and when it caught the lampad's hair, each strand seemed to glisten a plum purple. Aidox eyed the stunning looking women and their lithe bodies. Perhaps there were joys to be had in the underworld.

One by one, each of the departed lined up. They approached the ship, handed Charon their two coins and were escorted aboard by one of the lampads. Aidox did not wait, he pushed past the rest and took his position at the front. He stepped up but was stopped by a wet hand. Aidox looked at the lampad and growled.

"Commander Aidox," Kelaria spoke softly, her words were like the echoes of musical notes, dying in the distance and consumed by the shadows. "Slain on the battlefield."

"Make this quick," he ordered. "I will not be here long. The gates of the underworld are opening and I will return to the land of the living to seek my vengeance on all of mankind and those by whom I was slain."

"You were slain by Stellia, Daughter of Stellios, Scyronna, Daughter of Astyacho and Perigoss, Son of Hylas," she informed him.

Aidox roared in sadistic glee. Now he knew their names. Revenge would be his. Even if the giants failed, each of the three would be forced to the underworld eventually. He would wait for them here. He would have his revenge eventually and it would be beyond brutal.

Aidox thrust his coins at the ferryman and tried to push his way onto the barge but Kelaria would not allow him to pass. Aidox tried again, calling upon his giant strength but Kelaria moved not an inch.

"Kelaria," a hollow voice asked suddenly. "What are you doing?"

"I apologise, Charon," Kelari pleaded, never taking her eyes off of the Commander. "Please use the Commander's coins for your next wager. This gigas needs to be taught a lesson."

"What lesson is that?" Aidox scowled.

"There are some souls in this realm and the next that must go untouched. Not a finger is to be laid upon them and threatening them means you receive no warning. You simply get punished." Kelaria scolded. "You need to be punished."

"You mean to punish me?" Aidox laughed. "Which soul did I threaten?"

"You threatened the soul of Perigoss," Kelari said. "Never threaten my son again."

Kelaria grabbed Aidox, leapt off the barge and dove

into the River Styx, dragging the gigas commander with her. Aidox screamed as the corrupted, necrotic water swallowed him. As the hands of the unfortunate pawed at him, desperate to use him as a raft but in turn pulling him further and further down. All the while, the memories of his last moments assaulting his mind over and over.

Aside from the lampad, those who fell in the River Styx never escaped.

Charon looked at the water for a long, still moment before eyeing the coin in his hand. With a shrug, he pocketed the coin. Perhaps there was still a chance to place a wager. He was on a hot streak after all.

THE END

PERIGOSS, SCYRA AND STELLIA WILL RETURN

APPENDIX

THE GODS

- **Arachnil**: Goddess of Trickery
- **Brizzollo**: God of the Sea
- **Cetolla**: Goddess of Monsters
- **Cydomea**: Goddess of War
- **Haluta**: Goddess of Death
- **Hekation**: God of Magic
- **Opato**: God of Harvest
- **Psophious**: God of Knowledge
- **Syceux**: Goddess of Nature
- **Venodite**: Goddess of Love
- **Vulcaetus**: God of Fire
- **Yulorandia**: God of Polies

APPENDIX

THE POLIES

ATHONEA

THE BIRTHPLACE OF ERUDITION

CASTLEX

THE CONSECRATED COAST

HAKROS

THE LAND OF MYTH

OIBALOX

THE HOME OF MIGHT AND HONOUR

YASCURA

THE ROOTS OF THE WORLD

AUTHOR NOTES

It has been a long time since I've done this. In my defence, it has also been a long time since I wrote a book. So lets see if I still rememeber how to do this.

I started this book a couple years ago. I put it down and picked it up many times until I eventually was convinced to finish it. Needless to say, it is my first book since 2019.

Why is that?

Covid was not gentle to me.

Lockdown provided me with little time to work. As the world shut down, my RL employment got busier. Suddenly free time vanished. Lockdown also assaulted my tech. Two separate computers crashed on me in the span of four years. The first crash was devastating. I lost major chucks of Lightyears 2, Ben 4 and Mac 2, as well as other projects.

Needless to say, backing up has become my new religion. So here I am, back in the author world, writing a new book and moving back into the creative world.

Time has a way of taking from us. There were people in my life when I wrote this that are no longer around. Some have passed on and others have chosen to move on. However, time also has a habit of giving. I have new people in my life. People that now mean the world to me.

No man writes a book alone. Every story is product of the people around them. This book is as much theirs as it is mine. If that is true then I have a lot of people to thank (and hope none ask for their cut).

There are the female fans dubbed as the Gentle Girls (How did that name catch on?). Your legion is many and each is helpful and supportive. Thanks go to MM, KC CL, KF, and SC.

Through it all, there have been the pillars of my creation. These are the friends that have always been there and have never wavered. Cliff, Lenny, Jordan, Shannon, John, Adrienne, Kayla, Jay, Heidi, Sara and Ken – Thanks.

To My family: You were the ones who fed me books, kept me reading and encouraged me to create.

Mom: I read books to be like you. My humour is because of you and the reason I am the adult-ish I am today is because of you. I can never stop thanking you.

Val: I don't know where I'd be without you in my life.

Elder Kami Zid: All Hail!!

Vash, the Kitten Typhoon: Watch Out!

Thank you to everybody who helped me get back here today.

Larry Gent
Aug 2024

My name is Benedict Thompson and I am a superhero. With a single Touch, I can read an item's past. I can tell who used that pen before you, I can describe how that shoe was made and I can describe everything that has been done on that motel room bed.

The problem with having superpowers is that people want you to actually use them.

I just want to watch TV but here I am dealing with a movie-quoting assassin, murderous celebrities, kidnapped children and secret government conspiracies.

My family's in danger, my life is in ruins and worst of all, my TV is being ignored.

I miss my TV.

NOT EVERY

SUPERPOWER

IS A BLESSING

THE BENEDICT FORECASTS

Author **Larry Gent** transports you into a world spies, espionage and superpowers. Each book is an action-packed thriller that'll keep you on the edge of your seat.

Winner of the silver medal in the *Best in Halifax* award, the Benedict Forecasts deleve deeper into the ever growing Lycotta mystery

WHAT'S WORSE THEN BEING STUCK IN A VIDEO GAME AND NOT BEING ABLE TO LOG OUT?

My name is Rake and I'm stuck in a MMO. It wouldn't be so bad if I was in my max level main but I'm not. I'm stuck as my level 1 Rogue. I'm stuck in my bank alt.

Now I'm running for my life, I'm fighting to stay alive and I'm trying to figure out how the hell to get out of here.

Where's a GM when you need one?

HELP!

BEING STUCK IN YOUR BANK ALT!

Wörissa's Catalyst

ONLINE

Patch 1.01: New Game+
Patch 1.02: Escort Mission
Patch 1.03: Corpse Run
Patch 1.04: In Another Castle
Patch 1.05: Silent Protagonist

In this new series by Award Winning author Larry Gent, we dive in the action and mystery of the *Stuck Online* genre.

Follow Rake and company as they fight in a harsh digital world. If they're smart, they'll keep their lives. If they're lucky, they'll keep their sanity and if they're both, they just may find a way to log out.

TO ARMS, SOLDIER

LIGHTYEARS TO GO
BEFORE I SLEEP
ON SALE NOW

Allana Guiver was the Legendary Soldier that all of history knew. She won the great war but lost everything she knew and loved doing so.

400 years later, Major Guiver wakes up from cryo-sleep to find a world she doesn't reconize.

Earth is gone, humanity floats through space on a massive ship, searching for a new home and a new alien threat wants to rid the universe of every human.

Humanity needs their Legendary Soldier but how do you ask a woman who gave up every-thing to give up more?

YOU'RE NOT DONE YET

Photo by Lisa Liteplo

ABOUT THE AUTHOR

Larry Gent is a is a bottomless well of knowlegde on historical wars in worlds that are, sadly, fictional.

Larry is a enthusatic gamer whose dreams as a child was to be either a detective or a TARDIS Repair Man (it's like a VCR repair man except you just see the ending of the movie first). He got into writing to give back to the worlds he's enjoyed so much from.

A Perth, Ontario native, he lives in both Ottawa and Halifax where he works as a freelance writer and full-time dreamer. He lives with his wife Valérie and his owner Zid and Vash the cats.

Website:	Larrygent.com
Twitter:	@42webs
Instagram:	@xan_in_the_hat

9 781989 152072